NIGHTFALL

A WINTER CASE

JAMES BETHKE

CONTENTS

CHAPTER ONE: Traffic Jam 1

CHAPTER TWO: Free At Last 11

CHAPTER THREE: The Winter Case 17

CHAPTER FOUR: Beside The Woods 31

CHAPTER FIVE: When They Met 36

CHAPTER SIX: Search 48

CHAPTER SEVEN: Quick Stop 58

CHAPTER EIGHT: Blake Meets The Mother 62

CHAPTER NINE: Home Alone 70

CHAPTER TEN: Memories 76

CHAPTER ELEVEN: Veronica Torres 90

CHAPTER TWELVE: The Information 95

CHAPTER THIRTEEN: See You Later 100

CHAPTER FOURTEEN: Belmont Avenue 104

CHAPTER FIFTEEN: Upper Level 108

CHAPTER SIXTEEN: Nightfall 114

CHAPTER SEVENTEEN: Terrible News 123

CHAPTER EIGHTEEN: The Next Morning 134

CHAPTER NINETEEN: Dropped In *141*

CHAPTER TWENTY: Scope *151*

CHAPTER TWENTY-ONE: Lurking *155*

CHAPTER TWENTY-TWO: The Meeting *162*

CHAPTER TWENTY-THREE: Funeral *170*

CHAPTER TWENTY-FOUR: Counseling *178*

CHAPTER TWENTY-FIVE: The Gift *183*

CHAPTER TWENTY-SIX: The Call *191*

CHAPTER TWENTY-SEVEN: Woods Chase *195*

CHAPTER TWENTY-EIGHT: Hospital Visit *205*

CHAPTER TWENTY-NINE: Runner *215*

CHAPTER THIRTY: Prepare For War *227*

CHAPTER THIRTY-ONE: End To It All *232*

CHAPTER THIRTY-TWO: Christmas Day *244*

NIGHTFALL:
A WINTER CASE

CHAPTER ONE

Traffic Jam

Autumn was made up of pistol casings smacking onto the solid ground of a shooting range inside the city's police station. He spent the entire season with a small group of strangers learning how to handle a weapon, use self-defense, sustain a healthy physique, and acquire further knowledge on other police tactics.

Although it had been a crammed journey for the past few weeks, many were able to stick it through; choosing to ignore the bruises and headaches the course had come with. They were taught how to clear a room with weapons gripped out in front in several prototyped settings. It was quite an experience for them. Nothing they've undergone in their lifetime before. They hadn't realized just how easy it could be for someone to make a mistake in a search. Realistically, they would have all died their first time around in a real scenario.

Claustrophobic or not, every person in the force was expected to excel in a task involving crawling through a long stretched mock-up model of an air duct. Not everyone was able to make it across in a timely matter, but as the police instructor would say, "Practice makes perfect."

It was every Wednesday throughout; training was always held in the afternoon for two hours the least. There had been twenty people, putting in hard work and dripping sweat. But, nearly every law enforcement officer had paid more attention to this one particular individual for the past month and a half. They say the man was good, really good at every test thrown his way.

From a distance, a mildly gray-bearded African American male who had been wearing these perfectly blacked out shades in an agent suit and a fedora hat to match had scrutinized the fellow guy out on the floor of the shooting range, semi-impressed with a simper on his face. Even if the fellow man had not shot all of his rounds at the very center of each target sheet that hung yards away, he was still able to land most of his bullets nearby. It was the best those officers had seen from a 'beginner.'

A policeman stood beside the mysteriously discerning gentleman in the suit and muttered to him, "It looks like you did a good job in scooping him up from the old shooting range."

With a simper on his face and a gravelly tone, he solely replied with, "The man still needs more work." Then he had walked off just as he was adjusting his hat.

Suppose this mysterious man was expecting quite a bit more. There was something about him that made everyone in the room feel uneasy.

Many of the bullet holes appeared to be just a hairbreadth away from the bullseye. The twenty-year-old was proud but acted humble about it. He just couldn't be upset. He knew for a fact the program was made for him. The young male could perceive the eyes of several badged men on him most of the time, and the jealousy written all over the faces of those fresh recruits in the room gave him a malicious enjoyment. Those newbies were just nowhere near as good as he was with a gun. It could mainly be that he'd been training with cops since the summer, an entire season longer than most of the others.

To set one thing straight, the young man and these fresh recruits were not real cops, nor trying to be. This newly designed program that these people had gotten themselves into had been working them up to be like shadows in the night, to look out for their city. One thing to understand, the program was created to reduce crime rates without the need to hire on more police officers. In return for their attainments was a solid remittance distributed by the government of which designed the organization.

Surely, after completing their training, they would be given a police badge, unnoticeably different from the original form, but would look real to the majority of the public. To go along with the fake badge, a military pistol with no clip. A bit of currency would exchange for a full clip at the armory at the lowest level of the building. They will also be receiving a pair of handcuffs, but no uniform. Police uniforms would defeat the purpose of undercover work, and that's what this program was more about; taking undercover police work to a whole other level.

An agent wardrobe gets distributed out for those to use in the time in need. It also comes with a lovely brochure where the edges are wrapped in glossy smooth gold trim. 'Government Police Program,' the front read. Inside it stated exactly what's expected and why the government program was established. Also, mentioning the benefit of how after being enlisted two years could knock out a few college classes it would take to be a certified police officer if so desire to hop on board for the full job.

Now, this one young man didn't consider himself to be that hero everybody needs, nor was he looking to get acknowledged as a policeman. He just happened to be a money-hungry fellow living around the neighborhood with people who knew him as, Blake Anderson.

One afternoon after his two-hour training, just before he had left, an officer said to him, "Now that you've completed your basic training, you are only required to come in every other Wednesday."

"Sounds good to me," Blake spoke in a raspy voice, following up with a solid grin as he had taken a look back at the police officer following about a yard behind him.

When Blake exited the facility, the sun was lowering itself slowly behind the clouds. The blue skies he saw when he entered the police station had faded into an orange and pink glow. And a gentle breeze had pushed the clouds effortlessly.

It was beautiful, Blake thought.

On that late afternoon, he went to visit a nearby cemetery site. He parked his black Jetta off to the side of the grass, where he could see his father's headstone from the driver's seat. Blake quickly unclipped his seatbelt, then stepped out with eyes still glued to the ground. He motioned over and stood in front of the stone as his eyes squinted from the intense bright setting sun.

Right there he squatted down, taking a moment to cherish the times he'd had with his father as the wind brushed through his skin, dangling a red mirror plastic superman necklace from his neck.

Blake lamented as he remembered his father passing away while he was very young. He was only fourteen when he had lost him; barley a sophomore in high school at the time.

Memories flashed in his head of the last few days he'd seen him. Sadly, those days where hospital visits when Blake and his mother, (Elizabeth Anderson) stood beside him as he rested on a hospital bed back in his old hometown in Elgin. Despite his father's condition, he remembered his old man still holding a smile on his face; always was a positive man.

On top of the inscribed stone was his father's favorite cigarette pack, which had been left behind by a close relative. Forever, his father's now able to light as many as he wanted, without the worry about the consequences anymore.

As the necklace was swaying back and forth around his neck, he took it off and placed it in the center of a two-foot-high wooden Jesus piece planted inches deep into the ground, and he waited there in kneeling position for just a few more moments. Then he smiled.

It was soon enough when Blake stood tall, nearly teary-eyed when he had given himself another moment of silence as he kept his eyes low before he decided to stroll back over to his car. Shortly after, he drove home leaving behind the accessory while the sun reflected intensely off of it.

Several weeks later, while sitting in the middle of the Michigan Avenue Bridge, over the frozen lake on a snowy Saturday morning, Blake Anderson received a phone call from his lovely girlfriend. She was the woman that places her man before anyone and anything else. The one whose decision was to make her dark brown hair wavy every day; Emily Rae Stoner. Emily had always been the shortest girl around. Sitting at twenty-one years on this Earth, she only grew to be five foot tall. To Blake, he found it unique, and admirable.

Perfect timing it had been for her to dial him up, considering the man was stuck in traffic while one of the most famous Christmas songs of all time played in the background; 'Rocking Around the Christmas Tree.' It was practically the middle of December. Can't go wrong with a Christmas classic, the young man thought. And soon he realized he'd been swiftly bobbing his head and muttering some of the words to the song.

The snow had been falling slowly for a while. Blake Anderson witnessed the flakes glistening in the air as the sun attempted to peek itself through a layer of thick gray clouds. The weatherman from the radio had predicted the snow reaching an estimate of five inches in some areas that day, with continued snow showers throughout the week.

Having been stuck that early in the day was a poor start for Blake. Never had he been in a jam like this one before. It was Fifteen minutes since he'd been barricaded by cars all around, and it was apparent people were becoming quite aggravated. Several drivers honked their horns and seemed to be mouthing harsh things from their seats, and then there were others that were more on the calm side, tapping into the small keyboard of their expensive phones.

It appeared to him that there was no getting out anytime soon. He felt like a big dog in a tiny animal cage with over a dozen cars lined up ahead as well as behind him. The trapped individual could tell that there had been a minor car accident up ahead, with no medical attention at the moment. "Just my luck," he murmured.

The young male picked up that one of the victim's vehicle had a slight smoke out session while it seeped out from the motor through the bent hood of a white van. Based on the way the cars were angled, Blake presumed it was due to ice.

Slightly leaning back in the seat of his brand-new white Chrysler 300, he briefly sang along to the radio. While doing so, he slipped his ringing cell out from his pocket, then answered with undivided interest, "Hello babe, how's everything going?"

Setting his seat back even further to get comfortable, he listened on through his precious silver coated cell phone.

"What's that noise?" Emily wondered out loud. "It sounds like someone's honking at you."

"Yeah, I know, I'm stuck in traffic," Blake told her. "I was trying to pick up some stuff from the supermarket. It looks like it might take longer than I thought."

"Oh, that sucks." Emily laughed softly. "And are you really listening to that song?"

"What song? Wait, you could hear it?" Blake grinned. Then he quickly reaches for the volume nob to raise up the sound. "This is my winter jam!"

"You are such a dork," Emily giggled.

"Oh come on, you love this shit!"

"Yeah, and after hearing it on the radio about four times today, maybe not so much anymore."

And then Blake was quick to have lowered the volume.

"So, pretty lady, do tell me about your day so far," he smiled, broadly.

With his head tilted up, facing the ceiling, Emily had promptly notified Blake that she had been doing well at the moment, but mentioning with details about the rough week she'd been having earlier. Apparently, it consisted of a lot of hard work, as well as tears, as she strongly stated.

The young woman filled Blake in about how she'd been up late for several nights to get ahead of the game with her studies. It was her way of preparing herself for the end of the semester, as it was approaching quickly. She'd gotten most of her assignments achieved while finals were only a few days away. Even with all she'd crossed off her to-do list, she still felt unprepared for the most prominent examination of the year.

Talking away, Emily mentioned she had been preparing a meal with her mother since six o' clock in the morning. It was for this intended dinner that was scheduled for the three of them later in the evening. Emily had also brought up that the dinner rolls that she had been baking from scratch were giving her a hard time as she felt the first two batches might've been a bit overdone. She was also sure to mention she had been working up a sweat in a heated kitchen.

From the other side of the phone, Blake could hear laughter as Emily's mother taunted her for a quick second. Blake had let out a small chuckle in place. "I'm looking forward to meeting your mom finally, and having dinner with you guys," he said. "Although I must admit, I am kind of nervous."

Emily's hearty laugh could be heard beyond the phone if anyone were to be in the car with him. "There ain't nothing to worry about, but if you don't show up, my mom's gonna give you something to worry about," she humorously warned Blake.

"Aw, so does that mean I can't call in sick?" he kidded.

"You better come!"

Blake had settled her down as he promised Emily that he would be there by the evening. Making that commitment meant everything to her, it made her feel triumphantly happy. The bright expression on the woman's face became noticeable to her mother who had been standing just a few feet away. She had been standing next to the stove, melting butter to go along with her famous, traditional deluxe chocolate cake.

Beholding the smile on her daughter's face made Dana feel quite right about the boy behind the phone. All this talk about him had made Emily's mother feel thrilled to finally meet Blake.

Shortly enough, the two said their proper goodbyes. The whole 'I love you and I miss you' kind of deal. "I'll see you tonight, Emily," Blake told her. And shortly, she hung up with a smile that remained.

Emily's mother had taken a glance at her once again, and said to her daughter, "Seems you guys are taking this serious."

Emily slowly stepped up to the stove, peaking over at the steamy pot, then said, "I feel like he might be a keeper."

After taking in that last sentence, her mother carefully explained to Emily that all men come with disappointments. Additionally, the mother had informed her little daughter that every relationship would go through some type of trouble, but what matters is finding the one that's worth the suffering. Dana also hadn't forgotten to mention that getting comfortable too soon can screw with one's mind, leaving a person hurt.

"I do not want to see my little girl get her heart broken," Emily's mother told her.

"I understand, Mom," Emily sighed at the unwanted lecture she was receiving.

Meanwhile, being stuck in twenty-degree weather in his Chrysler for what had turned into twenty minutes became more unsettling after the call ended. There wasn't much to do at the moment. He gently set his phone down on his lap while he began moving his seat forward to take one long look out his windshield. During the whole conversation over the phone, not a single car had moved. He noticed there were multiple transportation service vehicles surrounding the area, losing their clients as people abandoned their rides and decided they would walk instead. Many others stuck in this horrible traffic continued honking their horns, which was utterly pointless. Either way, Blake joined in on the madness and pressed down on the center of the steering wheel as if he was running a part of a CPR procedure.

"Come on!" he called out from his seat. Then he rolled his window down halfway. "I got shit to do today, places to be, people to see. Hurry the f**k up!"

Suddenly, his phone rang once again. As he looked down at the caller ID, he saw that it was coming from an 'Unknown Caller.' Not knowing who it might be, the young man picked up and answered, "Hello?" with a grave tone in his voice.

"Are you coming in today?" a man spoke from the other side.

Luckily, Blake recognized that voice. Anyone could pick up on that voice anywhere. Blake cleared his throat, then informed the mysterious older gentleman that there would be a huge possibility he would show up late for the mandatory meeting that got suddenly dropped on him. Hearing the colossal breath exhale from the other side let off a vibe that the man was disappointed. "Ok, well, you must get here as soon as you can," the caller instructed.

"Yes, will do, Sir."

After hearing the end click of the call, Blake threw his head back. The thought of him getting ruled out of his second job dawned on him. Right there, he'd assumed that his boss would not be so understanding.

About a minute later, Blake heard the sirens cry from nearly a quarter mile behind him. The ambulance soon squeezed its way down the middle. As he watched the flashing red lights pass by, Blake let out a loud hysterical fake cry. It was his way of calming his nerves so that he wouldn't go insane, but then he realized that maybe he had. He just knew it would take a while before the roads would get to rolling again.

CHAPTER TWO

Free At Last

It took nearly fifteen minutes after the paramedics arrived before the roads were clear. Thankfully, no one in the area had signified any serious injuries, and everyone was finally able to get moving.

Blake felt as though a huge weight had lifted off his shoulders. He released a huge breath of relief, then rambled off about the time that was wasted. Being barricaded on his way to a meeting at his side job was such another letdown on his attendance performance. Sadly, his want for a perfect record was far gone from him since the start; way back in the summer.

Even if work wasn't on the schedule for the day, he was still unexpectedly set up for a one on one meeting with the man who made the phone call not long ago, and no matter what, he must show up, and be timely. As harsh as it may have been, that's the way things ran in this newly designed police program.

As he stepped on the gas, Blake could only anticipate that his boss would accept his late arrival once more. While driving through wild weather conditions with slow-moving vehicles up ahead, Blake had felt more irritated than ever. At that point, he underwent the same weight that gradually pressed down on his shoulders earlier.

"What are you doing you old hag?" Blake yelled straight through his windshield, aggressively tapping into his horn at an elderly lady driving fifteen miles per hour. "Move! Get the hell out the way! I'm gonna be late than a mother!"

It wasn't long before Blake was able to switch up his driving route, hoping he would get to his destination quicker. He swerved from lane to lane, passing by multiple vehicles driving way too slow for his taste. He had used the icy road conditions to his advantage. Especially, when turning the corners, and he remained in control at all times.

A little more intel on this skilled driver, Blake has been in many illegal street races which would allow him to time his lane switching perfectly in between vehicles. Some police officers in his old hometown might recognize him for that, considering he'd been pulled over quite a few times for his reckless driving.

Soon enough, the fretful man made a sharp right turn into a narrow entrance between two large red-bricked buildings that wrapped around the back. The entryway led him to a squared parking lot in the center, and there was only one narrow road that was designed to get in or out.

Not taking much time to find himself a space to park his Chrysler, he squeezed into the only available not so hot spot, and parked it. Anyone who lived in these apartments knew it was the worst place to park a car, especially on a rainy day. The concrete was sinking at the front, presenting a high rising water puddle. It was the main reason why the people who lived there neglected that particular space.

He was well aware of the dirty pool that rested just beneath the driver's side. Blake hadn't been too bothered at the moment about making the slightest mess on his recently purchased vehicle. *Nothing a slight rinse wouldn't fix,* he thought. All that mattered to him was being able to keep his job.

There had been a huge gap between the puddle and the sidewalk up front. Surely, he could've walked around the lot to avoid ruining his black dress pants, but Blake had grown impatient. He had only walked through the wide-spread puddle to the point where he was able to make a huge leap onto the cemented footpath. It wasn't long after when he felt his pants were drenched up past his ankles.

Unbearably cold. Those were the two words he used to describe in his head. Blake had taken a moment to shake off the access water in his pants, and he could feel his body beginning to shake uncontrollably as a rush of winter breeze ran through his spine.

As Blake shivered while he was passing down the walkway that led to the front door, he had taken a quick glimpse up at the sky as the snow shifted to a weakened snowfall. It settled him down a bit, but soon the worst part of the snow storm would change it all again.

Shortly, after lowering his eyes, he appeared appalled as he'd been looking at an old apartment building that he believed should have been taken down years ago. For some reason, the area around him reeked of sewer, but that didn't surprise him.

Observant, Blake realized these red bricks didn't appear so red after all. The outside of the building had many of them bricks chipped, with beaten windows, noticeably dated with many being held together by duct tape. Several windows looked as though they had made contact with a baseball at some point while no one wanted to replace them. Sadly, the city didn't want to fix anything at that location, not even the lumpy parking lot entrance.

The number of litterers living in the area had no respect for their home. Some plastic cups hung together like ornaments on a bush that most people now use as trash. It wouldn't surprise Blake if anyone used that particular plant as a urinal. He figured the bush was as old as the creepy looking apartment.

For this building the twenty-year-old was about to step into, wasn't just any old apartment building. This location acted as a substitute for the police station. Those who were part of the program would most definitely be sent there to meet with a man who's often described to have a stern voice that lived on the upper level. The same man that had been wearing the agent suit, eyes covered with shades, observing Blake from a distance back at the station weeks ago.

The way the procedure works, whenever the young man would receive a phone call from his boss asking if he could come in; it usually never meant a good sign. It would all just depend on the way the recruits take it. It mostly implied they were about to be introduced to an opportunity to make an extreme amount of cash for completing an allocation. Blake usually gets those calls often, although the level of difficulty varied. The amount of money served up by the government also depended on the challenge level.

One reason Blake had stuck around this long was because with each completed task, he usually earns himself a nice check to cash out.

All of the money that he'd been stocking up was well-deserved. It benefitted him since it gave him a chance to spoil his girlfriend, Emily. Emily, was always that motivation he needed. And he was willing to risk his life for their future so eventually, they could both be swimming in money someday. But it is not always guaranteed the agents would get the job done fast enough. About ninety percent of the time, it is the real police men who solves these cases, considering that they are more skilled while the agents usually have a lot more to learn.

On the downside, his girlfriend didn't know about any of this. This was his side job, and he was suited well to it, considering the skills this five-foot eight-man had which could be a living nightmare for most of those who break the law.

It still amazes Blake that he was recruited one day by a man hanging around inside a shooting range. It was the absolute, least expected thing that one would think would happen on a typical day.

Blake hadn't even known there was a new police program until a man in a black overcoat approached him.

The mysterious man in shades witnessed the determination in Blake's face, and the steady bullet holes all appearing close to each other. It would seem to the man that Blake had plenty of training at some point in his life. That's kind of how his recruiter discovered him.

The program was where most of his income had been coming from. But, not only does he spend his money on Emily, Blake has also done a little spoiling on himself too, which would explain the Chrysler he had bought three weeks ago. Everyone was lead to believe he was able to acquire such a thing from inheriting money from his old man.

Right off the bat as Blake had stepped inside the building, he noticed the horrible ceiling lighting. One of the LED lights flickered in the hall like a person with an uncontrollable eye twitch. The dim lights ran down the walkway and up the staircase. It would look as though he was in a horror film.

Beside him on his left was a huge stain from water damage on the wall. Old and rotten. It would appear as if someone had tossed coffee straight from their mug onto the beige wall. Some renters have joked around and shared that someone had gotten their brains blown out. Owners would tell visitors that so much, one would actually believe it.

To Blake, the place was just too dated and moldy, and down-right creepy. He could practically see the air bubbles seeping through, like coming across the skin of someone with a severe case of the chicken pox.

He let out a sudden dry heave. Everything about this apartment building was off-putting. It was evident that no one took the time to keep the halls and stairwells clean. The maroon carpet job beneath Blake's feet was tearing apart like it had been there since when the apartment was built.

The complex was the type of place that anyone would least expect to be gaining some serious income from, which made it a perfect place for a police hideout.

Blake walked across the hall, and the farther down he moved the more it reeked of old books. Blake sealed his mouth shut, breathing in as little as possible through his nose. The smell alone made the man want to turn back around and head for the door, but of course, that didn't happen. Nothing could turn him away from the new mission he may get assigned to; it could be worth a ton.

Blake moved up the flight of stairs as each step creaked beneath his feet. When he made his way up to the fourth floor, he hurriedly passed down the hall as his eyes scanned across for the room number, 127. Then, he found it.

CHAPTER THREE

The Winter Case

Blake knocked while he fidgeted with the car keys in his pocket. Standing out in front as late as he was, he did not know what to expect. Nothing scared him more than the man behind the old, rusted, burn stained door. He remembered agreeing to the terms before being enrolled in the program that he shall not miss a day, nor be excessively late under any circumstances. Harshly, it seemed that not even a sick relative is a good enough excuse to miss a meeting.

"Come on in!" the man hollered from the inside with a grave tone.

In the process of entering, Blake had to use a bit of force with his right shoulder to get the door to loosen up. When he pushed it through halfway, the door released a loud creaking sound. He had been looking straight ahead at his boss as he was entering, but the man had not bothered to look up.

His boss appeared to be engaging himself with a stack of papers on his desk with nothing but a desk lamp on and a small television playing in the background. It was an old, chipped, beat up wooden thing. The four-legged structure looked as though he had bought it cheap from a garage sale or maybe even unearthed at a spot where its previous owner abandoned it. The nameplate resting on the far right read the man's full name, Agent, Allen Polk Johnson, and those were the four words that gave Blake Anderson the shivers.

Allen's a highly ranked FBI Agent whose main duty had recently switched over to become the leader of the Government Police Program. With that included, he's been in law enforcement for nearly a decade longer than Blake had been on this Earth. It was certain the man had seen it all. Blood, bodies, people being murdered on sight. So, it was most definite to the young male that nothing could scare, Allen.

Shutting the door behind took more force than getting it to open. With both hands on the knob, Blake presses down, attempting to make as little noise as possible, but that did not go so well. With the force that Blake had against the thick old door, it roughly closed, shaking the walls that it shared, and Blake's teeth visibly clenched together as that was not his intention. First, his late arrival, and then his disruptive entrance. *What else could go wrong?* Blake wondered. Then, he thought, *getting terminated, of course.*

While he was taking such small footsteps further in, Blake began to feel odd as his palms were becoming sweaty. His boss remained with his bottom planted on a wheeled, cushioned desk chair while a writing utensil he had in his hand ran thoroughly through the papers resting over a beige folder.

Without looking up once through his prescription glasses, the man had said, "Agent Anderson, have a seat," as he had pointed at the chair up front with the back end of his pen.

The desk set up gave him a whole job interview vibe. He observed the room quickly as he was taking his seat, then he had noticed the laundry mess hanging freely all around. Suddenly, it looked more like a high school locker room to him. From casual clothing to business outfits, it was there.

He analyzed the layout of the room by looking at the couch, the floor, the dirty stove, and even on the man's small entertainment center which so happened to be playing an oldie, 'Leave It to Beaver.'

You name it; a clothing piece hung from it. If anything, there appeared to be more ties and white tank tops visible than anything else. Frightening enough, Blake remembered it being this way from his last visit, only that this time, the mess had gotten worse. He wasn't quite sure whether the laundry was dirty or not, but it made the room feel clustered and polluted.

The two closed curtains from a large window behind Allen wasn't making the room feel any better to Blake. Even with the lamp on near his face, the layout had still felt dull and unwelcoming. There was never a day Agent Johnson had those curtains open; it was all dark twenty-four seven with him.

Surely, Blake had taken a quick glance at the papers sitting on the man's desk while he sat himself down in the chair. He noticed right away they were someone's police records.

Blake could see the seriousness in his boss's eyes as they rapidly shifted from left to right. Briefly, Blake examined the scar on Allen's right cheekbone area. It certainly had a story behind it. With glasses that hung midway down the man's nose, Allen pushed them in towards his face as he began to skim over the same documents.

Between the two, the room was silent for another while. Blake hadn't gotten a clue as to how to open up. He'd hoped Allen would speak first, for all he just wanted was to know the reason why he'd been called in so early on a cold morning.

Twisting uncomfortably in his seat, Blake glanced over to his left, looking over at the corner where the little entertainment center sat. He'd wasted five long seconds just staring at the screen. After glancing back at his boss, the young male belatedly opened up with, "I must admit, you're the only black fellow I know that likes to watch, 'Leave It to Beaver.'"

Agent Johnson laughed softly in place while he scratched his mildly gray sideburns, eyes still pointed downward. Right then, Blake began to feel a bit agitated. He was hoping to get more out of his boss with that opener.

It almost worked, he felt.

A short while later, the man took off his glasses and began gritting the ends with his teeth.

"Why'd you call me in at this time?" Blake asked in a more serious matter.

Finally, Allen flashed his eyes upward, straight ahead at the puzzled twenty-year-old. If a look could kill, this would be the first ever in recorded history.

With Allen's hazel eyes making contact with Blake, he could feel his heart pumping harder and just a little bit faster. With each tap inside his chest, he felt as if it wanted to rip its way through his bone structure. It was quite odd. Allen was the only person that could make Blake feel any less than a human being at times.

The high-strung individual could instantly feel his lips becoming dry while the older, wiser gentleman was looking more concentrated than normal. Blake did what he could to avoid showing a drop of fear by not breaking the eye contact. He then followed up with slow breaths through his nose to keep his heart rate beating steadily at its regular pace.

Pulling the ends of his glasses out of his mouth, the man finally spoke. "How's Emily doing? She's doing all right?" Allen asked in a more in-depth tone while wiping his glasses with his dark blue tie.

As irrelevant as it felt to the discussion Blake was hoping for, the young man was stunned. Somehow, his boss knew about his relationship with a girl he was certain he had never mentioned to Allen before. Blake struggled to find the right words to follow up with as he had left his mouth open.

"Uh, I-" he stammered.

Blake spaced out into Allen's blue and white striped vertical button down.

"Emily's doing great. She's doing just fine. Eight months going strong now," Blake awkwardly answered. But, may I ask, how do you know about her?"

Allen raised an eyebrow with an odd grin. He placed both elbows on the desk with fingers crossed as he leaned forward and said, "That is the funny thing about being a great spy. Now, you all lucky I ain't no bad guy; tracking you down was too easy. In a job like this, always check your surroundings and always keep a low profile. I feel like every time I tell you to keep a low profile you go and make it more big."

Blake then gave a quick nod of his head as he continued to listen.

"I've known about you and Emily for about seven months now. From the time when you guys met up one afternoon near the outside mall just outside the little coffee shop back in June," Allen admitted. "Keep in mind a pot deal was going on at the time, close by and I made that arrest. Should have been you."

Once again, Blake didn't know how to respond to such words being thrown out to him. He had just gone from feeling worried to socially uncomfortable in a matter of seconds.

"Don't worry; I creep up on all my recruits. I needed to know if I have loyal people working for me. It's part of the gig. The administrators and I specifically informed the team that being in a relationship while on board for the job is a no-go," Allen strictly restated.

"Oh," Blake simply said in the softest voice as he was suddenly unable to make eye contact with Allen.

"Yeah, you broke that rule, and you came in late today, but not just today. You've been late three times in a row, now."

In an instant, the young man's eyelids stretched further away like Pangea. He never thought anyone had been keeping tabs on him. Suddenly, Blake was feeling concerned about his spot in the program, again.

"It's hard to get here last minute, especially in a snowstorm. You should open your curtains more often," Blake smart-mouthed.

"I know it's snowing you smart-ass. If you're working with me, you'll find a way to get here faster. Didn't we teach you to move quickly?" Allen spoke gravely. "And here's another thing, you've missed three of my calls, and someone else had to come in and do the work for you. Perhaps your little girlfriend had something to do with that?" Agent Allen Johnson assumed. "Being in a relationship causes distractions. The fewer distractions my recruits have, the better their performances are with their tasks. The last thing I expect to see is one of my agents dead, especially from careless mistakes. You guys are not highly trained enough like police officers. The recruits in this program are much more vulnerable to mistakes, and mistakes can lead to death."

Allen took a quick gulp to clear his throat, then he added, "Now, that's just one of the many reasons why a rule such as that was set & stoned. You all need to stay committed by showing us you can follow the rules. The government wants to make this new program work. And Chicago's the first to test this system out. A year in running now, and hopefully many more," Agent Allen Johnson explained. "The administrators don't want people that are going to get behind on work due to some kind of whack-ass commitment they have somewhere else, because lives could be at stake here. Now, typically I would cancel out any recruits from the system because of the dishonesty. Sadly, however, I am short staffed, and I've got a severe, most recent case up my ass to handout. It's so bad we've already got the swat team on it, and they are insisting that I get an agent of mine in on it as well."

Red flags began to wave inside Blake's head.

How bad could the mission be? Blake wondered.

Blake felt his left leg beginning to throb as his right foot was uncontrollably tapping lightly against the front leg of the desk. His lips became dry again. He tucked his lips into his mouth, swiping his tongue back and forth as he sat there in the awkward moment of silence.

Allen had skimmed through the papers again, then glanced right up at Blake, "Before I let you in, does Emily even know what you've been doing?"

Blake cleared his throat, and answered with complete honesty, "No, sir."

"That's healthy," Allen snickered with sarcasm.

"She thinks I only work at a donut shop, which is about three blocks away from where she lives," the young male clarified.

"Well, continue to keep this a secret. Otherwise, I am going to be forced out of my place again," Allen instructed. "Here's another reason why I say no relationships. I canceled out a guy about eight months ago for many reasons. Then, three days later, he came back with his crazy ass girlfriend and started blasting the hell out of my old place. They fired their guns all ballistic from outside my home. It left me this scar," his boss explained while tapping onto his right cheek. "Losing the ability to make an extreme amount of cash when you get so close, it does something to a person, and that's what it did to him," Agent Allen Johnson added.

For a second, Allen let out a huge breath. The whole, being a leader in the program was getting way into his head.

"Remember, you are working in a police program, and keeping shit low key is part of the deal, so don't screw shit up."

Blake nodded from his seat. "Yes sir, I understand."

Soon after, Allen added on what became a tough decision for a guy like Blake to take. He didn't dare give it a bit of thought before even speaking.

"Any dishonesty here will go unpunished, and sooner or later, you're going to lose the girl completely, or I ban you from ever coming back here again, losing the ability to make your wallet much fuller than what it would take you working any other job around the Chicagoland. You can also say goodbye to your wish of having that early retirement. If you break the rules, you get shitted on, I've made that clear since the beginning. Better hope the girl is worth it."

"She is," Blake interjected without any second thought just as he gave Allen a hard stare.

"You are one crazy son of a bitch," Agent Allen Johnson replied roughly. "I am going to give you time to think this through. I'll give you a week. You can't make me look bad."

The room then maintained silence for a second, and the two had looked away from each other. Blake took his most unobtrusive gulp before asking about his next possible case.

"So, what's the assignment about anyway? Or am I not getting one?" Blake wondered.

"Oh, I'ma assign you a task alright," Allen spoke with an impish grin on his face. "Since I don't have many people at your skill-set level available to me at the moment, I can rely on you, just this once to get this job done for me."

Blake smiled in a silly way as he dropped his head down. He had been thinking about the option that was given to him just a few seconds ago. There seemed to be a no win-win situation. No matter what, Blake was in trouble. Either he loses the ability to make enough money to last him up to his old days in a small deal of time, or keep the woman of his dreams, but also be serviceable for the majority of his life at some other place making a lot less than he would in the program.

At the back of his mind, Blake was sure leaving the woman of his dreams was a no-go, although it would be nice to stick with this current job for a while longer. But what if there was a way to keep both?

All that was left now was for one more case to be solved.

Allen soon leaned back in his seat with his arms crossed, licking his upper lip. "This case I am about to assign you is worth nearly twenty-five thousand dollars. It's to anyone who makes the arrest official arrest. Are you ready to hear it?" Allen asked.

Blake nodded his head looking more nervous than when he'd stepped in. "Yeah," the young male answered.

"They are calling it, 'The Winter Case,'" Allen addressed.

The middle-aged man swiped through some papers before placing them in order and straightening them up, soon topping it off with a paper clip on the upper left corner. Shortly after, Allen slid the papers that he placed above a beige folder on over in Blake's direction.

On the front sheet, resting on Allen's desk were mugshot photos of a male who appeared to be in his mid-thirties. He looked intimidating, with tattoo ink exposed all along his neck and down throughout his body.

Freaky looking individual, Blake thought to himself.

The tattoos running from his wrists and up both arms were of crazy skulls and graffiti. The name Amelia was inked on his whole right forearm while it spiraled around. And judging by the aspect of the man's eyes in those photos, he looked unstable, like he had gotten his picture taken just after sniffing a line of cocaine.

"Marco Fuentes, ex-gang member; highly suspected of taking the lives of many this past month. His mother suffered from multiple stab wounds along with his three-year-old daughter and a six-year-old boy. The kids were then finished off by being gunned down."

"What makes you think he's the one responsible?" Blake asked.

"His whole family was murdered, and Marco didn't call for help, he ran away."

Blake nodded his head, understanding where Allen was coming from, and it was a good observation, but Blake had always been the one that needed more information to believe entirely.

"His girlfriend, or whoever the hell that woman was to him, also suffered a brutal beating. She's nearly responsive again, so I advise you to visit her soon at one of the local hospitals and get something useful out of her. The name's written in the report along with the hospital she is currently staying. Now, I am going to need you to bring Marco in, pronto." Allen instructed.

"Alright, simple."

"It's not that simple," Agent Johnson spoke in a grave tone. Suddenly, Blake's eyebrows furrowed in confusion.

"The thing about this ex-gang member is that he may be rolling back to his old roots. Marco started out small with theft and graffiti since he was fourteen. Now, he has possibly moved onto more serious stuff like playing with weapons and killing for pleasure. You also might be dealing with several men that want to kill people like us. A few men in uniform were in the process of tracking Marco down when they got ambushed by two men in a rusty blue vehicle. One Hispanic male that's identified as Tony Garcia, and a large male of color by the name of Tommy Banks. Those two men used a semiautomatic gun and fired at the police from a rooftop. Right then and there, Marco made a run for it, and he went out of sight. It was as if it was rehearsed," Allen told Blake.

"Additionally, Tony and Tommy are strongly suspected of raping a fourteen-year-old girl a year ago in an alley. It was during a drug exchange, but ever since then they became a ghost, making their way through town in secret. Would be nice if they get captured too.

"So, no officers were killed during the ambush?" Blake asked.

"Luckily, no," Allen answered him.

Blake instantly became suspicious of it. Semi-automatic guns, a surprise attack from above, and no one killed, just three men that got away while every single officer was able to come home.

Allen paused to wipe his hand over his dry mouth before he continued. "Yesterday, five police officers chased Marco across town till he disappeared off into the woods. The man's a runner, a fast one. He left an officer injured as he was shoved down a staircase. His fingers were fractured then, and he was also left with a huge scar on the back of his head. The man had to get stitches," Allen informed. "Now, in the woods where Marco was last seen, you should be able to pick up tracks there. I've circled some areas on the paper tucked in the folder where we've already searched. Shouldn't be hard if you check the remaining areas today before this snowfall covers up the layer from the previous one."

Leaning forward, Blake sets his wrist down on the desk with fingers locking, "Alright," he said.

"Whether the suspect killed his family or not, the man has now got some serious weight on his back. Resisting arrest, running away, physically touching an officer, and putting my people in danger. We still need him brought in," Allen informed. "If later we see that he is not the killer, the case will still be up in the air along with the money, and you'll get it as soon as you find the real person."

"Crazy," Blake said. "I have never dealt with people with guns before."

"But I've seen you down at the range, Blake. You're a good shot. You just get distracted easily," Allen replied.

Allen's whimsical act then had him pick up a giant bottle of whiskey from the bottom right drawer and roughly set it on the wooden surface. Blake grinned as he watched the middle-aged man pour himself a drink till it reached the midpoint of his glass. "Care for a drink?" Allen asked.

"No thank you, I never really got into drinking myself," Blake replied.

"That's a good answer. You're underage anyways," Allen laughed for a solid second. "You thought I was actually going to let you get a taste?"

Blake smiled foolishly as he watched Allen taking a huge gulp from his glass. It was one of those grins where the young male hadn't known whether to take Allen serious at times or not. He'd been a little hesitant to laugh.

Allen exhaled just after he distant the glass from his mouth. With the glass still at hand, Allen began staring intensely into the young male's eyes once again. In that time, Agent Allen Johnson wondered if Blake would pull through with the whole operation, and prove to other's that Allen can manage the agents well. He discreetly had his doubts but held on to that little bit of hope that the job would get handled till full completion. "If you happen to catch Garcia and Mr. Banks, the government just might raise it up to fifty thousand dollars," Allen mentioned.

"I won't let you down, sir," Blake said anxiously.

"Bring them in as soon as possible, and don't wait too long, now. I don't want to hear anything about another innocent life being taken away again."

Blake felt a load of pressure dump on him. He had never felt this level of uncertainty about a case before. Sure, the young man had taken down a couple of crooks and even found a local missing boy, but this one felt different. This one sounded like a load of bullets with Blake's name on it.

"Got you, Sir," Blake promised

Allen took a huge gulp from his drinking glass and lets out another loud, delighted sigh. After setting his drink down, Allen slid the sheets back over to fit them nicely in the beige folder. After straightening them up once again, Allen closes the document, then hands it over to Blake. "This is your task, do not let me down," the middle-aged man instructed. "You're free to go now."

After getting up from his seat, he motioned on over to the door. Blake took a quick peek inside the folder as he walked with small steps. He flipped and flipped through the papers some more. He'd seen that there were a lot to read through. Chances were, he wouldn't even peruse half of what the folder held. He felt it was unnecessary.

Blake reached for the door handle, but before he crossed through that doorframe after using a ton of force to get it to open, the boss man called out to him. Blake could feel his ears flinch up in an instant.

"Agent, Anderson. Do not let me down. The picture is better without the girl."

With his back still facing Allen, Blake raises an eyebrow, gritting his bottom lip with his teeth with the temptation of saying something harsh in return. Blake bit his bottom lip and continued to move forward without saying a single word. He just shuts the door behind him as delicately as he could.

As soon as he was in the hall, Blake looked up and realized that one of his good fellows he met from the program had been waiting just outside the door. Matthew Dack. He'd worn the provided agent wardrobe; the white dress shirt, red tie, a black overcoat along with a top hat, dress pants and shoes to match.

Interesting enough, Blake had one just like it hidden in his car in a brown briefcase. Nicely sealed, ironed and ready to be put to use.

They both smiled with a subtle head nod as the two passed one another. And just before stepping into Allen's room, Matthew Dack looked all around him to see if anyone else was near just before shortly ramming his shoulder against the door just as Blake had earlier. Matthew seemed to have struggled a bit more than Blake had, but he made it in.

It hadn't been long before Blake was having second thoughts about his case. It was way out his level of expertise. He hadn't felt comfortable about any of it since the mention of the wanted man's name. Blake was close from throwing the whole operation to the nearest trash bin, but that meant losing his spot in the program before getting to see nightfall. The offer was too big just to push it away, so he pulled himself together and quickly loses the look that made him appear irritated. This was a mission he needed to pursue.

CHAPTER FOUR

Beside The Woods

A thick layer of dark gray clouds hovered over the city as Blake exited the building. The young male could perceive the second batch of the snowstorm approaching ahead. That was his cue to move along, quickly.

Blake wanted to seek shelter, fast. "What is going on with this weather today?" he shook his head in disgust.

Just before having to walk through that widespread puddle for the second time, he went over to see if he was able to enter through the passenger side where it was less steep, but just as expected earlier, the car parked next to him was too close to get the door to open. Blake shuffled back, then forded through the puddle again with a leap, creating a splash that drenched his clothing much higher than the last time.

Immediately, the heater blew at full blast as he remained seated in his parked car. He'd been thinking about a lot of things at the time. Surely, he the young male had let what Agent Allen Johnson said earlier, get to him. All Blake wanted was to have the ability to make enough money and retire at a very young age, to live happily ever after with his captivating girlfriend. Even if it meant risking his life a couple of times to do so. There was just no way he could leave her

Blake began taking a look through the folder that sat on his lap, he paid close attention to specific details. He skimmed through the text underneath the photographs.

'Undocumented immigrant.' Those were the first two bolded words he'd read.

Those files stated the following photos were taken three years ago from his last visit due to battery charges. He'd been locked away for physically and verbally abusing his current girlfriend, Veronica Torres. That's the name, Veronica, the woman currently under a roof lying on a hospital bed. She'd been beaten by what was strongly assumed to be Marco once again. It could have been possible that she may know where he may be hiding.

The file also contained more of his up-to-date information, giving out his height, which had been a good five foot eleven, approximately three inches taller than Blake. He had also picked up that Marco was thirteen years older than he was, and sat near two hundred and ten pounds, a huge difference compared to him.

The more he read on, the more intimated he felt, which lead him to think that for the first time ever, he may need to waste a bullet on a human being, which was something Blake felt he never fully prepared himself to do.

"Better not cross me," Blake muttered down at Marco's mugshot photos.

Soon enough, he shuts the folder, then tossed it onto the passenger seat. Not wishing to waste another minute, he quickly sets his car in reverse, then rolled out. It was back onto the icy streets again.

Taking in Allen's tip, he was on his short journey to the woods in search of those footprints or anything that would hopefully lead him to a hideout or something.

Throughout the drive, he imagined ways the whole operation could end. It could go quite simple, such as getting Marco into a pair of handcuffs, no blood, no resisting, no broken bones, or use of weapons. Just a smooth adventure down to the police station like a walk in a park. Which would be what he preferred.

The other way it could play out, which Blake was certain would most likely happen, Marco may show a ton of aggression. Blake wanted to be certain he gets credited and awarded for the arrest. That meant calling for assistance was his last resort. So, pushing Marco throughout the woods on their way to the station was in mind.

With Christmas right around the corner, it would be splendid to have the money roll in while he sits comfortably in a new soft chair with Emily on his lap. Just a little fantasy of his.

A couple of blocks out, the man had reached the location. As he pulled up alongside an empty street, he noticed that the only cars in sight had been the ones that were aligned, parked just as Blake was.

No vehicles were moving up or down the street for some time now. Perhaps most people wanted to stay away from the roads for the remainder of the day.

As soon as Blake powered down his vehicle, he could hear the loud screams of the swirling wind smacking onto his windshield. He then thought to himself if searching the woods for those prints was all that necessary. If anything, Blake wasn't so sure if Marco would still be there. He could be long gone, possibly snuck into another country by then.

It was assuredly not the time to be out, Blake was thinking.

After turning his head, peering through the passenger side window, he'd seen the small range woods that awaited his entrance.

"Damn, I do not want to do this shit now," the man complained.

Blake fished inside the glove compartment. He'd gone through some old copied paperwork from his previous tasks with the word 'captured' stamped in bolded red ink in front of each clipped packet. He kept them all in remembrance of his greatest accomplishments. Having the sight of that pile of papers nearby always provided a good feeling. It sets a smile on his face every time he opened the compartment. To him, it showed hard work and dedication, mostly done by himself. That was the beauty of the packets he collected. They were like trophies, but those papers were not what he had been looking for at the moment.

Shortly, he pulled out a metal seven-inch, glossy black, light-weight piece of machinery. Holding it by its handle felt cold against his skin. It felt a bit like sandpaper on the handgrip as his fingers hugged it. The rough-edged, uneven texture could even be observed by the naked eye. It was a guilty pleasure of his, to be able to get hold of one of them.

Blake was fascinated at how a small thing of such could make him feel so powerful. At that point, Blake was beginning to feel safe.

As he held onto his metal piece below chest level, he took a quick look around from the comfort of his seat. It was purposeful; an innocent bystander could be walking around the area. After all, the city was just beside him on his left.

No cars were strolling by, and still no pedestrians in sight. The only thing the twenty-year-old was seeing a lot of were the snowflakes from the suddenly weakened snowfall.

"Finally," he said with a delighted breath of relief.

It appeared as though the storm was dying out for good. As Blake looked over to his left, he could see the beautiful Willis Tower from miles away. It had been down the road that stretched as far as the eye could see as the snow danced its way to touch it.

Meanwhile, he placed the service pistol in between his legs to run a few check-ups. Blake first looked to see if the weapon was fully loaded. He released the latch and noticed the gun did in fact, contained the nine bullets it could hold.

Before putting his gun behind, in between his belt-line, he wanted to be sure the safety was on. Blake checked, and then looked again to be convinced. After figuring out that it was, he tucked it away, hovered over his gray quarter-zipped sweatshirt.

Blake had then picked up his badge from the glove compartment. He never knew what he would come across as he was about to begin his hike. With that, he'd taken a quick photo of Marco's mugshots with his cell phone just before stuffing the beige folder into the glove compartment.

A few seconds went by, and the wind roared lustily into his windshield once again.

"So much for a dying storm," Blake muttered.

CHAPTER FIVE

When They Met

Just as soon as Blake had stepped foot from his Chrysler he could feel the dab of wet flakes plummeting onto the top of his head, and his ears were the first of anything to freeze. He shuts his car door and walked up to the front of the vehicle, then he paused there for a second. The young male took that moment to look at the great big wall of nothing but thick dead trees.

When he took that stroll down a slight hill before entering the woods, Blake's one hope for that moment was not to slip on any ice. He kept an extra sharp eye on the ground, watching each step.

Upon entering the woods, he took a quick look around in every direction. He had been fascinated by the depth of the area. Most of what he could see were simply naked branches. And although they were dead, the sight was still one of the most beautiful things to him.

Even with the view being beyond amazing, Blake never thought it would be a scary place to walk through during the daytime until it came down to it. It was when the man first stepped inside that he felt a sense of paranoia, a strange feeling that someone or something would jump out at him. He glanced all around to be sure that the area was clear, and it was, for what Blake believed.

The further Blake walked through, that feeling of paranoia slowly dissolved like the first flake in a snowfall.

Then he had thought of something that soothed him, and that was Emily. The man so happened to be thinking about the time they first met, and he remembered every detail quite effortlessly.

The two met at a breakfast diner about eight and a half months ago. It was early in the morning, approximately nine-thirty. Emily was a waitress at the time, and as for Blake, he had been the fellow that had walked in on a perfect day, only anticipating a meal that consisted of plenty of pancakes and sausages. But just outside the diner before stepping in, before that thing happened where his whole life had changed in an instant, Blake had bumped into his dread headed friend, Terrance Patterson. Blake was quick to expose this smile on his face as soon as he spotted his friend walking down the broad sidewalk. Terrance had that effect on that people.

"Hey, my boy!" Terrance came forth for a special handshake while displaying a contagious smile. "What in the world? What have you been up to? I haven't seen you in a minute."

"Same old, same old," Blake chuckled.

"Still working' at that doughnut shop?" Terrance laughed. "Look, I got you, bro. If you ever need a job or anything, I got you. That's what friends are for."

"That's alright. I've actually found another gig."

"Oh snaps, that's awesome man, what is it?"

"I can't really say, but it's all fast-paced," Blake smiled as he'd been referring to his assignments from the Government Police Program.

"I get it, I get it," Terrance nodded with that same huge smile. "You some friendly neighborhood spider-freak ain't cha? Some double o' seven type shit?" Terrance Joked.

"Ha! funny!"

"I'm just messing with you, bro."

"I see you still selling on the streets," Blake laughed as he lowered his eyes down to the man's protruding hand pockets of a Bob Marley sweater. Almost instantly, Terrance chuckled, staggering in a circle, giving Blake the indication that it was indeed true.

"Look, you've helped me get through high school, and now that I've run into you, I must pay credit to where it's due. If you need some extra money, I got you. I can let you in on this."

"No thanks," Blake quickly declined. "And be careful, I don't want to have to arrest you."

And right away, Terrance had taken a step back with eyes widened.

"I'm joking!" Blake laughed.

"Jesus man!" Terrance was relieved. "I'm starting to believe that you should have been a cop. But all right, if you need something, anything at all, just let me know, my people and I got you."

Blake had taken his friend's offer into consideration just before they had departed ways, only the part where Blake would allow Terrance to help with any circumstances in return for getting him through high school. Indeed, it had been something to keep a mental note on about.

Moments on, Blake had come in through the main entrance on that beautiful, warm day, and he sat himself down at a small booth beside a huge window. The long stretched bar happened to be beside him, a couple of feet to the right. Blake initially thought about sitting there, but quickly decided against it. Instead, he remained right where he was, and he stared through that window as moments went on. He remembered the busy street, the crowd of people strolling by, and even the sun peeking halfway out from behind the clouds.

He continued to look out for a while longer, reflecting on the easy arrest he had made the previous day. That was until a woman in a bright yellow apron, holding a coffee pot came in and stood beside his table. But it wasn't Emily. It was this German lady with blonde curled hair and red lipstick who appeared to be in her mid-forties and quite delicate with her voice.

"Hi, my name is Kelly, I'll be your server for today. May I start you off with a cup of coffee this morning, sir?"

With a bright smile on Blake's face, he softly answered, "of course."

Promptly after approval, the waitress reached her arm over as she poured coffee into the man's mug, then she had asked a somewhat unusual question. "You are such a handsome looking fella; are you seeing anyone?"

As Blake remembered, he did this soft laugh, and told her, "No, I am actually a lone-wolf."

Shaking her head in disbelief. "No good," she told him with a suspicious grin on her face. She then went on to say, "I think I can arrange something for ya."

At that moment, the young male was left speechless. Blake tilted his head down, laughing with shrugged shoulders.

"I'll be back," she said to him.

As Kelly walked away, Blake was left feeling utterly confused. As he had been thinking to himself at the time, he assumed the waitress had been asking for someone else. Blake shifted that thought to the side as he remembered pulling up a menu that slanted on a stand near the edge of the table beneath the window.

As he skimmed through the menu, he heard this voice from a distance. It was what Blake had defined as a 'sexy voice.' He took a quick glance over to where it had been coming from, and was instantly amazed at what he saw.

This beautiful waitress behind the bar was catching up with an old guy friend of hers from her high school. He was seated down on the bar stool, resting his elbows on the wooden countertop with no intention of ordering a single thing. Very jock-like, very muscular and so smooth with his words. And there that girl was, giggling away at whatever was being said to her.

Blake looked away for a quick second, then he looked right back and noticed his waitress Kelly, breaking-in on the interaction between the two as she leaned in towards Emily's ear. As Kelly began mumbling, the young girl's eyes began to wander immediately around the restaurant. Blake was quick to assume Kelly had been talking about him.

Blake recalled having this weird gut feeling, and soon enough, Emily stopped to look past her friend, Trevor Banks and set her eyes on Blake. Right then and there, he rolled his eyes off to a different direction as he slowly turned his head elsewhere.

As he faced forward, this weird gut feeling had gotten worse. It was not a bad feeling at all. It became apparent to him that it was something he hadn't experienced in a long time. The young man did not have any clue on how to describe the feeling, but as a matter of fact, he enjoyed it.

Meanwhile, Blake kept thinking about the awkward eye contact the two had made a short while ago. He found himself to be more curious as to what they were saying to each other. Blake wanted to turn his head to the right again, to see if they were still talking. At that point, he was eighty percent sure they had been gossiping about him. It would make sense if he were correct, considering the forty-something-year-old woman had asked earlier about his current relationship status.

On the other hand, as Trevor remained seated on the high-rise seat at the bar, he turned his head to look over his shoulder. Without looking back, Blake was well aware of the jock fellow staring directly at him. Blake pretended to mind his own business by staring straight ahead at the empty booth in front of him as he drank his coffee, which he remembered being so warm and full of delight.

Trevor looked away after staring for a long minute with tensed eyebrows. From the table, Blake recalled having an impish grin on his face just before taking another sip from his mug. At that point, Blake was ninety percent sure he was the one getting talked about by the giggling females.

Soon enough, Kelly came back over to the table and asked the man if he was ready to have his order taken. Softly, Blake requested a pancake stack along with a side of sausage. Without having to jot down on her little notepad, she let his demand seep in and lock itself inside her head like a vacuum.

He then remembered after, when his waitress opened up with a shocking statement.

"You see that girl behind the counter over there?" she asked while referring to Emily. "She thinks you're quite the looker."

Blake then couldn't help but express a cheesy smile from where he sat.

"You should go over there and talk to her," she encouraged him. "Personally," Kelly adding in her input, "I do not want to see her get hurt," She glanced over to Trevor.

"Ah, got it.," Blake nodded, as his waitress began walking away.

Kelly made her way back behind the bar, and over to Emily. She whispered into the woman's ear for the second time.

Emily giggled while her hand was cupping her mouth, and she had looked straight ahead at Blake as he pretended to be unaware. The anxious man had been looking out the window again, and he noticed her staring right at him from the small reflection that appeared in the glass.

Blake soon figured it was time to do something daring. He took a glance back, and their eyes met, only this time, neither of the two looked away so quickly. He grinned at her, and as for Emily, she beamed right back.

Being seated between the two, Trevor witnessed their moment and began to feel uncomfortable. Without any further words said, the man had caused a scene as he roughly scooted out of his seat. The bar stool screeched against the floor when he began to storm out the exit. That's what had broken the eye contact between the two.

"Banks!' Kelly called out to him. "Trevor!"

As Emily watched her friend head out, she'd seen him forcefully push the door open as far as the brackets could hold. Blake too had seen it, as he had to look over his shoulder. Blake shook his head with disgusted look on his face as he was looking back down at his table.

"Pussy," he muttered with a smirk that shortly came after.

Meantime, as Blake waited for his order, he'd seen the eye-catching, young woman, and the hard work she was putting in all around.

All over the place she went, hurriedly taking orders from left to right. Her loose, drooping shoulders made her appear exhausted as she kept moving along at a pace to be certain everyone experienced the best service.

A minute had gone by when Blake observed straight ahead and noticed an elderly couple getting up from their small booth. Their table happened to be a few tables down from his. After putting on their light coats, the middle-aged man dug in his pocket for his wallet. As he slipped it out and rummaged through the leather slots, it appeared to Blake that the man had only taken out a single dollar. That bill was to be left behind as a tip. He tossed it over to the center of the table, and the couple walked out.

Seconds later, Blake caught Emily going back to that very table to fetch the checkbook. She looked at what was beside it, and her facial expression told it all. The young lady let out a heavy sigh as her doleful face was displayed.

For her being in that situation, he sensed her pain. He analyzed the look she expressed and was able to tell she was bothered by working at a dump, assuming that most of the people in the city would leave behind the same amount. Grabbing onto the dollar bill that rested on the surface, she shoved it in her pocket like it was a worthless receipt.

Soon enough, Blake was distracted by the mouth-watering food placed in front of him by his waitress, Kelly.

"Thank you," Blake said in a raspy voice.

Right away, the smell of that butter-like dish creeped up his nose, and he immediately drowned his pancakes with the old fashioned syrup. Watching the sticky golden-brown substance glisten and swarm down each layer was like heaven on a plate.

As he chowed down, he first tasted the sweetness that spread around his tongue, easily setting a smile on his face. Shortly Emily walked up to Blake's table. "How's everything?" she asked.

"This is orgasmic!" he complimented with a mouth half full, pointing at the dish with the end of his fork.

Looking up, desperately needing to know the woman's name, he scanned for a name tag in which she had pinned to her shirt. 'Stoner,' it read.

At that moment, Blake had asked for the woman's first name. "I'm a stoner as well. I've got plenty of bongs up in my truck," he jokingly teased. And surprisingly, she laughed at such a terrible introduction.

"The name is Emily," she said. "And oh boy, I've heard all the jokes." she playfully rolled her eyes.

The man then quickly introduced himself by stating his name. She let that five letter word seal itself inside her head. "Ok, got it," she said while keeping a straight face.

Emily had seemed pretty observant herself. She noticed the dark blue shirt Blake had underneath his other clothing. That's when she had asked, "Do you prefer the Chicago Cubs, or the White Sox?"

Blake grinned when he answered. "Cubs, definitely the Cubs."

At that instant, it appeared that her level of interest sparked up. She confessed her love for the Chicago Cubs team and how she nearly watched every game in the current season.

But of course, being the busy girl that she was, Emily had to return to what she'd been doing earlier; taking orders and wiping down tables.

After telling Blake that she had to dismiss herself, the young woman had first asked him if he needed a refill on his coffee. To be kind, Blake assured her that he had been 'okay," but Emily refused to walk off without giving him that refill.

Stepping a few feet away to the counter to retrieve what was then a full coffee pot; she walked straight back and poured some freshly brewed beverage into his mug.

"You didn't have to do that," he told her. "I could have asked the other lady to fetch me some more."

Without saying a word, Emily took a quick look into the man's eyes. Blake's senses told him to do the same. He remembered the feeling he received while doing so. The increased speed in his heart, the gut-twisting spirit, how hard it was to swallow his food, all of it. Soon enough, the beautiful waitress who had immediately gotten a hold of the young man's attention slowly stepped away and returned to the counter.

Suddenly, the gentleman realized he was craving something other than what was on his plate. He pushed his dish to the center of the table, half empty, as he anxiously planned the first official move.

A moment later, his waitress, Kelly, informed him about his bill making its way over to him. "I am going to let the tip go to her," she told Blake just as she glanced over at Emily. Right then and there, Blake immediately spiraled up with what he'd thought was a brilliant plan. It was as if Kelly had been fixing up a bit of foreplay.

His waitress disappeared off into the kitchen and seconds later, popped back out through the two-panel swinging doors, holding onto a leather flip book with his receipt attached. After being handed the booklet, he pulled out his wallet and paid the amount. He patted himself all over his jean pockets, searching for a pen. He glanced over his shoulder and discreetly lured his waitress back to the table.

Blake had asked the woman if she would lend him the writing utensil she had stuck deep in her hair. Being the lovely lady that Kelly was, and with no hesitation, she let him barrow it, quickly while she went on over to a table where a lovely young couple seated themselves.

Flipping the receipt to the blank side, Blake quickly jotted down what he still felt were his best few words yet. He'd kept it short and smooth, but still very moving. The young man then dragged out his wallet from his pocket once again and took out a single bill.

Shutting the booklet closed with the receipt inside, he pushed it off near the edge along with the pen. Blake had tucked in that green statement midway, underneath his half-empty mug. Shortly after, he got up from his seat, then ditched his table for the bathroom.

When he approached the men's room, he'd witnessed his waitress Kelly speaking to Emily, and she pointed at what was then an empty table.

The restrooms wrapped all the way around behind the bar. During his little stroll, Blake kept his head directed behind, observing Emily as she moved over to his booth.

First picking up the booklet, she held it in between her ribcage, then reached out towards the center of the table for her tip. Not fully paying attention she had assumed it was only a single.

Soon, she took a better look and was amazed when she realized what it was worth. A hundred-dollar bill. With her jaw stretching as broad as it could she had taken another look at it as she was in disbelief.

With eyes that wandered the place, she was hoping to have found the man that tipped so big. As for Blake, he made sure that he did not get spotted as he bounded into the men's room when her eyes almost reached him.

Emily tucked the money into the pocket of her black jeans. When she removed the booklet she had pressed against her ribcage, Emily noticed the pen ink bleeding through the receipt. That's what drew her attention to it.

When she pulled the printed strip entirely out from the leather booklet, she held it up in front and began reading it through. It was a matter of seconds before a smile sparked again. The receipt simply read, 'Thanks, Emily. Your hard work is appreciated. Hope to see you here again for a sweet deal, and I'm not talking about saving money or the hotcakes,' with a drawn wink face.

Meanwhile, Blake had been standing in front of a large bathroom mirror, and he realized he'd become this confused individual. He stood there nervously, looking straight into his reflection with both palms planted firmly on the sink counter.

In his mind, he processed how it could all play out once he stepped foot outside that bathroom door. He knew it would be a bad idea, considering the work the man does for a living. Blake just knew taking it a step further could jeopardize his job, his ability to make a fortune at a younger age according to Allen's number one rule.

After throwing all of that to the side, Blake busted through the door. He had taken a quick look around as he searched for Emily. He spotted her behind the bar again, pouring a middle-aged man some coffee that had just walked in.

He made his way over, standing beside the seated man. He prepared to keep it short and straightforward. He opened up with a soft greeting. That's when her smile instantly became brighter.

The man's level of confidence that day was off the radar. To cut it short, what the man did was very smooth, and he moved it along quickly. He asked for her number after a brief conversation, and with slight ease, he received it.

"I'll talk to you later tonight," he said, as he let his smile become visible.

Right after, he stepped away from the counter and began to walk towards the door, feeling more proud of himself than ever. Who would have thought that day would be the day he'd meet someone special? particularly at a breakfast diner.

Emily had a smile so cheesy that Kelly noticed it from afar as she kept herself occupied with a close customer. The two ladies then gave each other the thumbs up from across the room, which depicts a mission accomplished.

CHAPTER SIX

Search

Fast-paced, Blake nearly slid down a steep hill due to black ice. Thanks to his quick reflexes, he was able to immediately grab onto a thin tree branch leaning just off the edge. He had both hands cupped tightly around as he heeded at what would have been a disgusting twenty-foot drop.

A couple of quick breaths later, he pulled himself upward. After all the kicking and crawling, he made his way up to safety. He remained in place with his back pressed against the cold ground, catching his breath.

Shortly after he had regained some air into his lungs, he laughed loudly to the sky. When his laughter died out, he lied there calmly, letting the snow fall on his face. At that point, he was beginning to think his boss may be right; "Relationships causes distractions."

Soon he got up to his feet and walked over to where the ground was less steep. From there, he proceeded down with caution while sticking his arms out midway to allow himself to get a hold of anything to prevent a nasty tumble.

Thereupon, Blake advanced further into the woods when suddenly, he decided to change his course. Blake turned a left figuring he'd might find something there. It was a hunch he was basing his decisions on.

Blake soon realized something. He had been coming across a ton of plastic bags half buried in the snow from a grocery store nearby. It was like someone had been hauling food across. Not once. Multiple times it seemed.

He advanced onward as he continuously scanned his eyes left and right. Bad enough, the wind picked up again. Right then, Blake, faced away from the dominant force, tucking his head down with his chin pressing against his collarbone as it was slowing him down.

When the wind had weakened, he moved forward at a much faster pace. That's when he realized it was a race against time. The cold weather had made his fingers shake as they turned this blush red.

More time went by, and he'd found nothing. Blake needed to transfer over to Plan B, but he hadn't discovered what that was quite at the time. It felt nearly impossible to find footprints, hours deep in a snowstorm. All Blake witnessed was a sight of nothingness. No movement, no sounds, nothing. Not even a single squirrel in sight.

The wind picked up less frequently, but when it came, some were mildly cold, and some much worse. In fact, there were times when he wanted to turn back and head for his car because of it. The one thing that kept him moving was the money. He knew for sure he'd have a lifelong regret if he turned back then.

About a mile in, Blake discovered something unusual. He encountered three log cabins smack in the middle of the woods with trees circling the perimeter. It looked like a small village. There was a great deal of space as the three homes aligned horizontally with each other in the center of a circle, outlined with boulders.

Blake never knew there were homes this deep in the woods, and he was sure that most people in the city didn't know about it either. Residents in these small houses told Blake one thing, they must not enjoy people.

One way of telling these log cabins had owners in them was by the dim lighting that was shining through their small windows. For a moment, it occurred to him that Marco could potentially be staying inside one of these homes. Not a second later, he released that thought to the sky like ashes being blown away by a winter breeze. It was unlikely that Marco would have been hiding in one of these homes. It would have been all too easy, and something says that Marco is not that simple of a man.

As he stood there from a distance wholly taking in what he was seeing, he'd been amazed at those beautiful wooden structure. The three identical cabins looked as though they had everything in it. Food, running water, gas, electricity, and down to the cozy beds, and fireplaces.

Being the person that Blake was, he just couldn't pass up an opportunity to see what it was like on the inside. He walked closer to one of the homes, the one on the far right to be specific, when he came up with the idea of just how to get his free one-way ticket inside. Asking a couple of questions about his case, it was the perfect excuse, but still purposeful.

As he got closer to the side of the house, he'd seen several bicycles on a small bike rack, all with a resettable cable combination lock wrapped around each one. He assumed that this was the only way to transport through the woods, and it then caught his attention. There were narrow bike trails that lead in and out the circle.

Blake became aware of one thing as he viewed the rack. It appeared as though one of the cables had been torn apart and left hanging in a space that could fit just one more bike. The cord looked as if someone had snipped it with a hand shear.

Forgotten combo, or a stolen bike? Blake asked himself.

Blake had also seen an old cell tower sign tucked beside one of the bikes. He assumed those owners had salvaged it long ago in the area, but it still wasn't clear if a signal could even be reached at this point in the woods.

Meanwhile, as he made his way over to the front, he'd seen a well put, custom sized tiny doorstep. Blake causally walked up, gently knocking on the door.

He quietly waited as he took a look around from behind him, remaining alert for Marco.

As he waited just outside the door, he could hear mumbles of a male and female from the inside. It sounded as though they were communicating with each other.

The voices became louder and clearer as they were seemingly getting closer. Blake heard a male's voice asking who it could be at the door.

"Open it and find out," the woman replied.

With such few words, Blake heard a slight accent in her voice. Blake took a guess and assumed the woman was from the Philippine descent.

A moment later, the door opened midway. The homeowner poked his head out to take a quick look at Blake. It would appear that he was expecting someone he knew. The man inside seemed stunned with eyes that grew.

"May I help you, Sir?" the owner asked Blake.

Judging by the looks of the man, Blake would say he shared the same background as the woman, and he looked to be somewhere in his early fifties.

Blake exposed his badge from underneath his sweatshirt as he declared to ask a couple of questions about his case. It didn't take much after that to be let inside the man's home.

"Come in, come in," the owner said, repeatedly.

When Blake stepped foot inside, he instantly felt the cozy heat in every inch of his face. And it all came off of the blaze from the chimney that was located a few feet to the left. The woman he heard speaking earlier was standing right beside the fireplace with her arms folded. She had a heavy brow, and from the looks of it, she meant business. The way the woman was standing made it seem like she was expecting some crook to be outside their door. She was ready to take action.

"It's a police officer" the owner informed his wife.

"Something like that," Blake smiled. "I won't take up too much of your time. I just need to ask you guys a couple of things before I head out."

The male owner of the house shuts the door behind Blake as he was about three yards in. While so, Blake took a swift look around. He realized it was better than he had imagined.

It's incredible, he thought.

At the back of his mind, Blake considered buying a cabin as beautiful as theirs someday. The wooden structure of the house, along with the floor looked glossy as if every inch had recently gotten smothered with wax.

The lighting from the chandelier above created more of a gleaming shine on the floor all throughout. When having thought about it, it was mainly just a great big room. Open concept.

To the left was what the owners considered the kitchen area, neatly organized. All the essentials were lined up against the wall; the stainless steel stove, the two-door fridge, everything. A cherry red wooden cabinetry was hugging each appliance with a shiny wooden countertop finish. Custom made.

Above the kitchen sink that lied in between the refrigerator and stove was a small window. The glass had been patched up with duct tape to cover the baseball-sized hole in it. When Blake first saw it, he hadn't thought much of it, except for the possibility that someone from the outside may have caused it.

To the center of the great big room was the seating area. All futons were in the form of an open square. There was no television in sight. To Blake, it would seem as though the couple enjoyed many quiet and peaceful moments.

In the center of the seating area was a rectangular one-foot high coffee table with a variety of magazines resting on the surface. Magazines were their way of occupying their time, and they varied from healthy living to cookbook reads.

"Nice home you got here," Blake said graciously. Without a word said, the male owner smiled with closed lips.

Soon enough, the male house owner escorted Blake to the seats. Blake sat towards the end of the futon as the middle-aged man was taking his place, leaning his side against the armrest of a separate futon, placing himself diagonally from Blake as he waited for the discussion to begin.

Blake opened up firstly by complimenting the room temperature of the house, considering it was freezing outside. With a great big smile on his face, the owner repeated the words, "thank you," like a broken record. He must have thanked the young man four times within' the same breath.

The wife joined in, sitting beside her spouse with her knee pressing up against his. She held her cell phone tightly in her hand. Right then it was evident that a signal could be reached. It was a good sign. But Blake had been glancing at her phone as if she was ready to make a call to the police or something. Like she hadn't trusted Blake at all.

He proceeded onward. Blake had pulled out his cell and displayed the two a photographic image. "Have you seen this man?" Blake asked.

They laid their pupils on the screen, and their eyelids stretched at that precise moment. As the two took a closer look, Blake presumed they'd come across him before.

Blake paid closer attention to the expression on their faces. They appeared frightened, angry and surprised all at once. "What is it?" Blake asked.

The woman gulped before she had answered. "We saw him a couple of days ago."

"He came here asking for a place to stay, and I told him no," the male owner said. "He raised his voice at me after I told him to leave. There was no way I was going to let a guy come inside my home looking like he did."

Remaining quiet, Blake continued to listen.

"He got into it with my wife, and he pushed her onto the floor and ran out. He threw a huge rock at my window too," the middle-aged man affirmed as he pointed above the kitchen sink. "I also noticed earlier that he took one of our bikes."

At that moment, Blake could not believe what he had been hearing. He was unquestionably in a jovial mood since he'd visited those lovely people. It was then that the wise twenty-year-old suggested that they keep their windows and doors locked at all times from then on out, and to have a weapon and a handy phone nearby.

Pulling up his fraudulent business card, Blake handed one over to the male. The cabin owner took it and examined the printed words. "Chi-City Florist?" the confused man asked.

Blake snickered where he sat and said, "That's just to throw people off, I guess you could say, I am working undercover right now."

The owner nodded his head but did not give Blake the indication that he understood entirely. The middle-aged man took another look at the card. The way he had his upper lip overlapping the bottom made it seem as though he had wanted to say something more.

"Is everything ok?" Blake asked.

The room went silent for a moment.

The older gentleman opened his mouth as he was about to speak. "We see him on a regular basis," the woman chimed. "We think he may be living somewhere here in the woods."

"What makes you think he's living out here in the woods?" Blake asked.

"I always catch him walking with a bag of groceries outside my house. He looks back at the house like he knows when we are watching," she answered.

"But he didn't bother you guys after the first incident?" Blake wondered.

"No, but I don't like him crossing through our yard," she replied.

"That should be the least of your worries," Blake stated. "Why haven't you contacted the police prior?"

"We didn't think anyone would come all this way to help us," the male owner said.

Shortly, Blake remembered coming across a few plastic bags along the way. Chances were mild that most of them could have been from Marco. If what they had been saying was true, it could have been logical that Marco's hideaway was near.

"When was the last time you saw him?" Blake asked.

"Yesterday," the male's voice shook.

"And around what time do you guys usually see him?"

"It's a different time every day," the male's wife addressed to Blake.

"Well, he knows for sure someone is watching so perhaps that is why he is constantly switching up his order of routine," the young man inferred. "He must be hiding somewhere that he is able to see far from."

"Are there any ditches or caves nearby that you guys may know about?" Blake wondered.

Both had shaken their heads.

"What about a hangout spot, aren't there kids that come by to hang around here like after school or something? Like maybe a tree house or some special pond nearby?"

Still, nothing from the owners.

"Well, it's a good thing that Marco didn't," Blake paused for a second. "I am just glad you two are safe."

Blake went on. "Marco is a troubled individual. His mind is not in the right place right now, and he is firmly believed to have killed his family. So what I need you guys to do is to be more alert. As long as you keep your doors locked and not agitate him, you guys should be ok."

Taking in what Blake had been telling them made the two appear more worried. Scaring them was not his intention, but rather to prepare themselves from keeping the worst from happening, as he mentioned to the owners. "You guys are my watchers, now you don't have to call the police when you spot him, you can call me as well," Blake said. "The card I gave you earlier, it's got a temporary number linked to it. You call it and it automatically goes to me."

The two nodded their heads in understanding.

With the only intent to gather information along with the additional short tour of the beautiful home, Blake announced his departure. He seemingly collected everything he needed to know from them. As soon as he stood up, he was thanked by the man and woman for an unexpected, but surely needed visit.

As he was moving towards the door, Blake said, "Again, if you see anything, you can call the number on the card, immediately. Put it on your phones, and it should be ready with one push of the button."

"Ok, sounds good," the older gentleman said.

Surely, Blake felt more relaxed about the situation after communicating with the house owners and grasping that he'd got himself a couple of watchers. It seemed soon enough he will receive the reward.

He made his exit. As the door closed behind him, he had paused out on those tiny doorsteps as he had been analyzing the area once again. He felt the fading heat from his cheeks slowly cooling down by the winter breeze.

There were many places to hide in the woods. There was always that bit of chance that the wanted man was near, and Blake wanted to be sure that leaving these house owners alone was a good idea.

Blake stood there a while longer as he slipped up his cell from his pocket. He dialed Allen on his private phone and waited for a pickup. Allen had not answered, so the young male left a voice message instead. He waited for the beep, then he spoke clearly into the phone he held near his mouth. "I need someone to do a security camera check at the closest mini-mart nearby. We may have a lead on Marco Fuentes." Then Blake clicked end.

After he scoped the area one last time, Blake felt somewhat sure Marco wasn't around. He stepped down and planted his feet firmly on the ground from those steps and stared straight up into the naked tree branches.

A couple more seconds went by, and he realized it was the calmest he'd been. Nothing out of the ordinary, so he trailed off into the direction where he'd come from, and soon noticed the snowstorm had finally died down.

CHAPTER SEVEN

Quick Stop

Walking away with more knowledge set a bright smile on the young man's face.

He'd soon decided to call it a day and head back to his car after a half an hour more of trailing through the woods. It was officially time to do what Blake had intended to do for the day. To prepare himself for the good impression he was hoping to make on the woman who gave birth to his lovely girlfriend.

The evening dinner was approaching quickly. Blake, later reached a point in the woods where his car came into sight through the broad peak between the trees. There that beauty rested with a quarter inch of snow hovering over it.

Unfortunately, he'd left his snow brush in his garage back at home. He had to use his arm sleeve of his quarter-zip to wipe across the hood of his Chrysler. He repeated the process on all windows before hopping inside, leaving his car with a decent clean.

Finally, in the comfort of his seat as the heater blew at full blast, Blake stared blankly at the steering wheel for a solid minute. This feeling was creeping in him. He could feel it inside, the hunch that the hunting trip would end sooner than expected. It seemed that everything had been running well at the moment.

It was before he made his way over to the Stoner's residence when Blake thought it would be a nice gesture to bring something to the table. It would create this great first impression. That was the main goal for the night. *It just wouldn't feel right to show up empty handed,* Blake kept thinking to himself.

With no experience in fixing up something, and no particular dish to prepare for the evening, it was best to make his way over to the closest food market – as he had intended to earlier before Allen had called him.

Making his way into the parking lot of a mini-mart, Blake realized he had entered into a chaotic holiday mess. The lot was full all the way around. More vehicles were coming in than leaving. As a result, finding a parking spot was a hassle. Pods of people moved along in every direction as they were rolling their carts along. From the looks of their fully loaded shopping carts, it would appear as though they had been stocking up for the entire season.

Great Christmas deals must be active in this place, Blake thought.

The impatient man circled the lot three times before finding an open space. He automatically pulled in after someone who was in the process of leaving. Blake soon realized he'd beaten a person who'd been waiting for the same exact spot.

An angry woman behind the wheel of a blue minivan annoyingly tapped onto her horn as she rolled by slowly. Blake laughed evilly, feeling no pity for what was then her situation.

In response, the woman made sure Blake had witnessed her flipping him the bird. "Yeah that's real mature," he muttered sarcastically as he quickly rolled his window down. "Shove those fingers up your ass!"

After he'd roll the window back up, he laughed, nearly sliding off his seat. He then came to realize that the holiday spirit seeped its way inside of him.

It was more than just any ordinary parking spot. With a car as new as his, parking next to a newly purchased black hummer made him feel quite comfortable leaving it right where it stood. He figured parking next to a new vehicle would lessen the possibility of his ride getting banged up or scratched by careless people.

The first thing Blake noticed when he walked through those automatic doors were the huge lines at the registers. Irritatingly, there were only three out of eight lanes open. He shook his head as he moved along. He couldn't waste any time, so he walked with purpose to the freezer section with a sudden idea of what he wanted to get.

He'd been on the lookout for a key lime pie. It was Emily's mother's absolute favorite dessert, as Blake remembered being told once while on a date.

He passed down the freezer section as he scanned the aisle. It was a bit of a challenge as a group of six-year-olds was chasing each other around chaotically in the center. The kids appeared to be playing tag aggressively, repeatedly shoving each other into the freezer doors. "Where the hell are their mothers?" Blake whispered to himself.

Blake shrugged. Time meant everything. Blake zigzagged his way carefully through the group of kids. "Get the hell out of the way," Blake mumbled through his teeth.

And that was it. Blake made it across that little obstacle and proceeded to the freezer door. Blake grabbed the bright green box as he carefully examined it. Blake just couldn't help but expose a cheesy smile. He was so sure of a near perfect impression.

Easy trip. He made his way over to the registers and waited in one of the three busy lines. In place, the young male noticed the most adorable thing smiling and giggling back at him from a blue stroller at an aisle beside him. A baby girl. Her mother was occupied, flipping through a magazine she'd picked up off the rack beside her.

He witnessed this genuinely happy baby with big blue eyes, staring straight at him, and it made him realize that someday he wanted kids of his own.

While he waited for the line to move, Blake dreamt of his future child. He pictured it would have big brown eyes, that would look like Emily's. Surely one day Blake would work his way up to that point and start a little family, but that was an entirely different goal. Right then at that moment, he only wanted to worry about making a good impression, capturing Marco, and possibly even keeping his spot in the Government Police Program.

CHAPTER EIGHT

Blake Meets The Mother

Emily spotted Blake slowly pulling into the driveway as she had been peeking through the closed living room curtain of a huge window. "He's here!" Emily called out to her mother as she jumped off the couch with exhilaration.

In the time that Blake was sitting in his vehicle, he sensed this shaky sensation in his hands as they were gripped firmly onto the steering wheel. He couldn't tell whether it was from the chill interior of his car, or the nerve wrecking appearance he was about to make. It was absolutely nothing Blake experienced before, and the man wanted to make this one right.

So it began, it was the moment he'd been waiting for; it had finally come, and luckily for him, he'd made it on time. Blake shuts off his Chrysler to step out and quickly wipe off any fuzz and other residues that could be sticking onto his clothing. Blake wanted to be sure he looked as crisp and clean as he possibly could.

As he motioned over to the passenger side door of his car, Blake opened then reached in for the bright green dessert box resting over the seat. He quickly examined to see if the package was in excellent condition before proceeding.

There on her doorstep, he stood there nervously just after he gave the door a couple of knocks.

Right away, someone answered. It was as if they had been standing behind the door the whole time. And there Emily was, looking as stunning as ever.

Surprisingly, the young woman had her hair curled. Blake had no idea Emily would prepare herself the way she did for the night. She'd worn a red long sleeved dress that reached about an inch above her kneecaps. The curvature of her body in that dress had made it difficult for him to breathe, and the smile she let visible to Blake along with her stare down with those brown eyes were making it worse on him in the best of ways.

He was at a loss for words for a couple of seconds. It was as if he'd seen Emily again for the first time.

Blake worried he'd been a tad underdressed. It was the same quarter zipped sweater he'd worn during the whole stroll through the woods and all.

A moment later, the mother came by and stood beside her daughter and rested a hand on Emily's shoulder. She wore a floral shirt and white pants with some polished brown dress shoes. And they've shown the brightest of smiles.

The happy young fellow standing just outside reached his arm out to properly introduce himself with a solid handshake. "Hi, I'm Blake, Blake Anderson."

"So, you must be the boy I've heard so much about," Emily's mother grinned. "I'm Dana."

"Nice to meet you. And is that so?" Blake smiled awkwardly. "I sure hope she didn't mention anything bad about me."

Right off the bat, there were many simpers and waves of laughter. It was apparent the three were excited about that precious moment.

"Here, I got you this," Blake handed over the box. "I heard it was your favorite."

Dana's eyes bulged as she held it up front with both hands. "Gracias," she said. Then she immediately laughed, "Thank you, I mean. I'm sorry. Spanish was my first language, and if my Spanish slips, don't be alarmed. I am just warning you"

"That's ok," Blake assured. "Although it may not look like it, I am half Hispanic."

"That's right! Emily did mention that in the very beginning," Dana stated.

Blake smiled broadly, and the three continued with the small talk for another moment.

While Dana went on, Blake discreetly looked in between the two and peeked inside the house. He first noticed the grand staircase that curved its way up.

"Why don't you come on in?" Dana finally recommended. "It's a bit chilly outside."

Slowly, Blake stepped his foot into the house, and he took a quick observation all around. Over to his left, he'd seen the living room, no Christmas tree in sight. He wondered then why they hadn't set it up yet. He'd just been staring into the fireplace where he thought the tree should have been. But the living room itself was enormous and detailed, coated in white paint all the way around.

The lighting was crisp clear and bright. Back tracking to the family room, it had been everything Blake would want in his living space. In fact, it was the only room in the house with a dim light which gave a little romantic, cozy feel to it.

Those quick moments inside Emily's house, he became astounded by the layout. The living room itself along with the curved grand stairway that led to an upper-level balcony was mind-blowing enough; there was no need to see more. Blake immediately fell in love with the place. The whole set up made him picture how his dream house would look, and it quickly eliminated the idea that he had about wanting a cabin as he'd seen in the woods earlier.

"Wow, your house looks lovely," Blake complimented.

"Thank you. It wasn't easy doing this all alone," Dana replied.

"It's a good thing you have Emily."

"You're right," Dana muttered.

It wasn't long before the three got to stuff their faces. It was a long day, and the man had built up an appetite. They laughed loudly at the huge dinner table.

At first, the whole seating arrangement felt a bit odd to the young man. The table could fit up to ten, maybe even a few more, but there were only three for the evening.

Blake sat off to the side across from Dana, and Emily sat at the edge between the two, beaming away. It hadn't taken long before the young male grew comfortable at the table, communicating like it was his own family gathered at the table.

For that special night, it was like Blake stole the show as he'd been rambling on to Dana about a hilarious moment he'd shared with Emily. Going into details, he explained about the afternoon Blake came to pick Emily up after her classes. "I used to drive a Volkswagen Jetta, and there was another one similar to mine two cars down, and she goes inside the wrong one," Blake laughed, trying to keep himself together.

Dana had a shocked look on her face, desperately trying not to crack a smile. "Oh, my gosh, Emily," she shook her head.

Blake went on. "Emily immediately gets out of the stranger's car and apologizes to the woman that was behind the wheel. I could see Emily laughing with her face as red as a tomato."

Chuckling in her seat, Emily blushed on the spot as her mother teased her for a second.

It was evident to Blake that everything had been running smoothly. The nervous sensation he came in with drifted away like the smoke from the finished candle sitting at the center of the table. The room smelled of apple pie for a while; then the smoke invaded the sweet scent.

Meanwhile, based on the questions Dana had been asking Blake after his little story, the young male felt he was on the right path. The woman seemed genuinely interested in his life.

"So where do you work Mr. Anderson?" she asked.

"I work at a doughnut shop three blocks from here." And Dana was shocked.

"That's where I used to work. When I was this little sixteen-year-old, I started there, but it was a pizza place at the time."

"And what do you do now?" Blake asked.

"I'm a receptionist. It's located just by Belmont Avenue," Dana replied before stuffing her face with her homemade mashed potatoes.

Blake was intrigued, and right then he realized she appeared gregarious to him.

"You like it there?" he asked

"I like the pay, but I get frustrated with my co-workers there. They're immature."

"Oh, I know the feeling," Blake cracked.

Soon after about an hour, the evening dinner was drawing to an end. Blake took the last bite of Dana's deluxe chocolate cake, then insisted on grouping together the dishes and wiping them off in the kitchen sink. Dana practically jumped out of her seat to make sure that he had not.

Not long afterwards, Blake decided to take his leave. Emily wasn't up for it, but Blake informed the women that it would be a splendid idea for him to hit the bed as soon as possible due to the early shift he had coming in the morning. That's when he said his proper goodbye to Dana.

Dana thanked him for coming over, as well as bringing in her absolute favorite, key lime pie.

Blake laughed softly. "No problem," he muttered.

Dana then swiftly made her way to the other side of the table and gave him a sort of handshake followed by a solid half hug. It was at that moment he felt the respect between mother and daughter's love interest.

When Blake was halfway out the front door, Emily picked up an oversized purple coat from one of the hooks near the entrance. She closed the door behind as she threw it over her shoulder and caught up with Blake.

The two had been walking side by side down the pathway that led to her driveway.

"Well, what do you think?" Emily asked.

"It went much better than I expected," Blake replied.

The young woman was with smiles after his last statement.

"I like her. Your mom's nice."

"Maybe you can come over more often now," Emily winked.

Blake beamed as he reached for the car door.

After making himself comfortable in his seat, Emily shuts the door beside him as she peered down at him. Blake started his vehicle and quickly rolled down his window to say, "I'll be coming over more often. That's a promise."

Emily nodded her head uncontrollably. "Looking forward to it," she said.

"I'll see you soon, beautiful," Blake smiled.

He then began to back out of the driveway as Emily gradually headed for the back of the house. She stopped at the corner for a second to watch his vehicle drive down the street until it was out of sight.

Moments after, she accessed back through the kitchen door with a smile that remained, and her mother looked over her shoulder as she was washing dishes and just said, "Well done, Emily."

Emily looked up at her mother with no idea what she meant. "With what?" she asked confusedly.

"I think you've found a good guy. He's the first guy that I like for you," Dana praised.

Emily's eyelids stretched apart. She said it. Blake's been the first guy she approved of, and the young woman was enjoying every moment of it.

"If I see something I like, I'll even get him something for Christmas," Dana told her daughter. And it all sounded right with Emily.

"That's a good idea," Emily responded with a solid nod.

Meanwhile, as the young male was behind the wheel, a ring had come from his pants pocket. He slid up his cell and answered immediately without checking the caller I.D.

"Hello?" Blake answered.

"We think we may have found something here," Allen spoke.

"What do you mean?"

"Well, we reviewed the security cameras like you suggested and found that the person of interest has a routine here. Every day, same time, the same person in a black beanie and a white t-shirt crosses through the parking lot, entering into the store with no transportation. I guess the man never gets cold."

"Tattoos? Were there any tattoos? We need to be sure that he is our guy," Blake worried.

"The angles are all off. Can't really tell through these footages."

"So what's the play?" Blake wondered.

"Best believe I'm gonna have my agents up in there. The FBI will be there too, posted up in parking lot waiting for his ass to show up at the store again. But I'm gonna make sure my agents get credited for the arrest."

"Alright, that sounds good to me," Blake lied.

"And if tomorrow we catch him, Blake, you'll get half the cut for helping us. Take care now, Agent."

The call ended where Blake remained with his left hand on the steering wheel, zoning through the windshield as he reflected off of what Allen had just said to him. It bothered the young man. He didn't want to split the cut. He wanted the money all to himself, and receive full credit for capturing Chicago's most wanted man. That instant he thought to himself that he should have never let anyone else get information on his lead.

CHAPTER NINE

Home Alone

The following morning, Blake was up and ready to head out before the sunrise. It was that time to head on for work behind the counter at the donut shop. It was the one place he least wanted to go to at the moment. He'd rather sit in his recliner with a bowl of cereal watching old cartoons in the living room than to take orders for once.

Four hours into his shift, Blake had gotten a phone call. While his phone vibrated in his pocket, he worried that it could be from Agent Johnson. It was bad timing; there was no way Blake could ditch work because Allen needed something.

Luckily, it wasn't him. Blake had slipped his phone halfway out his pocket to see that the incoming call had been coming from Emily.

The shop wasn't busy for the moment.

A young blonde co-worker with her hair tied in a ponytail kindly took over the register after Blake requested a moment to step out. After the time of her approval, Blake immediately stepped into a small storage room in the back to answer the call.

For some odd reason, Blake assumed something terrible had happened, but it came nothing close to that. In fact, Emily called to inform Blake that she would be home alone for quite some time in the afternoon. She had also mentioned that it would be an excellent idea for him to visit later, considering her mother will be at the office for the remainder of the day.

Blake couldn't help but express this huge smile on his face. Never once had he been invited to her house alone while only being accompanied by a woman holding so much attraction. Young Blake Anderson did not know what to expect.

Emily went on to inform Blake of the primary goal she had set herself for the day. Being more than halfway through December, she wanted to set up the Christmas tree in the living room, along with the other decorative items around the house, and she highly requested for his help.

Blake was undoubtedly up to the idea. With a great big smile on his face, he lets her in on the plan that he'll show up right after work.

In such short notice, Blake had to wrap up the conversation there.

With a few hours left on the clock, Blake said his goodbyes and promptly clicked the end button just before stepping back out onto the floor.

Blake had met up with his co-worker near the registers. That's when he suggested he'd wipe down windows and tables for the remainder of the day. He figured time would pass much quicker if he had occupied himself with a line-up of duties, but he found himself to be checking back at the clock on the wall irregularly as he impatiently waited to punch-out.

Some hours have passed, and there were only a few minutes left. Blake slowly began taking his headset piece out and apron, dropping it off at the front counter after asking if his co-worker could set it aside for him.

Before he knew it, his shift had ended. Perhaps the lack of customers the shop had earlier that day dragged those remaining four hours. Blake clocked out on the dot and threw his black cap into the waste bin inside the employee storage room before heading out the door in a hurry.

Blake wildly made his exit from the parking lot as the people from the inside could hear the loud screeching sounds of his Chrysler when he'd made a sharp turn at a corner. It indeed set multiple heads in the building to look out the window as Blake zipped across the lot in his Chrysler. His co-worker that was stuck behind at the shop shook her head, grinning at the crazed man as he rolled out of sight.

Just before arriving at Emily's house, Blake made a last minute decision to make a quick stop over at one of the local Jewelry warehouses. It was a crazy feeling for him that she may just be the one. With her luscious hair and sparkly brown eyes, it was immediate when the young male felt this strong attachment. Blake knew there would be something special from the start. And Christmas would be the day he planned to pop the most important question.

When Blake entered the building, he realized the shop was much more significant than he had thought. It stretched quite a way with well over a thousand shiny items encased in a glass surface. He also noticed about six different surveillance cameras pointing directly at him at the entrance. Right there he knew, it was the real deal.

Blake searched for the one he'd seen before on a website. His hand glided down through the edge of the glass case as his eyes scanned over the huge selection they had in stock.

With some unfortunates, he hadn't found the one he was looking for, but he sure saw something else that was quite eye-catching. A princess cut diamond ring with a silver band.

It was immediately when Blake had it escorted to the register by a worker there. The lady that rang him up from behind the counter smiled and told him, "good luck," just after she had bagged his purchased item.

Blake hadn't said a word back, but he smiled nervously as he was motioning away. He hadn't realized until then about how Emily could turn him down.

Would it be too soon? Blake wondered.

Five minutes later, Blake carefully pulls into the driveway of Emily's home. That's when he hid the bagged ring under the passenger seat before he stepped out of the car.

Soon he had paced his way to her front doorstep, and she'd open up before he was able to knock. He was just about an inch away from touching the door when suddenly, she rushed in with a leap; both legs wrapped around his waist as he staggered from the unexpected weight thrown onto him.

When he reached full steadiness on his feet, Blake motioned his way inside with her still latched onto him. Blake kicked his leg back, shutting the door behind as he made his way over to the living room. Emily noticed Blake was leading her towards the comfy brown couch that sat right below the huge front window. That's when she held on for dear life.

Blake could feel that his knees had been touching the bottom front frame of the sofa. He attempted to slam her on the cushion, but instead, also non-intentionally brought him down with her. Emily chuckled in place as her legs remained around his waist.

Blake found himself to be face planted in her chest. When he lifted his head, he stared into her eyes. At that moment, he smiled a closed lip smile.

Emily cupped her hands behind his neck and pulled him close. Their lips met, and he could feel his chest become a drum pad.

Blake guided his hand to her pelvis, then gradually worked his way inside her Christmas sweater and up to her breasts. They could feel the warmth of their bodies as they continued lip locking, intensely. Blake could feel her tongue working its way around his lips, and their breathing became heavy. The nearly breathless man then moves his front, pressing against her thighs through her tight brown leggings.

Shortly, the two paused. They initially agreed on it being too inappropriate for the living room. The two figured it wouldn't be wise to escalate things on the same couch that

Emily's mother would routinely kick back in to enjoy her favorite Spanish shows after a day in the office.

At that point, Emily gently pushed Blake aside as she hopped out the sofa to lure the male upstairs. And although the two were up in her room, it wasn't for anything explicit. Her room happened to have the only access to the attic, which contained all the decorative items. The snowman, stuffed toys, the wire lightings, the ornaments, and even the huge box that rested the Christmas tree.

With Blake's lean, vein protruding biceps, he gripped the huge box by the handles with slight ease.

"Let's get started," he muttered as a grin formed on his face.

Blake walked the box over to the edge of the staircase and tossed it at the midpoint, then watches it slid the rest of the way down. Emily couldn't help but come up from behind and squeeze his arm. It was something about it that made him laugh.

Going back to her room, they gathered all the things they needed, and that was when the actual fun began. With a Christmas soundtrack playing, they backed each other up by removing the coffee table that sat in the center of the living room and setting it elsewhere. The two then opened up the big box and began setting up the tree near the fireplace. It must've taken at least ten minutes to bend and unwind most of the branches.

Up next was setting up the lights. Emily kicked back at the couch near the window as she sipped on some hot chocolate she'd just stirred up in the kitchen. She watched as Blake was becoming a tad frustrated with the tangled wires. Setting up the lights was Blake's least favorite part as he remembered from his childhood days, but he knew the clear lights would blow his mind away once it's put together and lit up in the night.

Much sooner than expected, he got the job done. The two then moved onto the ornaments. Emily set her mug down on the floor and jumped back in to help by flipping the lid of the carrier open. As she reached into the bin, Blake came from behind to wrap his arms around her waist. He lifted her a foot off the floor and playfully threw her over to the side, having her back on the couch again. Blake flinched his head back as he thought he might've used more force than what he had intended to.

Meanwhile, they joked and giggled through the whole process of decorating by pushing and shoving one another. It became a little aggressive as Emily pushed Blake, using both hands which almost had him fall onto the floor and nearly destroying one of the cheap made, sparkly ornaments he held. Blake released this look of panic in his eyes for a second. It soon made that moment memorable as Emily wrapped her arm around her abdominal as she laughed to the floor.

After about a minute of pulling herself back together, they continued working on the tree. With Blake being a few inches taller than she was, he was the one to hang the majority of the ornaments near the peak. Blake teased her because of it, which had the woman reaching his way to backhand his arm.

Last but not least, the star to go on top. With Emily being as short as she was, Blake did the honor of ducking down and swarming in and under her legs. Using the force of his knees, he lifted her up off the rug like he'd been lifting a barbell as her legs hung off his shoulders.

With a sweet and innocent gesture such as that, a bright smile was brought to her face as she placed the star on top. And with Blake's daring move, he spun her up in the air like a part of a cheerleading routine and catches her with both arms out. Emily panicked a second, and her laughter followed. The young woman gave him a solid punch to the chest, and Blake couldn't help but giggle.

Soon enough, the two realized the white flaky substance that began to sway its way down to the ground again. The view was wondrous through the huge living room window. The only thing unsettling about it for Blake was having to go outside eventually.

They peeked out for a moment longer and enjoyed the sight. It was the first time in years they felt the holiday spirit kick back into them, and they were enjoying every precious second of it.

Night rolled by quickly, and the snowfall hit its end. The curtains closed, the Christmas tree lit up, dim lights in the living room on, and Emily's head nestling on Blake's chest as they shared the recliner. They've been stuffing their faces with their favorite ice cream. They ate straight from a cup sized container. Blake happened to be chowing down on some cookies & cream. Emily, on the other hand, was more of a chocolate kind of person. She devours her chocolate on top of chocolate as brownie bits scattered inside hers.

As they ate away, not minding the mild brain-freeze, their attention was set on the small television as it aired a Christmas classic, the very first Home Alone movie from the nineties. They laughed where they sat, in absolute comfort.

Although Emily's mother was gone most of the day, the house looked as if she'd been away for a week. Everything from pizza boxes, bags of candy, specifically gummy worms, soda cans, and an empty eggnog carton were all laid out on the coffee table.

CHAPTER TEN

Memories

As the two shared a space on the recliner, Emily came up with this splendid idea of sharing a favorite memory they've had together within the last couple of months. Emily was so eager to go first. She didn't need time to think. She'd already had one in mind, and she kept it simple.

Emily brought up the day when she met Blake at the diner. It was when all of her happiness began, as the young woman stated. Emily was using words such as smooth, calm and charming to describe her first impression of him, and that's when Blake couldn't help but smile as he caressed the strands of hair falling over her forehead.

While going against the rules of her own game, Emily quickly transferred onto another memory that popped into her head as opposed to Blake going right next.

In her memory, they were at a water park on a warm summer's day having the time of their lives. Blake was so vulnerable then. She recalled a specific moment when she caught Blake off guard by pushing him off a ledge that sent him smacking in cold water. "Ha, ha!" Blake responded sarcastically.

Emily had to be given a minute to settle as she had been laughing with her hand cupping her mouth. After so, Blake realized then it was his turn.

He kept silent as he looked up at the ceiling, taking a moment to think of a favorite memory. Then, it came to him.

Blake began talking about the night after the day they met, but before that, Emily made herself more comfortable in the chair so that she could listen in more carefully for details. She knew it was going to be a story worth hearing time after time again.

After that day they met at the diner, Blake dialed her up on his cell, and she picked up rather quickly. She's stated once before that it was a surprise to her, for she didn't think he'd call. As for Blake, he didn't think she'd answer.

During their short phone conversation from that night, Blake had asked if she would join him for a little stroll through the city and perhaps get some ice cream.

At first, she seemed hesitant over the phone, and that was when Blake recalled feeling his heart pumping aggressively in his chest. More than a full twenty-four hours passed since Emily had last seen the guy. If anything, she wasn't quite sure what she remembered of him.

Is it worth it? She asked herself.

"Sure, I'll go," the young woman told Blake as he remembered.

Immediately, Blake reached up and squeezed his flushed cheeks downward in attempt to control the broad smile that had overtaken him. It has indeed been a long time since someone sparked his interest near this level.

While still on the line, there came a decision that it would be best to meet somewhere in the city rather than meeting at one's house. It was best to play it safe, they both agreed.

The two then settled that they would meet in front of the diner where she had worked during the time, and to his surprise, Emily was there before him by a minute.

That night, Blake pulled up to the curb in his Jetta. He'd seen her looking his way with a green sweatshirt overlapping her arm. Blake had been feeling crisp-clean in a red t-shirt with his old superman neckless exposed over it, and pair of ripped blue jeans.

Blake approached her, and he couldn't help but look pleased as he was looking into her big, brown eyes.

"I can't believe you showed up," Blake remembered first saying.

"Why wouldn't I?" Emily asked, following up with a grin.

"Come with me," Blake jerked his head to the town sitting beside him, followed by a smooth, half smile.

So, they began their stroll as Blake led the way, guiding her through a crosswalk leading into the next block. They stopped at an ice cream shop a few buildings down as Blake promised. He had ordered himself the cookie dough ice cream in the largest cup size the place had to offer. As for Emily, she requested a small cup of coffee flavor. In a flash, Blake could feel his nose crinkle in disgust since being the coffee flavor would fall in a list of his least likely to choose.

They took it to-go and ventured through the city with no destination in mind. It was side by side, Emily, and Blake. They were chatting it up, quickly becoming comfortable with one another.

"You studying something?" Emily questioned.

Blake gave himself a brief second to think about his answer. "No, I'm very indecisive at the moment. I'm thinking about taking it easy for a little while before even thinking about stepping my foot on another college campus," Blake responded.

The expression she had on her face as her eyes widened told him she had quite the opposite in mind. "What about you?" Blake asked.

"Well," she began, "I love working with kids, and I love helping people out, so I was thinking about becoming a physical therapist. It pays well, so why not?"

Blake grinned at the thought of her becoming one. "That's nice; I can picture it already," Blake told her. "If you are fully committed to it, I don't see how it can be a problem. I know you can do it."

In an instant, she smiled. It was like she needed that bit of encouragement to pursue her goals even further. So far then, she'd been quite impressed with his way of words. They had somehow taken effect on the woman, and Blake had seen it through her eyes.

Just after their little career path discussion, Emily went on to talk about other things. "Do you live with your parents?"

"No, I live by myself in a small two-story rental house. I moved out of my mom's not so long ago," Blake addressed.

"Oh, I see," Emily replied.

"My parents separated when I was seven, but my father died of lung cancer when I was fourteen," he added.

"Oh my, I'm sorry to hear that," she said. "My parents split, too, so I just live with my mom for now."

After Emily stuffed a spoonful of ice cream into her mouth, she proceeded to know more. She asked the one question Blake was sure she'd ask: "What do you look for in a girl?"

The way she mumbled made Blake assume that she was hesitant about asking him. "Well, I look for a girl with ass and brains," he joked.

She laughed. "You're so lame."

"I'm kidding," Blake shakes his head. "I look for that kind of girl who stays at home as opposed to someone who goes out every night. A kind of girl who can be respectful to herself and others. A girl who strives and has a good sense of humor. The ones with big, brown eyes. The ones that I could get lost in every time I look at them."

Emily quickly turned away for a moment. Blake didn't have to look directly to his side to know she'd been hiding a smile. That's when he became confident about being on the right track with her.

Soon he realized the evening had turned into a session of a twenty-one questions game. His mind went blank for a moment. He hadn't gotten an idea of what to ask Emily next, so he retrieved her question over to her. "What about you?" he asked. "What do you look for in a guy?"

She blushed for a quick second as she dipped her head down, staring at her feet as it was advancing slowly down the sidewalk. "Well, muscles are a huge plus," she giggled.

"Interesting," Blake smiled broadly.

"I'm serious," she grinned, nearly laughing again. "I like a guy who is willing to put effort into seeing me and showing me that he cares, so constant reassurance is a big thing for me. I'd like him to fight for me. I need him to win me. I want someone who's a sweetheart, a man who's funny, strong, good with people, intellectual and, of course, charming."

It was at that point on their little date that Blake remembered feeling like she'd been describing everything about him by the sound of her soft voice. It seemed specific.

"Where did you get your necklace? I like it," Emily told him.

"I got it from my dad when I was a little kid," Blake replied. "Superman used to be my favorite superhero. I hadn't worn it much until my father passed away."

"Oh, well, it's an awesome necklace. It's like it has a message behind it as if your dad wanted to remind you to stay strong and have hope," Emily explained.

"That's what I thought, too," Blake muttered before quickly switching the subject. "So what do your parents do?"

"My father was a marine. I'm not sure what he does now," she said. "And my mom is a hotel receptionist."

Nodding his head with an intrigued expression, Blake had simply replied with, "Marine? I respect that."

"And what about kids, you ever thought about having kids of your own?"

"Oh yeah, in the far future," he laughed.

"I like the name Camilla for a girl. It's a weird thing, I know, but that's my wish."

"Is that so?" Blake smiled. "It's not weird at all. I like that name too, maybe not as much as the name Abigail, but it's up there on my list."

Emily laughed at the ground. "You're probably thinking I'm weird for talking about kids. It's just for making conversation."

Blake glanced over at her with all smiles, "It doesn't bother me at all," Blake assured her.

A quick thirty minutes have gone by, and they knew it was that time to call it a night. They met back in front of the diner, and he offered Emily a ride home.

The drive from the diner to her house took approximately five minutes. He pulled the Jetta to the curb up front and was amazed at such beautiful curb appeal. Much wealthier than what Blake was used to.

As Emily reached for the door handle, Blake was quick to say, "I just wanted to let you know that I had a great time with you tonight, in the softest voice."

Blake remembered Emily saying, "I'll see you soon."

At the time, Blake didn't have a clue if she meant it as she was pushing the door wide open. Emily soon dipped her head back in before closing and said, "You should text me when you get home."

"For sure," Blake nodded.

And that was the memory. Emily was very pleased with how happy he looked talking about that night. "It was one of the greatest nights of my life," Blake stated.

Right then and there, Emily smiled as her fingers tapped on his chest like a piano with her head nestled. The two were caught up in a moment as they gazed into each other's eyes when unexpectedly, Emily had come up with this crazy idea as Blake would describe. "Come upstairs with me, I got a little surprise for you," Emily smiled oddly as she was quick to hop out the recliner.

Blake then couldn't help but smile. It was evident he wasn't sure where this would go, but he followed her up the stairs anyway while her hand reached behind for his.

"I don't know about this, Emily," Blake said worriedly. "What if your mom comes home early? and if she catches us up here, she'll kill us."

"Stop worrying," Emily laughed as the two continued stepping upward. "Sometimes in life, you got to do things differently for a different outcome. Otherwise, things will always stay the same, and you'll just end up being disappointed."

"Damn," Blake grinned. "That's an interesting way of viewing things. But I am not seeing the relevancy in that."

Emily looked back at Blake, and expressed a suspicious smirk on her face. Right then, Blake was more concerned about being on the upper level, but at the same time getting this uncontrollable, tingly, growing feeling all inside his pants.

When they stood out front her bedroom door as she slowly twisted the knob, Blake was still unsure what her intentions were, but his heart kept beating fast, and he figured, nothing appropriate could come from sneaking in a bedroom, especially at late hours.

And just as Blake expected, Emily was walking towards the bed, and she sat on the edge with her ankles crossed. She stared straight ahead at the door to see that the worried, but smiley man stuck back a few feet.

"Come here," Emily softly ordered.

Blake did just that. He stepped in slowly and sat right beside her with his legs hanging off the edge of the bed frame. Emily had then faced Blake with a seductive gaze as her fingers had gently crawled up his sweater like a spider to his lips, then she brushed back down to his collarbone to where she'd been stretching the neck hole of his shirt away from his skin.

Emily had then released it. She got up on her feet to push Blake flat on the bed, taking in full control of whatever she had planned.

"Wait right here," Emily told him as she headed over to her small bathroom, closing the door behind her leaving Blake feeling teased on the soft mattress draped in thick blue sheets.

As he lied on the bed staring at the ceiling alone, he rubbed eyes gently to see if he would wake up, from what Blake was expecting to be a dream.

Nearly five minutes later, Blake heard the lock set being unreleased just before the doorknob was twisted open. Right away, Blake flipped his head back up and switched his attention ahead while the bathroom light was immediately turned off.

Once Emily had revealed herself, Blake froze where he sat. Emily had switched out of her comfy clothes and placed something a bit more seductive.

She wore black lacy lingerie with a matching see-through robe. She stepped on over with slow steps with the sway of her hips that nearly gave Blake a panic attack in the best of ways. Blake covered his mouth in amazement. It was evident the man was speechless.

Blake sat up on the bed as she stepped up in front of him. She dropped her robe straight down onto the floor. "You like?" Emily smiled with closed lips.

"Oh, hell yeah," Blake whispered in between her lacy bra cupped breast with lips watered down.

Gently, Emily pushes Blake to lay flat, but he had decided to crawl with his elbows back to the very center of the bed. Emily followed in, growing closer to Blake as he soon switched his attention from her face, over to her rear as he admired the way her body fitted perfectly in her outfit. The young male couldn't help but get his hands on her bottom as she sat just below his waist. She rocked her body slowly against his front, and Blake could feel his heart increasing its speed. He ran his hands up to her breast and crests them in his palms, and her breathing immediately became heavy.

Emily arched her body down to give Blake a wet kiss on the lips.

He pulled back for a second, "This is crazy, Emily," Blake whispered worriedly as he laughed after. "We are going to get caught."

"Just shut up," Emily grinned as she had reached under his shirt to slip it right off.

She swung his t-shirt around until she released it, sending it flying across the room, then placing her fingers on his chest, and slowly guiding them down to his toned stomach.

Emily dipped her head down to kiss on his body when suddenly, Blake pulled her face in to give her a quick peck on the lips. That little bit of contact instantly escalated everything. Blake then smoothly crested the back of her head while they continued lip-locking. He gripped her bottom tightly with both hands as she was lifted up and flipped onto her back for him to climb over.

Emily giggled in total surprise as Blake ran his tongue from in between her breast and down to her waist. Right there he got a hold of the lace-line of her underwear and slowly pulled it off with his teeth. That's when Emily sat midway up as she quickly unclipped her bra and tossed it aside.

Not a minute had gone by before Blake and Emily were naked in her bed while the heavily breathing man slowly thrust on top of her. Her knees pointed to the ceiling as Blake kissed all over her neck. Emily's wide open, heavy exhaling mouth could be sensed through Blake's ear as he continued to work his torso.

Shortly, Emily was on top with the bedcovers hovered over, and Blake stared at her beautiful hair that fell over her face. It was at that moment when Blake realized there were a ton of things to love more about her.

Later, the two laid beside each other, nearly breathless as they gazed up at the ceiling with a silly smile on their face. "So," Emily began. "Was I really your first girl, of doing all of this?"

"Yeah," Blake answered softly. "And does this make me your first, too?"

"Yes." She confirmed. "You're lucky though because I told you we were going to wait until we were married."

Blake then rotated on his side and faced Emily with his palm supporting his head while he gazed straight into her brown eyes. "Don't worry," he told her. "I will never switch up on you, no matter what."

Immediately, Emily simpered as she looked over at his tired eyes. "I love you, Blake. I mean it, and I wish you the best possible future. I want to encourage you to go back to school and get that college diploma."

"That's the plan," Blake promised, and he leaned in for a kiss on the lips.

"I don't know who you think I am, but I am a man of my word, and when I say I'm going to get stuff done I will," Blake said, looking pleased.

"Well good, but you're gonna have to prove that to me," Emily smiled under the covers.

Several minutes later, Blake and Emily got themselves dressed and hung back downstairs again. Emily laughed as she jokingly said, "I think I'll be walking funny tomorrow morning." Blake then couldn't help but grin as he looked back at her.

Shortly after, they got back to resting in that recliner together while the television up front was still on. Soon, Blake got to asking something that was on his mind for a while. "That guy at the diner, are you sure he wasn't more to you than just a friend?"

"I mean, I liked Trevor, but we never really went out like that."

"Really?" Blake asked in total surprise.

"He was a good friend to me, but he was too cocky, and that's like a major turn off," Emily clarified.

"Well, I sure am glad I came in when I did," Blake stated, then he gave a big wet one on her forehead.
Then unexpectedly, a loud bell rang from the dining room, indicating the clock reached its hour mark. It startled the two as they hadn't been keeping track of the time. It was that point for Blake to start making his way out the door. Emily's mother was just starting to head over to the house.

"Oh yeah," Emily laughed. "I set the volume up, so I know when it's time for you to start heading out."

Worriedly, Blake had hopped out the recliner as soon as Emily got off, and no more than a minute later, Blake was at the door, receiving a quick goodbye kiss from Emily. Then he was out.

Meanwhile, miles away, there were quite a few police officers and the agents of the Government Police Program having a stakeout in front of the grocery store near the woods. They'd been there since the morning, all because of what Blake had told Allen.

Sitting in non-conspicuous vehicles, they were all determined to catch Marco before he entered the store. They observed at the front entrance for a male that fits the description. Not a single person that walked through the lot was unlooked. Marco could be disguised as anyone by then.

It was during that late night when they'd spotted a male crossing through the lot with arms tucked in his white shirt, no coat. That was the first exact sign that they had been looking for, "We got him', we got him'!" a person spoke into a walkie-talkie.

The cops immediately took action just after the agents were told to stick behind and remain in their seats.

Several police officers stepped out of the vehicles, and in a flash had their guns raised, pointed directly at the man's back. "Freeze!" a male officer called out with a voice that shook the man walking closer to the entrance.

The startled individual turned around and immediately stuck his arms out, raising them up in the air as the cops gathered closely. Once they all had circled him, they soon realized it wasn't the person they were looking for, It was just some random shopper looking to buy cigarettes and potato chips, and that meant Marco could be anywhere.

"Damn," one of the men in uniform muttered while furiously shaking his head.

A split second later, an orange curly haired officer pulled out his walkie-talkie and spoke clearly into it. "False alarm, Marco is still on the loose."

From the other line, it was evident that Allen was agitated from where he sat in his apartment. "You guys are gonna have to dig deeper," Allen instructed just after he let out a heavy exhale.

With clenched teeth, the orange curly haired officer was short away from slamming his hand-held radio to the concrete ground. "Let go guys!" the curly haired man instructed. "He's not coming. He knew we would be here."

CHAPTER ELEVEN

Veronica Torres

After work the following day, Blake drove home for a quick minute. He switched out of the clothes he'd worn at work and threw on something more formal. After rummaging through his closet, he settled on a short sleeve baby blue button down with extra tightness on the sleeves and a pair of khakis. He kicked off his casual footwear and replaced them with glossy black dress shoes. It didn't take long before he felt more mature, like someone people could trust.

Last but not least, he threw on his favorite gray quarter zipped sweater on top. And that was that. He was ready.

Downstairs, he grabbed the beige folder and car keys from the dining table and sped walked across the house, heading straight out the front door to his vehicle. It was time to make his way to the hospital listed in the file given by Allen. And it was located just a few miles away.

On the way, he began to feel a bit anxious. The last thing he wanted was to discover the woman was utterly useless to his case. He needed all the information he could get. He checked himself in at the front desk and requested the room number the woman was recuperating in. The choleric lady behind the glass said, "Room number, B196."

She rolled her eyes as she slipped him a visitor bracelet beneath the glass slot. His eyebrows pinched together as he wanted to say something harsh, but luckily one of the lovelier nurses took it upon herself to escort him to his desired location. Perhaps she insisted on taking him there because of his charming good looks, or maybe it was part of the job description. Then potentially, it might have just been to get him further away from her rude co-worker. Either way, Blake was glad he didn't have to spend time waiting out on the main floor or waste precious time becoming lost in the great big building.

After traversing several flights of stairs and down the hallway, the woman stopped in the middle and pointed. "There you go. She's right in there."

The nurse walked off as Blake slowly moved closer to the slightly opened door. He could sense that he was a little anxious to see the woman's current condition.

While peering into the room, he could see Veronica lying in bed. She appeared to be sleeping, and still in a critical state with her head all banged up and bruised with colors from purple to green. Her lips were puffy and split down the middle. Her cheekbones were swollen and wounded as well. Who knew how many other injuries ran down her body?

It was a known fact the woman had more injuries than Blake could imagine. A moment passed by, and her eyes flickered open. She saw a man standing outside the door, watching her. She lifted her head for a better view and to convince herself that someone was indeed standing up front. She opened her mouth to speak, but no sound came out. Her mind appeared to have gone blank for a moment.

"Who are you?" she asked, finally.

Blake stepped in.

"Agent Anderson," he said. "But you can just call me Blake."

As he had taken a little closer look at the woman, a nasty feeling started in the pit of his stomach. Whatever it was, it bubbled inside of him. It was sickening for him to believe that someone would beat a woman half to death.

However, despite all the scratches, bruises, and bumps, to Blake, she remained this attractive and innocent looking lady.

As he pulled a seat close beside her bed, she asked, "Are you one of Marco's friends? You here to finish the job for him?"

She coughed uncontrollably, clutching her abdomen. It was apparent to Blake that the woman had suffered several blows to the stomach. "No," Blake answered in response to her question. "But I may be the guy to save you, to find justice, to give you the revenge you deserve. But I am going to need your help, though."

"Is that so?" she choked up for a moment.

She turned her head away from Blake and began to bawl on the spot. He could hear her sniffling away into the aqua blue bed sheets. His mouth dropped half way open; he realized he was at a loss for words.

"It's all my fault," she cried.

Confused, he asked, "Now why would you think that?"

She faced the ceiling, about to open up, but was hesitant.

"What happened?" Blake asked as delicately as a mouse.

She explained how it all happened because she had opened her big mouth. Surprising to Blake, It would appear that Veronica was about to pour out what was on her mind, including the reason she blamed herself for the death of her family.

Veronica licked at the salty tears that had dropped onto her lips. Gradually, she attempted to give Blake an insight into everything she remembered from that night. "After the first time he'd beaten me," she began, "He got locked up for a while, then deported all the way to Mexico. I didn't find out until recently that he had a kid there with someone else. He talked to me about how it bothered him, about the bad things he did over there."

"Now, is that something you can share with me?" Blake asked softly.

"I can try," the recovering woman stated.

Blake listened in more carefully. It seemed she was about to reach the climax of her tale. "My ex-boyfriend wanted to fix things when he came back. Marco led me to believe that he'd changed. To make a long story short, Marco told me a few days ago that it was his fault his son got killed. The son I didn't even know he had. He said it was a mistake, but he never went into full details about it. He never wanted to talk much about the things he did on the other side of the border."

Hearing her side of the story made Blake's blood boil, and he had found out something new, though. The file never mentioned anything about a third child.

"The loss of his son was probably the reason he came back. He needed a place to stay. That moment he told me, I didn't know what to think. He made me promise not to tell anyone."

A short pause later, after taking in a huge gulp, she proceeded. "Later that night, I found myself home alone with the kids. I didn't know where he'd run off to, but I scooped up the kids, got in my car, and drove to his mom's house. While I was over there, I sat her down and told her everything he'd said to me. His mother worried about him. She's always been worrying about him."

Choking up again, she took a moment to pull herself together. The bright ceilings became blurry and digitalized as her eyes welled up. Veronica cleared her throat again, and then went on, "I guess he followed me there because somehow he knew I'd been at his mom's house. And that's when..."

Blake looked down at his shoes, feeling like he was about to break. He knew the direction this next scene was going to play out, and that's what made his teeth clench behind his sealed lips. Blake hadn't realized his fist was ready until the man felt his arm shaking. He immediately releases it and made his hand sprawl on his kneecap.

"Marco came in wearing all black, including a full ski mask. He killed my children. He murdered his mother, and he beat me non-stop," She groaned.

That's when Blake felt more discomfort in his gut. Part of him wanted to cry with her, and a part of him wanted to release his rage on Marco as soon as he gets to him.

"Files state that there were huge holes in the walls of the living room, and in one of the bedrooms upstairs. Not quite sure if he was looking… for something."

"I have no clue," Veronica stated.

CHAPTER TWELVE

The Information

Blake had given Veronica a moment to hold herself back together again. It was an awkward stage for the young male to see a woman who'd been going through so much, and not knowing what to say. He never considered himself to be good with words. His mind would run dry with no complete thought process.

Either way, he began being vocal with the woman with anything little he could spiral up in his head. "It's not your fault. None of it is. It's not your fault Marco turned out to be a criminal."

Shortly, Blake felt a burning sensation in his eyes. He couldn't tell whether it was the lighting, the aroma of the floor cleaners in the room, or that he wanted to ball out with her.

He turned his head to the side, hiding away the face so blue. He took deep breaths till his eyes had gotten better. As bad as he didn't want to bother the woman, some things needed to be said and done. Blake went on requesting as much information as he could get, as much as he was allowed by the woman.

Veronica remained still with her back planted firmly on the mattress and head facing upward in silence. The woman's eyes showed a bit of thought process as she zones into the ceiling. Blake assumed she'd been imaging how that night had played out.

"I'm sorry to keep bothering you, but is there anything you can give me about his whereabouts, like a family members address? A friend's house? Or some hideaway? anything?" Blake asked.

A huge sigh had come out of Veronica. "I don't know why I am telling you all of this. I don't even know who you are. What are you, a cop?"

"Something like that," Blake answered.

"Then what? You ain't shown me no badge, no nothing."

Blake shook his head, not anticipating this type of conversation. He then realized he'd forgotten his badge at the car. "I'm with an agency that works for the police, and I just so happen to be the guy that was sent down here to save you along with the people of the city," Blake informed.

Although the woman didn't seem a hundred percent convinced, she went ahead and gave him his request for answers. She figured what more could she lose. Veronica stated Marco had always been the kind of guy to run away from his problems. The type to disappear for minutes, hours, days even, and then come back home to her as if nothing happened in the first place.

"He likes to hike out in the woods," pausing for a moment, "And spend a lot of time there. It's like he lived there more than our actual home," she said. "I remember him telling me that he would sleep on the ground, against a tree, sleeping away whatever he was dealing with."

"So, after all of this, you think there's a possibility that he's out in the woods right now?" Blake wondered.

"Either that, or he's in some upper-level attic in an abandoned diner."

After that last statement from Veronica, Blake's eyes crinkled in confusion. "Why there?" he asked.

"Besides the fact that it is an abandoned building, it is also one of the cities blind spots. Cameras placed in only half the block. Marco figured no one would bother him there," Veronica explained.

"And he trusted you enough to tell you about it?"

Laughing softly, she said, "It became normal for Marco to avoid problems back at home. He wanted me not to worry about him leaving the house, and that he won't be so far away."

As the woman was sharing this information with Blake, he was feeling more comfortable with the next step to his case as he feels closer to making his final move on the hunt.

With a glowering look, he sets a serious tone in his voice when he asked, "May I know the name of this street?" Veronica had turned her head, facing towards Blake, finally. Right, then and there she had gotten sidetracked. With her mouth halfway open, all that she said was, "wow."

Blake's face crinkled again, "Wow, what?" he asked.

Unexpectedly, the woman complimented the young male's features. Blake immediately felt flattered as he laughed softly with rosy colored cheeks. Veronica then apologized for the little attitude that leaked out earlier. Shortly, she goes on ahead with a voice so light, pointing out to the young male about his level of integrity, and how the woman admired it. Veronica then stated she'd always had trouble putting the right people in her life. "I wish I could have met someone like you," Veronica said.

Blake broke the solemn face he had on and then smirked on the spot. "Oh please, you barely know me," he grinned.

Transferring back to the main discussion that Blake intended to get to from the beginning; she began, meeting him eye to eye and whispers, "I hope you catch him."

She had clenched her eyebrows tightly together. "I pray that you make him suffer as my kids have suffered. I want him to cry as my children have cried." She then raised her voice a little higher, "I want you to look him dead in the eyes and let him know it's his last day to breathe!"

"No worries here. Marco's not gonna like where he's gonna to go next."

It didn't take much for the woman to have faith in him. Veronica faced upward, back at the ceiling again when she thanked the man, looking more relaxed then. She took it as a promise, a pledge that Marco won't see another day. Blake understood her pain. She had so much; it felt as if it was drenching onto him.

Although the broken woman felt as though killing a human being is the way to go, it was still unlawful. Blake was just going to wait till he becomes the target.

"Listen, if you want me to find him, how about that address I asked you earlier?"

Veronica laughed in place, but before she could answer, they were interrupted by a nurse who stepped foot inside the room. A woman in scrubs came in for a little checkup, delivering the best bedside manner as she could. The nurse examined her body language, her pulse rate and notified the woman her food was on its way.

Assuming Blake would stay awhile, the lovely nurse handed him a remote that controlled the small TV that hung in the top corner of the room. He would've rejected, but he wanted to minimize as much useless conversation as possible.

Then shortly after, the nurse had walked out.

Turning his head back to Veronica, he waited for the answer. "Alright," She opened up with a voice whose throat seemed to have been a little clogged.

After taking a huge gulp, she told Blake "It's on Belmont Avenue." Turning her head back to the man, "Belmont Avenue," Veronica repeated. "It should be the only place on the street with a closed diner, I can't quite remember the building number, but it shouldn't be hard to find," She informed.

Instantly, the street name sounded familiar. He was sure he'd heard about it before, but he couldn't put his finger on it. Without anything left in mind to say, Blake announced of his departure. Everything he needed to know, he had then at that moment.

"Thank you for everything," Blake said. "This hunt might be easier than what the police and I have anticipated."

Blake then got up from the chair and hands over the remote. As she reached, she grabbed hold of his hand. While looking up with eyes that quickly enlarged themselves, she stared straight into his eyes, and Veronica warned him of something, "Be careful."

Nodding his head as he gently pulls his hand away, "I will," he told her. "I'll stop by to check up on you," Blake promised as he walked away. And moments later, he disappeared off into the hallway.

CHAPTER THIRTEEN

See You Later

An hour had passed after that little hospital visit, and Blake had this repeated vision in his head of the stare that he was received by Veronica when she told him, "Be careful." The woman was indeed shaken up by any mention of tracking down Marco, which made it certain, Marco deserved first place in the Chicago's most wanted list.

For the time being, Blake decided it was best that he made a quick stop over to the stoner's residents. No one expected him to show. After giving the door a couple of knocks, the mother opened up. Dana appeared to be surprised, yet occupied like she had a busy day ahead of her.

Dana immediately called out to Emily, informing her about Blake's presence.

One look at Emily's mother it would seem as though the woman was ready to head out for another day at the office. Dana had worn her black dress shoes, black dress pants, and a black blouse to go with her red crop top.

Having been that she was dolled up, Blake realized then where Emily had gotten her good looks from, and it was one of those moments where Blake was able to see Emily's smile within her mother's.

Wrapped around her arm were a few documents and papers that looked vital. To keep the conversation short, she announced her departure and stepped through the door frame, giving the male a quick, solid half hug with her free arm. "Sorry I have to leave so soon, but I have to stop by the office right now," Dana told him.

Taking a quick glance back at the mother as she walked over to her Acura TSX sitting in the driveway, he soaked in all the positive energy floating in the air along with the fancy cologne she had on. It was only the second day they'd come across each other and Blake evidently felt accepted. He'd been surprised that Emily's mother allowed the two to be alone in the house together. There was no greater feeling than that. He felt trusted.

Blake stepped foot inside as he shut the door behind. No more than a second later, Emily came sprinting with arms wide open.

Blake wrapped her tightly in his arms, and he dragged it on. This one was different, Emily thought to herself. This one felt more powerful, and a little bit tighter, almost as if he'd not seen her in the longest time, or like he'd been going away for a while. Emily was ready to release, but Blake held on for another moment longer.

Soon he dropped his arms down, and he gazed into her eyes. "I'm going to miss you, beautiful," he said.

Caught off guard, Emily gave Blake this look of confusion. Her eyebrows pinched midway as she said, "Going to miss me, where are you going?"

Right then and there, Blake shook his head with utter word misplacement as if he were rewinding the last couple of seconds. "No," he paused. "I meant to say that I've been missing you, and I am going to miss you again and again, and again."

Emily slowly rocked her head back and forth, going along with what he was saying. She followed it with a soft laugh, although it wasn't genuine. It was just her way of convincing Blake that she believed.

Getting sidetracked for a moment, they could hear the weather forecaster from the television in the living room mentioning a Chicago snowfall. It stated that the area could expect a couple of inches of snow later in the evening. Snowfall can be a great thing, but for those two, they'd had enough in one week.

He remained looking hypnotized as he stared off into the television. Emily called for his attention, followed by a few snaps of her fingers an inch away from his ear. The male flinched, nearly swiping her arm away. Emily then began asking for the reason for his unexpected arrival with squinted eyes as she raises suspicion.

Blake smiled with closed lips and said in a gentle voice, "I just wanted to stop by and see you, maybe even sit down and have a cup of coffee with you."

Emily tilted her head for a second with her lips pressed tightly together. For a moment she hadn't had a clue as in what to say afterward. The twenty-one-year-old woman was not exactly sure if Blake had been telling the whole truth, but for the second time, she went along with it.

A bit after, she grabbed hold of his left hand and pulled him into the kitchen. Brewing enough for the two, they sat across from each other at the small kitchen table with mugs in place on some coasters. The young woman informed him about the level of stress she'd been having since the start of her day. It was all because of the first final which would begin in no later than an hour. Her mind was completely chaotic inside, and Blake could see it through her eyes. Emily had got to the point where she'd been asking Blake silly things like, "What if I don't pass? What if I can't move to the next level? What if I don't make it?"

Of course, after her minor meltdown, Blake persuaded her into thinking positively. "No worries," he said, "Once you see that test, you're going to feel a lot better. I know you're gonna do just fine."

"Thank you. Means a lot to me, Blake," Emily responded after taking a sip of her coffee.

Thirty minutes went by of Blake helping Emily with her studies, enjoying much laughter along the way, when

Blake decided to head out. He kissed Emily on the forehead goodbye and slowly motioned away while staring into her eyes for another long second. "I love you, darling," he said.

As she stared right back, she retrieved the same message to him. Then out he went.

Emily stuck back beside the closed door as she worried about him of his strange behavior.

Later that day, Blake drove to the gravesite to come across his father's tombstone while daylight slowly faded into night.

All the way from his last visit, Blake's Superman necklace still hung on the cross, and he was quite impressed. Blake figured it would've been long gone by then. With a dejected look on his face, he reached to smother his fingers on it, and he then smiled for a brief second. Why does death feel so near? He wondered. Blake couldn't help but think going after Marco would mean guns would go ablaze.

"Someday I'll get to see you again, Dad," he muttered to the stone right below him as he was kneeled down on the icy ground. He had then stared off into the carved stone for twenty minutes straight as the winter breeze picked up. Then it was back on the road again.

CHAPTER FOURTEEN

Belmont Avenue

The night was approaching quickly, and Blake felt strongly about the possibility that Marco would be at that vacant diner. He hadn't heard anything from the Philippines living in the cabin in the woods, so that brought up the percentage that he may be hiding somewhere in the upper level.

With the snow beginning to fall lightly, there was no way Marco would spend hours outside. He would most likely be in some form of shelter. All the more signs he was there, and Blake was starting to feel big-headed.

Blake threw on a bulletproof vest over his white V-neck, then his favorite quarter zip sweater right above it. He soon pulled out his gun that was tucked away in his bedside, checking to clarify that there were all nine bullets inside, even though he was sure he hadn't wasted a shot recently. After doing so, he clipped his gun together and slipped it into the belt strap that he decided to use for the night.

As he searched within his cluttered closet, he had picked up a black duffle bag. He threw the strap over his shoulder and traveled downstairs into the basement. As soon as he reached the bottom, he flipped up the switch on the wall.

A light filled the room, and there was a vast area of nothingness. All that was there was a desk, upon which rested Blake's father's old tools, and a few feet from that was a huge, thin-structured, wooden crate lying on the concrete floor. It

had been there since August; a raffle made by Agent
Johnson. Allen had also shipped the same winning prize to a
few others as well.

Up until this day, Blake had not open to see the
beauty that rested inside, but he knew what lied inside, and
Allen was very much the one person that could access the
hundreds that hung on a rack at the station.

Taking a quick look, Blake estimated the wooden
crate to be about three feet high, five feet in length, and
approximately two feet in width. At that moment, it became
evident that it was the day to open it up, finally.

Blake walked over to the tool desk and picked up a
wrench. It was shortly after when he stood in front of the
crate to begin popping the top loose, detaching many hinges
around it.

Promptly, he forcefully flipped the lid off to the side as
it came smacking loudly against the concrete floor while an
echo-filled the room. And with such pace, Blake moved
along, popping all four sides and disconnecting the hinges
with ease.

At last, there that beauty rested on a little display
mount: a black-coated sniper, almost ready to be put to use.
He took a slow step forward and reached his arms out inside,
gripping the gun from both ends just as he gently lifted it up
from its base. Blake held it upward, straight from his face as
he stared through the eyepiece. He felt secured and
confident. His first thought was, powerful and deadly. Just
owning one of these things had made him feel like a beast,
and he was about to roll out.

After he had loaded six rounds into his sniper, Blake
quickly stuffed it into his duffle bag. He had bent the little
stand that came with it into shape and packed it in as well.

He zipped the bag shut, and took it along with him up
the stairs and into the trunk of his car. He had then swiftly
hopped into the front seat as he started up the engine to let it
run awhile. As the inside slowly heated up, the young fellow

whipped out his phone and wrote a quick text to his lover, a little piece of motivation, wishing Emily the best of luck on her finals.

After he allowed enough time to let the Chrysler warm up, he drove out for another adventure of the day. To Belmont Avenue, he went.

On his way there, rather than thinking about all the terrible things that could happen within the next few minutes, Blake was mainly thinking about coming home to Emily and celebrating their accomplishments.

With only ten minutes out driving, Blake had made it to his destination. Instead of parking out front or anywhere near the building, he parked his Chrysler on an entirely different block, on the street to the left of Belmont alongside a curb of some old building and an alleyway that could lead him directly to the block he needed to be.

It was a small town. Most of the buildings connected and stood up the same height as one another. Blake hopped out the car and noticed just how quiet the area was around him. Blake closed his vehicle door beside him with slight force and began to take a short walk.

He had cut in between the two brick buildings and got onto Belmont. The only thing then left to do was walk down the street and find the closed diner.

An easy task for the young man it was. Not a minute went by, and he'd found the place. One look at the building, he noticed the bottom windows were boarded up, but the upper level wasn't. Blake took the next moment to get down to business as he quickly pressed his body against the brick wall to not allow anyone to see him from the windows above.

As quietly as he could, he opened the front door and whipped out his gun from his side. Secondly, he had slipped out his phone to use as a light source and scanned the dark room. There was no sign of anybody inside; the bottom floor was still. There was just a bunch of old dusty tables and a long stretch bar in the back. Very few bottles of fine liquor left on the shelf behind it. There was a good chance the drinks had not yet expired. The man was tempted to give them a try; he kept eyeballing the glasses just as he scanned the room from top to bottom, left and right.

To the left was a staircase against a wall of faded yellow floral design wallpaper. Blake looked straight up from the bottom. Suddenly, he got an odd feeling in the pit of his stomach, and his heart began to pound irregularly. He was having this sense of paranoia again. The last thing the man wanted was to make himself vulnerable to a surprise attack.

Moving upward on those creaky steps, Blake made sure that if anyone else were to be in the building, they know of his arrival. About halfway way up the staircase, he called out, "Hello!"

Seconds later, a small wooden creak came from the upstairs. It instantly caught Blake's attention. Right then, his eyes widened like a cat's senses, and he called out again, "If you're up there, we have to talk!"

Blake remained still with his pistol pointed upward, waiting for a response, or even another sign of movement at least. He gave it another few seconds when suddenly, he heard a clearer creak sound. At that moment, it became apparent that something was up there and moving.

CHAPTER FIFTEEN

Upper Level

Blake proceeded up the stairs with red flags that flashed in his head. Three-quarters of the way up, he realized that there was lighter bleeding through the upper-level windows from the light poles shinning across the street.

When Blake reached the top, he slowly stepped foot inside the room. He happened to have stumbled across an area with multiple support beams and columns in the area. There may have been about six columns, two rows of three to be precise and parallel with each other with at least eight feet of space in between the rows. There were a few more of those small, circled tables scattered around the room all draped with white cloth. The wooden floors appeared to be dated and filthy with dust and shoeprints all over, and the prints all seemed to have been made by the same person.

As he proceeded forward, he noticed that nearly every step he took caused a loud creak sound, making it that much harder to sneak around. It was the very reason he had given himself away in the first place.

Blake continued to move in with caution as he scanned the area from left to right, pointing his weapon in all different directions with his finger ready on the trigger. He shifted to the left and took a look beyond one of the columns. Blake then spotted a man standing by one of the windows. The person had his back facing Blake as he gazed through the glass, looking over the beautifully lit city. His shaved head and tattoos exposed on both of his arms told Blake one thing, it was indeed, Marco. The familiar ink job of the name 'Amelia' that spiraled around his forearm made sure of it.

Blake stepped a few feet closer, but still kept his distance, then he called out to him. The tall man in front of the window ignored him, and that was one sure way of ticking off Blake.

The young man had gone for another attempt, "Marco!" he called out. "You have to come with me. The police and I got a couple of questions for you."

Marco's ears pushed upward like a reaction to a cat's sensitive hearing. This time Blake was sure he had projected loud enough. There was like this switch that had gone off inside his head. Blake had immediately gotten agitated.

On the third attempt, Blake spoke even clearer, "Marco!"

He paused for a quick second. "You speak English? Come on. Let's go. They're waiting for you down at the police station!"

The sound of the wind shook the old wooden-framed windows. It was the only thing they could hear in a moment of silence between the two. At that instant, Blake looked beside him in both directions to be sure Marco hadn't gotten a couple of friends with him, Tony Garcia, and Tommy Banks from the ambush scene. Marco was appearing to be calm for being alone in a room with a gun being pointed at him.

Breathing in through his nose, Blake held himself back with all of his might as he was tempted to pull the trigger. There was nothing more aggravating to him than some no good man disobeying his direct orders. He had thought of everything terrible Veronica had told him about Marco, and it should have been enough for him to tackle the wanted man down, directly.

Suddenly, Blake seemed to have got the crazed individual's attention. Marco rotated his head slowly as his traps protruded even more through his black tank top. When his head was halfway around, he first uttered, "Did that bitch tell you where I was hiding?"

With an opener such as that, Blake was caught off guard. It took more than a few seconds to come up with something to say, until he belatedly replied, "No, no one told me. It was just that easy to find you."

"Kind of hard to believe a person who pretends to be a cop. Now, I know that bitch told you where I was." Marco spoke with an increasing tone of his voice.

"Doesn't matter," Blake said. "Either way, you're coming with me so please just put your arms behind your back and do not try anything."

Although Blake had presumed this man would not follow his instructions so swiftly, he thought it'd be worth a try. Either way, it was a part of the job procedure.

The older, intimidating man had not attempted to comply with Blake's commands, and remained by the window, peering out while the snow plummeted to the street below.

"Chances are she's kept in a hospital bed still," Marco muttered. "I should've finished her off myself. I knew her dumbass would snitch. I ain't stupid."

Blake cringed at Marco's last statement. His foul mouth was like the Earth's rotation, it never stopped. "Look," Blake began. "She didn't tell me anything. Now do as I say and there won't be any further problems."

Finally rotating full way around, Marco began to stare straight ahead at Blake with a clenched fist and pinched eyebrows. "So, you're just going to lie to me like that?" Marco asked. "You that same punk I've seen out in them woods!"

"Yeah, that was me. So what? I've found you, and now you're gonna have to leave with me," Blake addressed for what felt like the twentieth time.

"You see? Veronica done did snitch on me, telling you where I'd be! She's the only bitch that knows where I stay," Marco explained in an aggressively increasing tone in his voice. "There's no use for you here. So how about you turn the hell around, and don't come back."

"I'm afraid I can't do that. You left a woman with nothing. You killed everyone except her, why is that?" Blake wondered.

Marco's nose creased while his eyebrows pinched. "I'm through with you guys, all this cop bullshit, pretending like you guys are doing the world a favor. Y'all don't help me for shit. Just get out of here. Don't make me have to knock you out!"

Evidently, the tension rose quickly, and Blake could feel it spreading in the air like storm clouds. His one focus at the moment was not to press the trigger, just yet.

"Just knock it off!" Blake raised his voice. "I'm trying to help you, sir, don't make this difficult for me!"

"Where's your badge?" Marco wondered.

"Wanna see it?" Blake asked as he was about to reach behind his back pockets.

"Don't do that shit," Marco demanded.

"I was just trying to show you my badge, sir."

"Try anything, and Veronica will be dead too," Marco blustered, followed by a heavy breath release through his nose.

Blake took a step closer.

"Don't," Marco instructed. "You come any closer, you'll be a dead man," he warned.

Blake had no intention of fully listening to the crazed man. The young male went against Marco's warning by gaining a few extra steps closer. That's when Marco threw his arms behind him, reaching in for something, fast paced.

Blake had no choice but to lift his weapon up at chest level. At that moment Blake's heart had felt the rush of adrenaline.

As Blake attempted to aim his pistol directly at the man's face, Marco whipped out his firearm and shot two rounds towards him. With Blake's quick reflexes, he dropped himself to the floor and quickly presses down on the trigger, twice. Blake landed on his bottom, both missing their marks by an inch as Marco was quick to have shifted over and ducking right. The bullets chipped the brick wall behind Marco as he tensed up his body.

In an instant, Blake rolled over to his right as he continued to get fired at by Marco who hadn't been watching where he was shooting at, having Blake scrape his knees on protruding nails while doing so.

The room sounded like a dozen firecrackers going off at once. Blake was headed for the column on his right, dodging multiple bullets as it smacked loudly against the hardwood. The man could practically feel the vibration of the floors as he rolled through. Blake soon reached what he considered his safe zone, but it was only safe for a matter of seconds.

While Blake hid behind the column, Marco continued to fire without any leverage. The bullets smacking against the column had Blake feeling the vibration running down his back once again. Blake witnessed chunks of wood being blown out from behind. At that point, he was surprised to be still alive, yet he was beginning to feel he might get hit at any moment as the column was chipping into nothing.

One for sure thing was, Blake had to act quickly, so he reached for a small table on his right and used that extra bit of force from his arms to knock it down on its side, and roll it to the left part of the room.

While the table wheeled on its side through the floor, Blake dived behind it, moving along wherever it led him.

Marco fired three remaining bullets at the surface as the steel rounds bled through the top of the furniture. It was such a relief he was still in one piece. It worked. He made his way over to another column. As Blake made himself invisible, hiding behind another one of his safe zones, he slowly maintained his breathing in the intense fire out.

Marco repeatedly pressed on the trigger, but no bullets were spewing out. It was all just clicking sounds. To Blake, it seemed like he'd been out, and that was a good sound to him. That's when he took his chance to get back at the crazed man.

As fast as Marco could, he ran straight to his right as he made his attempt to escape through the other access door that Blake hadn't witnessed before. Blake shifted his body out from behind the column as quickly as he could and began to fire at Marco, but the man too fast. Marco busted out the door and to a staircase that led directly to the main floor.

Blake furiously hammered his fist into the column with the gun still in his hand. Allen wasn't kidding when he stated Marco was a runner. There was no way Blake was letting him off that easy, so he went after him.

"Crap! You're not gonna run away from me," Blake spoke with a face of determination.

CHAPTER SIXTEEN

Nightfall

By the time Blake reached the staircase, Marco had already made it to the bottom. He ran across the main floor and headed for the entrance and began to run through the snow-filled street as Blake followed.

With weapons fully exposed in their hands, the two had not a single care for who saw. No motor vehicles were rolling by, and no pedestrians in sight. Everyone appeared to have been locked and cuddled up in their homes or staying late at the office as the weather worsened by the minute.

Running as fast as they both could, the snow annoyingly plummeted their faces, nearly blinded them. Shortly, it occurred to Blake that he was out of bullets too. As he ran fast, he checked the weapon chamber for certainty. Empty. Just his luck.

Blake continued to chase him down about a block and a half straight, till Marco decided to change his course. He turned left, running in an alley between two brick buildings. Coincidentally, it was the same shortcut Blake had crossed through earlier to get to Belmont. The crazed man cut through the street up ahead just after passing Blake's Chrysler and ran into another alley, only this time, there was a dead end of solid red bricks as the walls shared in the back. For a second, Marco panicked as he looked all around for an escape. So far, Marco's only alternative was to hide and take cover behind a huge green dumpster that leaned beside the building on the left.

It became apparent to the young man that Marco was fooled. As easy as it may have seemed for Blake to walk down that alley and take him down directly, there was an odd, uncomfortable feeling about it. In the back of his mind, Blake couldn't help but think that it could be a setup. For all he knew, Marco could have been loading up his pistol chamber at that very moment.

One downside, Blake hadn't prepared himself with a spare magazine loader on him. For then, he just had to play it safe and play it smart, and it sure was a good thing Blake parked where he had. He shifted himself a few feet to the right to pop his trunk and quickly toss his pistol inside, although he knew his spare rounds was sitting inside. Instead, Blake reached for his duffle bag and threw the strap over his shoulder.

Just as Blake quietly shuts the trunk closed, he continually looked beside him into the alley across the street as he hunches back over to the shortcut where he had just come out from and stood beside a rusty, steel ladder nailed to a brick wall of some three-story building.

As he looked up, it seemed that people had access to the rooftop. It was without a second thought when Blake decided to climb up the ladder as fast as he could with the added weight from the bag. The ice beneath his feet was limiting his speed. With each footing, he made sure to grip the bars firmly to prevent a nasty slip. As he continued climbing, Blake paid close attention across the street on his left to be sure Marco didn't attempt to escape, let alone poke his head out from the dumpster to see what Blake had been doing.

After making it all the way to the top, there must have been at least two inches of snow beneath his feet. He tossed the bag down and lugged it through the winter mix. He began losing feeling in his ankles, but that was the least of his worries.

Straight ahead he noticed a brick border that rose about a foot high that wrapped its way almost entirely along the perimeter of the building. It served a purpose for the young male as he planned on posting out for a while. What a shame Blake wasn't able to enjoy the fantastic view from above like the man would have rather done. Instead, he had to pay close attention to one particular spot with no estimate of how long it would take.

When he stepped closer to the front ledge wall, he kept an eye out onto the street below. It was the perfect place to settle. It had all the right vantage points he felt he needed, and right away, Blake got down to business. He kneeled down to unpack as he consistently watched over the ledge wall and on over to his unfastened bag.

He then whipped out the sniper rifle, which was a minor struggle. Blake thought he had almost needed to tear the opening further apart to free the weapon.

One sure thing, Blake was confident Marco had still been hiding behind the dumpster. He was feeling right about the next step to the improvised plan. There was only one way for Marco to get out, and that was walking back out into the street.

"When he comes out, he can kiss his legs goodbye," Blake muttered with an impish grin as he quickly unfolded his little weapon stand.

He then sets the weapon stand up to the approximate height of the ledge, and everything in that moment became all too fascinating to him. He had this smile as though he was able to collect the prize by the end of the day, and maybe even sail off to a beach with lovely Emily by sunrise.

Swiftly, he had set his sniper on top, and he then put himself in a comfortable kneeling position. When he peeked through the eyepiece of his sniper, he adjusted the angle of the weapon in between the two buildings. At that point,

Blake unintentionally had this grin on his face. He couldn't hide it even if he wanted to.

While expecting Marco to make a run for it very shortly, there was this taste of victory sitting at the tip of his tongue, and the man was enjoying every second of it. It was as if the money was practically his already, Blake could feel it. It was just a few moments away.

Blake could picture himself on a cruise ship, sailing off into the Pacific with no destination in mind. Just Emily and him, enjoying the warm weather, the ocean view, and the beautifully lit, pink sunset with just the right music blasting in the background. Indeed, in his fantasy there were people on the ship as well, but Emily was the primary focus. It had almost seemed perfect. All Blake needed to see was his woman smiling back at him.

"Come on," Blake murmured as he focused the clarity of his weapon. "Whether you become sleepy, hungry, thirsty, or have to take a shit, you're gonna have to come out eventually."

Time and time went on, and he had become a tad impatient as he could feel the adrenaline rush creeping underneath his skin again. "Come on you sick, bastard," he mumbled as his finger itched to pull the trigger.

Momentarily, he perceived the snowflakes that began to fall delicately from the sky which proceeded to smack against his face, irritatingly. With his hand, he had to wipe across consistently, and he hadn't realized how cold his cheeks were until then.

Without expecting a sign of movement the very next second, Marco must have finally built up the courage to make himself visible to the city. He popped out of the alley, and halted right out front, looking both directions. Right then and there, Blake quickly adjusted his vantage point to the man's knees as his eye sockets became huge and breathing became heavy.

Blake must have had an overload of excitement since, by some misfortune, he managed to tip his sniper over the ledge, but with his quick reflexes, he caught it with the tip of his finger. Somehow he got a hold of it by the trigger handle with his middle finger. That's when the gun sounded into the Chicago sky, nearly shooting himself in the head.
One bullet wasted, there was no doubt Marco didn't hear a weapon just go off. At that moment, Marco was making another run for it. He was unsure of where the gunfire had come from, and that's when the crazed man felt he needed to move in any direction.

As he witnessed Marco running down the broad sidewalk at such speed, Blake quickly pulled his weapon back up and held the back end against his face again. With shaky kneeling posture, his gun followed the man precisely. Blake had this look in his eyes as he hesitated to press his finger down. With each passing second, he could feel his heart pounding with more force in his chest. Soon, Marco turned left, leaping onto a door of some building. As the runaway man reached for the handle, it was that time for Blake to make a final decision on whether to take the shot.

Struggling with the door handle for a second, Marco got it to open. As Blake took a huge gulp, his index finger quickly pressed down on the trigger as he targeted towards the center of Marco's back.

As the crazed individual flipped the entryway barrier wide open, Marco jolted inside. The loud thunderclap of the sniper sounded, and for some strange reason, the tattooed man shifted his body to the left, as if he'd been getting out the way of something else. Somehow Blake was confident the bullet had made contact, but not with Marco. Blake watched as his mind processes it in slow motion.

It would appear to Blake that a woman bystander with shopping bags had dropped onto the floor a few feet ahead of a blue carpeted staircase as Marco reached for another door right beside it. It couldn't be, could it?

Blake didn't want to say it, but all signs pointed in a negative direction.

Everything in that moment was going fast. The front door was closing behind Marco, and he was losing sight of the inside. With eyes that bulged out of its socket, Blake began to have this immediate sick feeling inside. He began expressing this panic look on his face as his breathing had gotten worse. And suddenly, Blake had this urge to throw up. He kept thinking to himself that something was not right; something went wrong, terribly wrong.

"Oh no," the man's voice shook as he slowly looked away from the eyepiece of his gun.

Soon enough Blake ditched his sniper out on the rooftop and rushed down the ladder. As the perturbed male made his way down, he'd hope that nothing played out like how he thought he'd seen it.

The young man was in such a hurry that he hadn't checked both ways before crossing the street. A stranger in a minivan passing by had almost side swapped Blake as he did not react to it. Blake just kept it moving while the driver annoyingly tapped onto their horn.

Quickly, the concerned man reached out for the door handle, and Blake realized then that it was much harder to swallow. Upon entering, he looked down at his hand as it shook against the handle. He'd been struggling to keep it steady, but just after twisting the knob fully, he realized it was then that time for the moment of truth.

Blake opened up slowly, but something had stopped it midway. He took his time to poke his head in to see what had been blocking the door from opening properly.

Taking a look down below to see that a woman was indeed lying flat on the floor, cupping her chest with both hands while bleeding out, the man had this instant paralyzed feeling in the knees. Using a bit more force, the man carefully squeezed himself through and stepped over to kneel beside the woman.

Glancing near her heart to what was no doubt a bullet wound, Blake's assumption led him to think he had caused her incident.

"Oh my god," he whispered in panic.

A thought had crept into his mind that she looked familiar from somewhere. Then Blake realized it was Emily's mother. Hit with double the shock Blake was in fear for his life.

In a fast-paced moment like this, it was hard to tell who the woman was at first with her eyes welled up and with the blood smears on her cheeks.

Tears quickly filled his eyes. With one arm he reached out for hers. He held on tightly to Dana's drenched hand as he took a moment to sob loudly. Shortly, Dana began choking on her blood.

"Oh God," Blake panicked as he attempted to roll her on her side. "Don't worry. You're going to be ok! You're going to be ok. I am going to get you help."

With his free hand, Blake reached for the phone in his pocket. Luckily for him, he had emergency help on speed dial. One push of the button and Blake's automatically connected to a nine-one-one operator.

With a voice that shook, he reported the incident, leaving behind the part where he'd been the one behind the gun. Blake instructed them that medical assistance needed to be on their way as quickly as they could. Blake then paused, sealing his lips as he was breathing in and out through his nose to have a decent steadiness in his voice as he remained on the line.

Blake gave the operator the address of his current location. He then waited as he stared at the woman whose eyes continued to drown in tears.

Shortly after being notified that help was on its way, Blake quickly shut down his phone and slipped it back into his pocket with blood smears on his hand.

"Blake," the woman muttered in total confusion.

"What? What is it?"

Dana was having trouble keeping her eyes open, and Blake's head had been covering the LED lights like a solar eclipse. She was losing visual quick.

"My daughter means the world to me. Please take care of my baby," she begged.

Dana faced towards Blake as she looked straight into his eyes. She begged him again, "Please?"
Blake shut his eyelids as a stream of tears fell from his right eye. He nodded his head, and told her, "Of course."

As Blake took a moment to wipe his nose across his shoulder, he noticed a big yellow shopping bag that had been kicked over to the corner along with her work papers. The bag appeared to have a wrapped gift or two in it.

"Do one more thing for me," Dana opened up. "Tell my little girl, that I love her. And not to worry about me."

"Yes, of course," Blake promised.

Then, he looked straight at the center of the woman's chest as a blood puddle built on it. The nasty feeling of wanting to vomit kept creeping up in his system. There was no separate explanation. He caused all of this.

The young male could see it happening now, going from the hunter to the hunted. His mind had become insane. Blake imagined the next few weeks, years even, tucking and hiding away from the world. He figured hibernating somewhere in a cave, or hiding out in a ditch somewhere would be reasonable, but that plan meant excluding Emily from his life, forever.

Squeezing tightly in his hand she gasped for air, "Help me," she said. Putting an even tighter squeeze, she repeated herself, "Help me," then she was cut off, she was out. Her eyes shut, and not a single part of her body was moving. Blake began to panic more, internally. With both arms, he reached out for the woman's shoulders with high raised eyelids and then began to shake her around a bit.

"Don't!" he screamed. "Wake up! Emily needs you. Your daughter needs you!"

"Dana, I-"

Interrupted by the sirens which startled the man, he could see the flashing red and white lights creeping beneath the door. Blake immediately tucked in two of his fingers into the wound to scissor up the easily traceable shell. He gagged as he slightly dug into her chest, and with some more unfortunates, he couldn't reach. His stomach reflexes and the limited time made him stop. The man pulled away as he gawked at the body, then he heard the commotion from the people outside.

While he paid close attention, it seemed as though the paramedic's group were rapidly approaching the door. That was the moment he had let go of the woman's hand and began making his escape. Blake headed for the other door, the same in which Marco escaped from as he used the sleeve of his sweatshirt to twist the knob open. Then he disappeared behind it.

CHAPTER SEVENTEEN

Terrible News

Ten thirty that night, Blake was sitting just across the emergency room on an old metal bench. Worriedly, he waited as he held onto his favorite quarter zipped sweater, balled up in his left hand. Blake hadn't noticed the tiny blood stains on it before entering with it. He'd only abandoned his bulletproof vest in his vehicle just before putting his sweater back on, therefore, inside the center, he had tightly clench onto the fabric to keep the quarter zip from unfolding.

As Blake shook in his seat, the male thought to himself how everything had pinned out a while ago, about the talk between Marco and him, and of course every bullet they zipped out of their firearms. But somehow, the paranoid individual was led to believe that there was a chance she'd still be alive in there. And he was right, but perhaps not for long. Emily's been inside the room with her mother, already. One downside is that the workers weren't allowing any others in at the time.

The same nauseating feeling kept sneaking its way into his system. At that point, Blake leaned back where he sat and tilted his head against the wall. While doing so, he shuts his eyes for a second as he took a couple of deep breaths. Steadily, the young male could feel it working, but what he wanted to happen was to hear that Dana would be ok.

As he remained seated for a moment longer, Blake heard the door up front opening up. Immediately, he dropped his head down and set his attention directly on the doctor who'd been exiting the room. The male wore those dark blue scrubs, holding a clipboard against his ribcage.

The doctor stepped up, standing in the center of the hall as he stared straight down at Blake in silence. After he had briefly analyzed the look on the professional's face, it told him enough. Whatever was about to come out of his mouth was all just terrible news. "Do you have any relations with Dana Stoner?" the doctor opened up.

"No, Sir," Blake answered.

"Well, unfortunately, we cannot allow any other visitors inside the emergency room at this hour. We're bending the rules a bit by having someone in there right now. I'm sorry."

Instantly, Blake got up off the bench. "She's practically my mother in law, and my girlfriend is inside with her," his lips quivered.

The troubled man shifted his head slightly to the right as he attempted to peek within the small square window on the door. From his angle, Blake couldn't see inside all that well, but he noticed the massive machine that operated on Dana but had not been able to spot her.

"I think you should really let me in. My girlfriend needs me," Blake begged.

Surprisingly, it didn't take much for the doctor to agree to the terms of letting the desperate man gain access inside. Right away, Blake made his way around him as he aimed his hand for the doorknob.

"Hold on for a sec—" the doctor commanded.

Blake then paused in front of the door as he had dropped his hand down, to face the person with all the answers he was hoping to get shortly. After the professional had taken a little gander at his clipboard, he had dropped his arm off to the side, and he says, "It's about that time to open the curtains and let through whatever is in store for us next, as I always say."

Blake gawked in confusion, not exactly sure what he had meant by it, but it slowly began to make sense as the doctor went on. "I can no longer bury the truth from Emily. I'm afraid it's that time to prepare ourselves for the unfortunate, Sir."

Blake immediately dropped his head down to the bright white marble tiled floors. He shook his head, and then asks the doctor, "How much of a chance does she have?"

"Looking at it this way, my workers and I are doing the best of our ability in a situation like this to help her pull through. Whoever shot her was looking for a way to kill her instantly."

At that very moment, Blake had the feeling he wanted to spew all over the polished floors. Blake could feel the nasty intensity settling in his throat.

"Surprisingly, we were able to get her heart pumping again," the doctor stated. "Dana is unresponsive at the moment, and my workers and I can only keep her insides unclogged for so little at a time, that is until she passes out again. She's experiencing a Tracheal Rupture with more severe issues within' the wound. The impact tore a massive hole through her windpipe causing an excessive amount of blood to be released, making it difficult for her breathe. I need you to understand that our procedure is a messy one."

"How much of a chance she got then?" Blake asked for the second time.

After he let out a heavy exhale, the doctor spoke in a way that he could only do to a seemingly desperate man. "Well, looking at the results, and if I have to give out a percentage, I'd say she realistically got about a five percent chance of making it. The machine that is currently operating on her is the only thing keeping her alive right now. My co-workers and I are talking about just letting her go through with it until she no longer can. I'm sorry."

After the last statement from the doctor, Blake couldn't help but blurt out, "No!"

His voice startled the doctor, having him flinch a step backward. "You're going to do whatever it takes to save her! You must save her!" Blake begged.

At that moment, Blake's expression exposed fury as he stared directly into the doctor's eyes. "Look, I'm doing the best of what I could do," the man informed.

As the professional went on, Blake had gotten into shock mode, and that's when he had heard unusual things come out of the doctor's mouth.

Blake somehow managed to hear the doctor yell, "No! It's your fault! You shot her!"

Blake flinched his head back, confused, but somehow knew the man in the scrubs wasn't speaking in such a way. It was as if his evil conscience possessed the doctor.

The man had then stepped up closer to Blake with eyes deadlier than a psychopath's and says, "You shot her, you took that shot, and now she's going to die! You're never going to see her again!"

Blake had tuned back into reality for a moment as the doctor was seemingly gentle with his words, "I'm sorry for this uneventful situation you have on your shoulders. If there was a way, believe me, I would go for it."

Having entered into shock mode again, "She's gonna die! That poor woman is going to die, and you are going to have to live with that for the rest of your miserable life!" A short pause later, he heard, "Emily will leave you if you're lucky, or maybe she'll just kill you herself," the man grinned.

Blake again snapped back to reality, and the doctor softly finished up with, "The best thing I can do for you is to tell you to walk straight into that room," pointing at the door behind Blake, "And be there for her. Right now, she needs you."

Then shortly after, the expert in the scrubs motioned away with hopes that Blake would be comforting to Emily as soon as he stepped foot into that room.

Blake remained in place for a brief second as he stared down at his feet. He had taken that moment to exhale the huge load building in his chest. The doctor was indeed right, Emily was going to need someone with her through the whole process, and Blake got right into it.

Shortly, the frightened male had spun around and walked right in that room. The first thing Blake noticed was Emily sitting beside the bed as she held her mother's hand. She'd taken a look his way to see who'd been stepping in; looking disappointed when she realized it was Blake. Emily lets out a heavy sigh. Perhaps she was expecting a doctor with what should be good news.

Emily faced towards her mother with eyes full while it shattered Blake on the inside all over again. Just as Blake expected, Emily didn't bother to get up from her seat. Understandable, he thought. Her attention was on her mother as a ton of tubing ran in and out her body.

Blake nervously moved closer to Emily, gently coming up from behind as he wrapped his arms around her for comfort.

"I'm so sorry," his voice shook as he near her ear.

Emily remained quiet, and Blake was getting a sense that she may have been on to him, but how? Thinking it more through, *how could it be possible for her to know so soon?*

Meanwhile, Marco's been standing just outside the building with fury in his eyes. Somehow, the crazed man knew Blake would be there. He had thought about going all ballistic inside, destroying everything and possibly injuring everyone in sight, but he held himself back. All he wanted was Blake's head on a stick.

Marco remained posted on a corner across the street behind a street-pole, eyeballing the hospital as the cold Chicago wind brushed through his face.

Since Blake, he may have to begin his journey of uncovering a new location to hide out. Marco Fuentes soon decided to let Blake have another night at rest, and save what's coming to him for a different day.

As for the young male who had been sitting against the wall, resting firmly on the bench from the opposite side of the room from Emily– who'd also been scanning the whole area, he kept silence. The only thing making a sound was the heart monitor, and the beeping was steadily giving the man anxiety. The thought of the machine going off at any moment was leaving him sick in his seat.

As he examined Emily, he paid close attention to her facial features. All tears were dried up. The tone she had been setting didn't show any sign of awareness as to what happened. She appeared clueless.

Emily brainstormed any possible way the incident could have played out, thinking that someone might've been after her mother, or someone just decided to rob her, and she refused. Her mind was asking all sorts of questions like, "Whom?" and "Why?" but sadly the man inside the room with her may have had all the answers to them.

How do you break it to the woman of your dreams that her mother is lying on a hospital bed on the verge of death, and it's your entire fault? Blake wondered.

That question hit the man roughly. He knew it was something that will stick with him, forever.

Later on, they got to talking. Emily had finally spoken with such delicacy in her voice. She pinned out a memory she had of her and her mother as if the situation wasn't already sad enough. The woman carried on to explain about a time she was just this little girl without much knowledge of the outside world. It was the period when her father was still in the picture, living in the same household and all. It was the time that her mother and father were romantically clinging to each other with every possible second that they could.

"Back then the family seemed happy as if nothing could break them," Emily stated. "The time was just perfect then."

The memory that consisted of the three together was the day of her fourth birthday party. She explained to Blake with a half-smile on her face that she had been sitting at the dining room table at her old home with her mother's arms wrapped around her shoulders as a lit cake rested just inches away. A woman, having assumed it was one of her mother's friends' that stood in front of the table, held a camcorder in her hand. Even up until then, she knew she had the footage concealed in a tape somewhere in her current home, possibly in a box in the attic somewhere.

Little Emily blew the candles on her cake as a group of kids she didn't recall, cheered and applauded on. Oddly, the group of random kids was looking jollier than Emily had. "What you wish for honey?" her mother spoke.

Emily explained to Blake that she hadn't opened up to her mother at the moment. She wanted to keep her wish a secret. Coincidently, her dream just happened to have stepped foot inside the dining room. It was her father clothed in his dress blues with badges pinned to his chest pocket.

As soon as he was spotted, Emily leaped out of her seat and ran around the table to give him a warm welcome home. Little Emily was filling up with tears in an instant, as well as her father. He was on a short visit. The man only managed to get less than a week to stay. In fact, he had reached back to the US a week before, just after his eight-month deployment overseas. It was Dana's idea to have scooped him up from the airport for a birthday surprise, and of course, it was a success.

As she reflected more off of that night, she remembered her parents getting along well. The two clinked their glasses half full of some fine wine and giggled at nearly everything each other had said. The moment was great. Seeing her mother smile in such a way was something little Emily could not forget. It was something she hardly recognized anymore.

"That's a beautiful moment," Blake grinned. "Hold onto that."

Emily smiled back just as Blake began to open up. He even glanced over at Dana with a fierce look in his eyes. "All the memories I had with my father, I was just this little boy. He wasn't much in the picture either."

"And that's the reason why you never talked about your parents much?" Emily asked.

"Yup," Blake answered dryly. "He was always this drunken mess. I recall the one time when I was five years old, and he put his hands on my mother. I was angry, confused, and afraid. I didn't know what to do."

Emily sat there with her mouth half open, speechless as Blake continued. "They were yelling at each other about something. Next thing I knew my mom got shoved onto the couch. My father was about to swing at her, but he hadn't. And no matter what, my mother still loved him, even if she knew she couldn't be with him."

"It's sad things had to go down that way. I'm here for you if anything," Emily replied.

"Thank you," Blake murmured. "And I'm sorry Emily," Blake added as he glimpsed over to the woman on the bed.

Unintentionally, Emily smacked her lips. "I never really understood why people say they are sorry when a loved one is dying. It's not like it's their fault. It's not your fault Blake," Emily cleared.

Feeling sick to his stomach again, Blake rested his arm on his abdomen. With eyelids stretched, the last five words that she said reverberated in his head, and that's when the floors looked wobbly to him. The man was sweating where he sat, and this time the sickening feeling was worse. His face expressed it with his pale skin and weak eyes. His heart began to beat faster than usual, and the neck hole of his shirt was starting to damp. Emily noticed something had immediately triggered something odd with him. "Please excuse me," Blake told her as he got up from his seat and rushes out the room.

With fast-moving feet, he moved down the hall and entered the nearest bathroom. Inside, the male panted as he walked in circles. He continued the process to keep his beating heart down to a steady rate, and it worked within' long seconds. Blake then stared straight into the huge mirror above the sink counter for a moment.

Bent over, Blake ran the sink on full speed and smothered cold water onto his face with cupped hands, when suddenly, his attention switched over to the door as he heard plenty of movement coming from the hall. Blake immediately shuts off the water as he heard voices and running feet zipping nearby. Apparently, something was happening to someone on that particular side of the building. Blake wanted to be mistaken, but all signs pointed towards something wrong.

The concerned male wanted to check to see what it was, so he stepped out of the bathroom and observed where a group of nurses had rushed off to, and he became so weak. It appeared to him that a group of workers was entering the same room as Emily's mother as he stared down the hall. His eyes bulged from its socket, and right away he had paced himself down.

The closer he got, the more he could hear the heart monitor. He lowered his speedy paste as he reached close enough to the room, and heard one of the male doctors say, "we're going to lose her. We're losing her fast!"

Blake peeked into the room as Emily watched from the side.

One of the nurses turned their attention over to Emily, and that woman immediately escorted her out by physically grabbing onto her wrist and led her out through the doorframe. In an instant, Blake reached out for Emily as the nurse forced her his way. No more than a second later, one of the crew members had closed the door to the room and slid the huge curtain all the way around the bed. "We're losing her. We're losing her!" one of the male doctors called out.

Blinded from the outside was making them feel more uneasy as they could hear all the commotion from within'. Emily was in desperate need of getting back into the room, but the young male held onto her tightly as she attempted to force herself free from his arms.

"Emily, wait. Stop!" Blake commanded.

The young woman kept going at it. She was doing everything she could to release herself from his arms by biting, scratching, pinching. Nothing's been working, so without a second thought, she had stomped her foot as hard as she could, directly onto his toes. It caught Blake off guard as he screamed on the inside. His eyes widened as he had lost control of his feet, having them come crashing into the wall behind them.

Blake never lost his hold on her. Eventually realizing that she had gone insane, she took a breather, pressing her back against his body.

With a distressed look left on her face, she stared at the door as she waited to hear what seemed to be inevitable. She got up slowly with her hair in her face and hands shaking. Blake got up as well, feeling minor pain in the nail of his big toe. He could tell that there was a bruising sensation growing in his feet.

Expressing physical pain, Blake didn't dare let Emily try to get into that room. The machine was still sounding. Blake had reached out to grab her by the arm, softly tugging her back in his direction.

Unfortunately, about a minute later, the machine had stopped beeping. The two heard the flatline of the monitor, and their hearts sank in a flash. Blake and Emily faced straight ahead at the door without blinking an eye, waiting for someone to open up the door.

Blake was possibly feeling much worse than she did. At that moment, Emily cried out loudly as she dropped down onto white marbled floors. Blake went crashing down onto his knees beside her as he tried lifting her up. Emily had lied in the center of the hall, while one of the doctor's assistants came out. It was confirmed. Dana's gone.

CHAPTER EIGHTEEN

The Next Morning

Emily didn't get home till 3:30 in the morning the following day, and she had made it there by herself. Once she got up to her bedroom, she had crashed onto her bed without any bother to change into her comfy sleep clothes.

She didn't get much sleep that day. Her eyes drenched in every moment that she wakes up, and every time that she did, she asked herself, "Is this real? is she really, gone?"

Sadly, the more times that she awakens in her sleep, the more she evolved to the realization that her mother will no longer come home through those doors again.

The clock beside her nightstand read 4:33 am. It was infuriating to see that the time was passing slowly. She had let out all of her emotions onto her pillow as she dabbed her eyes on the bed sheet.

With the house being all quiet and lonesome, she began to process a little as to how she was going to be able to carry herself up from the situation. Eventually, the bills will stock up. It dawned on her how she was going to lose the house someday, and her mother's vehicles that sat out in the driveway.

Emily began to think more of her future when suddenly, a knock had come from the front door downstairs. It was quite early for someone to be beating against the door, so she remained rested on her bed until another knock came.

She grunted as she leaped off the mattress and went to gander at who lied behind the entryway.

    The house was considered pitch black. She hadn't bothered to turn on the lights due to her wanting people to believe that no one was home. Emily watched her step carefully with each move that she made as she proceeded down the stairs while her hand guided down the railing.

    When she reached midway down, she paused as she had thought to herself that maybe, just maybe the person had left. Then a second later, more pounding came at the door as it startled the woman.

    It wasn't a typical three-door knock. Whoever stood outside, really wanted the owners to hear from every room in the house. Her heart raced in an instant as the obnoxious knocking vibrated the shared wall along with the hanging picture frames. In the back of her mind, Emily's first guess was the police or some nasty crook with the decency to knock.

    She tiptoed her way down over to the door and pressed her eye against the peephole. The fearful woman let off a huge sigh of relief. She opened up, and in that very instant, she was grabbed by the shoulder. Emily found herself to be buried in Blake's chest as he hurried in for a tight hug.

    They soon stepped apart from each other, and Blake took one look at her as she glanced off into the floor. "My God," he said. "I know you're hurt right now, but just know that I am here for you, every step of the way."

    At that point, Blake understood that the woman didn't want to be vocal. She licked her lips and stepped in closer to him and placed her head on his chest again. With all that went on in the night, Blake assumed she was drained, so he grabbed her by the hand and guided Emily up to her bedroom.

    Upstairs, he lied beside her, and she felt this instant comfort as if it had gotten a little easier to fall asleep. Emily rested her head on his chest with her knee nestled on his leg as he laid flat on his back. She was practically sprawled on top of him as he stared straight up at the ceiling with an arm supporting the back of his head, and the other running through her hair, slowly causing her to fall asleep.

After a while, Blake glanced downward, and he'd seen that her eyes held shut. Emily's cheeks appeared damped, so he had made a small loving gesture by using his other hand to wipe away her mid-dry tears.

A few minutes later, Emily rotated away, sound asleep. Blake, on the other hand, was wide awake. He realized then that he was, in fact, the one having trouble sleeping.

Blake had thought to himself thoroughly about the unfortunate occurrence of which happened hours ago. The more time that passed by, the higher the percentage of hope he had that just maybe, Marco had been the one to fire the bullet that pierced her chest, but it wasn't enough belief to ease so much of the sickening feeling he felt inside.

More time had gone by, and he took one look at Emily. He sat up on the bed, carefully hopping off the mattress, and just as if it was his house he took a walk down the stairs and headed to the kitchen to open up the huge stainless steel fridge door to grab what he felt he needed at the moment. It was a couple of bottles of Coronas resting on the door shelf. He'd taken two and made his way back up the stairs.

After he entered back into Emily's room, Blake didn't go straight to the bed; he had actually stepped out through the French doors into a small outside balcony. It was below freezing temperature, and the man happened to be out with just a pair of jeans and a white t-shirt.

The broken man chugged away his bottle as he sat up on the stone ledge, not having a single care that he could lose his balance and potentially plummet to his death.

As he took a huge gulp of his yellow drink, he stared straight out into the beautifully lit full moon through the thin cloud strays. Sadly, the young man couldn't admire it as much as he would. Flashing images of the horrid night rummaged through his head, the bullets, and the grin on Marco's face before he had fired that first shot, the chase down the snowy street, the blood, and a close woman who suffered.

A time came while he was outside when he thought of how he jeopardized the mission, the mission that Agent Johnson had assigned him. As good as it sounded in the beginning to gain such income and helping out the city, Blake had felt it lost its value. With the passing of Emily's mother, going through with the operation will not be about the money or fancy vacations anymore. This time, Blake felt it is about vengeance, for Emily. It helped to place plenty of blame on Marco so that he'd ease some of the pain on himself. It worked for a short minute, but at the end of the day, he was more than halfway sure it was his bullet.

On a night like this, he thought perhaps telling what seemed to be the truth would be the best idea; turning himself in.

Although it was scary, he did not want to pull through with it, yet. Until then, he had to pretend he wasn't guilty, even if all evidence led the law to him.

Blake took another huge gulp of his drink. He figured that running away was the way to go, only until he came up with a plan to move forward in the best way possible. The hardest thing to do of all is admitting to Emily that he potentially killed her mother.

Six thirty in the morning, Emily had woken up feeling a nasty cramp in the back of her neck. As she sat up and rubbed her neck, she took a look beside her bed and noticed that Blake wasn't there. The young lady's eyes scanned the room, wondering where he'd gone off too. She figured he might've been out on the balcony, or downstairs watching some television.

Emily hopped out of bed with her eyes looking red. She walked up to the French doors and took a look through the glass from left to right, and she hadn't seen him there. With her head turned behind she called out to him, but no answer.

The concerned woman stepped out of her room and took a look around from the upstairs balcony as she repeatedly called out to him. She was getting nothing in return, leaving her to wonder where he'd gone off to this early in the morning. Knowing Blake's work schedule, it was not on his agenda to be at the donut shop.

Emily continued her search and checked all throughout the main floor to see if Blake decided to pass out on the living room couch or whatnot, but still no sight of him. Soon enough there had come a knocking on the front door, assuming it was him again. Emily rushed in without peeping through the door hole, and when she opened up, she came across these two men in uniform. She'd first seen the shiny golden-yellow badge pinned to their chest pockets. They appeared to have had a grave expression on their faces, with determination, and ready to unload some substantial information.

"You must be Emily?" A male officer with small orange curls had said.

"Yeah, that's me," she answered worriedly.

"It may be best to let us in to talk," the man suggested.

Right away, Emily approved of the idea and invited the two inside. She escorted them to the dining room table for what she felt was a good place to discuss, and within' five minutes in, the second man in uniform unfolds a piece of paper straight out of his pocket. He was mildly beefy and bald, but excessively sweet. Often he would tilt his head down and lurch forward with bubbled cheeks with what seemed to be trapped air building inside of him. He slid the sheet across the table as he burped with his mouthed closed.

From her first glance, she'd seen what looked to be two photocopied images of a man with tattoos all over his neck. Emily adjusted her body by leaning her chest closer to the table to get a better look.

"You see this man right here?" the pudgy gentleman asked as he began tapping lightly with his index finger onto the paper. "Surveillance showed suspicious activity around town last night. Marco Fuentes, that man you see in these photos is an extreme psychopath. I need you to be aware that he's still running around in our area."

Emily nodded her head, feeling the goosebumps that instantly ran through her arms.

The pudgy officer went on, "From last night's footage we'd seen what appeared to be a guy chasing Marco down on Belmont Avenue."

"He was spotted running in between two buildings which lead to the street of your mother's workplace," the curly haired man budded In. "Sadly, surveillance didn't pick up what happened on the other side of the block, but we firmly agree that Marco's our guy."

At that moment, Emily's face had gotten pale. The two men seated at the table could see the discomfort in her eyes. It was all too soon for her. She looked up at one of the officer's and said, "And the other guy?"

"We got an idea, and he just might be one of our fellow, undercover, agents," the orange haired man guessed.

The bubbled cheeked man jumped back into the discussion, "Excuse me, Miss. By any chance did your mother have any problems with anybody, potentially sparking up the tension Marco had for him to go after her?"

Emily's eyes widened in an instant. She threw herself back in her seat with an eyebrow raised. "No, my mother got along with everybody," she replied.

"Cause thinking more in-depth, Marco seems to be going off on people he mostly sees on a day to day basis, not strangers," the chubby officer added.

"Yeah well, with Marco running around, we got guards with heavy armor and weapons strolling through the town to find him, but till then I would feel comfortable if you stay at a friend's house or have someone to look out after you. You know anybody that can keep you company?" the curly haired man asked.

With dolorous eyes, she looked at him, and answered, "Yeah, I believe I know somebody that would."

Leaving the discussion there, the two announced their departure, and they all got up from their seats. The rounded man faced Emily and gave her his condolences. "I am sorry about what happened." Then he hugged her with twitchy eyes that almost released the waterworks. "We'll get this guy out of the streets soon," he promised her.

Then shortly after, Emily stuck behind with bloodshot eyes, watching the two men step out the front till they closed the door behind them.

CHAPTER NINETEEN

Dropped In

The evening skies crept up in such a hurry, but for Emily, it was a different story. It had been a long day of moping and crying as it felt like three days were combining into one. The majority of Emily's day had been slipping away at the main entrance area resting on a futon, covered in a blue cotton blanket, sobbing as used tissues lied on the coffee table.

She had been zoning in at the small television up front, not paying a single attention to what was airing on the screen. There were moments when she'd catch herself staring blankly into space, thinking about that night at the hospital when the heart monitor hit its flatline.

For one more times sake, she had dialed up Blake's cell. Unfortunately, he had not picked up once again. A whole day was washing away, and she began to worry more about him. She had set her phone on the cushion, facedown, knowing that it wouldn't keep her from checking back at it every minute.

Soon, a knock came to the front door as the person gave the knob a little twist. Emily smiled as she had an idea of who it was. The young woman trusted her instinct and opened wide without peeking through the eye hole. Her eyes widened as soon as she spotted her father, Richard Smith standing right up front. It was exactly who'd she thought it would be.

Without a word said, he had stepped in and immediately dropped his luggage to the side just before the two went crashing into each other, and she had given him a warm welcome home, just as she did when she was this little girl from her fourth birthday party.

"I'm so sorry about your mother, honey," her father's voice shook as he crests the back of her head.

Quickly enough, the salt like water drops streamed down from the corner of her eyes and had soaked into his blue jean jacket, and the red and black checkerboard coat he had underneath it.

"I'm sorry if I'm ruining your jacket," Emily sniffed.

And Richard was quick to say, "No, that's fine. I don't care about the stupid jacket," in the lightest tone he could set his deep voice. "You say it like I hadn't seen you throw up on my shirt before," in reference to when she was this infant.

"Dad," Emily prolonged in which she then followed with a soft laugh afterward.

Later, they sat on the futon together. Richard had explained to Emily about how his day had gone. "As soon as you called me this morning, I got on a plane and flew all the way here from my condo in New York."

"What's it like over there?" Emily wanted to know.

"Busy," Richard replied. Sniffling away, "I can't believe this. How could this have happened?" he murmured.

"Someone shot her when she was leaving the office," Emily bawled.

Richard dipped his head down. "God, I miss her so much," he sheds a tear.

Watching her father have this water stream running down his cheeks has made her feel weak. She wanted to seem stable enough by not breaking in front of him at the moment. It was interesting to see that after all these years he still felt a little thing towards Dana. It was safe to say his feelings had never really left. Emily could see it in his eyes as he continued the waterworks. "I miss your mother so much, Emily," his speech shook. "I'm sorry that I was barely there for you guys. I was just so caught up with work and-"

"Don't," Emily interrupted. "It's okay."

Richard had done a hard sniff, attempting to keep his emotional expression down to a minimal. Then gravely he asked, "Well, did they find out who did it?"

"No," Emily answered. "But from what the police had been telling me, they claim that they have an idea of the suspect already."

Immediately, Richard let out a heavy exhale that showed he had built up a bit of steam as he was stared down at his feet. Emily could see it through her father's throbbing veins of his forearms- elbows placed on his knees while he clenches his fist mid-way, and releases it in a continuous motion like he'd been messing with a squeeze toy.

"So, what's gonna happen, you're gonna look for the man that did it?" Emily asked.

Before he answered, Emily could see her father's eyes which displayed a bit of thought process. "My old life is done. I don't want to relive what I've done in Afghanistan."

"I understand," Emily wept. "Cops are most likely going to lock him up, but I would most rather have him be dead."

"Crazy," Richard said with a grin on his face. "You truly are my daughter."

Meanwhile, he scooted in closer and sets his arm over Emily's shoulder to cherish that particular moment he'd gone over a decade without experiencing. It felt good. It had brought back old memories.

"We'll figure something out," Richard stated.

Later on, her father had asked if she was feeling hungry, assuming that she hadn't gotten anything to eat.

"No, I'm good," she answered.

The man himself wasn't feeling much towards food at the moment either. It was hard to think about anything else after the passing of a loved one beating in the center of their heads.

Shortly on, her father announced that he needed to crash somewhere soon, suggesting that he could sleep on the futon for the night, or one of the couches out in the living room. Traveling for hours on a plane has made the man want to doze off early in the evening. He had also made another suggestion, which she should get some rest, as well as her eyes, looked weary.

Slow paced, Emily, got up from the seat and heads for the staircase shortly after saying, "Goodnight dad."

Three steps up she stopped to look back at her father. "You want to sleep in mom's room?" She asked softly.

"Yes," he replied with a slight grin on his face.

The two then began walking up the grand staircase as she guided him to the room. Her father had already felt this burning sensation in his eyes as he was preventing the tears from becoming visibly noticeable to his daughter. Emily glanced off to her side as her father followed, and she could perceive that he was anxious to see the room.

"Well, there it is," Emily pointed at the bedroom door that was left slightly open. Her father did the honor of stepping up closer and gently pushing the door back. As it creaked open wide, the first thing he noticed was the purple wallpaper that surrounded the place, and then that queen-sized bed that rested on a black, leather full bed frame.

Her father walked in while Emily stuck behind. Richard took a quick look around; he glanced up at the window, the carpet job, the wallpaper work, and the crisped clean espresso mirror dresser beside the bed along with Dana's variety of makeup collections resting on top. The surface had everything from lipsticks to nail polishes, spray bottles to foundation, and the vast selection of makeup brushes tucked inside a small vase. Dana had nearly everything a woman could dream of having as a part of their collection, like cosmetic heaven.

Richard turned to face Emily as her shoulder leaned on the hinges of the doorframe. "Did she have someone help her with all of this?" he asked while looking corner to corner, amazed at the job taken place in that particular room.
"No," Emily smiled. "She did everything. I helped out a little, but she set everything up and picked everything out herself."

"Wow," her father said just as he rotated his head around again. "This house is astonishing. I remember promising your mother that I'd get her a home like this for the three of us, but she did it without me. She did it herself," he laughed softly.

The man had then stepped closer to the dresser. Richard snooped at what else could be resting on the surface, watching out for anything he didn't catch earlier from the first look. As he analyzed more, he was at the realization that he had not been looking for anything in particular, but maybe just some photographs, a note with an unknown phone number printed on it or anything along those lines. Then there it was up front, sticking onto the mirror dresser. A blue sticky note that had been split horizontally with a number on it.

Richard sighed in place, almost instantly. "You alright?" Emily asked.

"Has your mother introduced you to any new guy in her life?"

"No," Emily replied. "She dated others in the past, but nothing serious. None of them could even make it a month with her. I guess she was just never over you," the young woman smiled. "The number you see on that paper is from the office of her workplace. No need to worry about it."
Right away, her father obtained this massive smile on his face. "It's great to see you, all grown up and shit," Richard smirked. "Such a shame your mother didn't let you keep my last name," he cracked a bigger smile.

"Thank you," his daughter beamed. "It's good to see you too."

And as her father stared off into the bed beside him, it gave her an immediate indication that he was about ready to take a snooze. "Well, I'm going to be up in my room, I'll see you in the morning dad." She told him just as she had begun to move out of sight.

"See you in the morning," he called out.

Soon enough, Emily crashed her face into the pillow in her room.

Meanwhile, Richard kicked off his shoes and climbed on top of Dana's bed. As he lied there, he stared straight off into the ceiling, and a rampage of memories that he'd missed dawned on him. The regret of not attempting to make the relationship work in the past has bothered him more than ever. Would she still be alive if I was still around? Richard thought to himself.

When he rolled off to his side, he happened to have found a long hair string that lied on the bed cover. He pinched his fingers together as he pulled it up and analyzed it. It was hers, Dana's. The male's face turned pouty in a second. He fought back the tears, but that familiar perfume smell on the sheets wasn't making it any easy for him. It was his favorite smell, apple cinnamon.

After a few more seconds at rest, Richard hopped out of bed with the face that quickly turned to anger. He began to look all over the room. From the closet to Dana's drawers. It wasn't until he rummaged through the bottom desk drawer when he'd found what he was looking for, and it was the address of Dana's workplace printed in the handbook. At that point, the man realized he had lied to Emily when he said earlier, "My old life is done."

It was not intentional. Richard just figured it was most important to him to go back to hunting mode, just as he had done overseas. But one shall pray that the man would make the right choices when he finds him- if he finds him, and not take a life away as he is not the Marine spending the next few months in Afghanistan, anymore.

Inside Emily's room, she relaxed on her bed with her eyes wide open. It was the second day she had trouble sleeping. It was only a few minutes later when the young woman hopped out of her bed and took a little stroll over to the entrance of the attic, and stepped foot inside the semi-dark room. She looked, corner to corner while her legs carried her further in.

After she had passed a ton of unpacked boxes from her move-in day, she was quick to have located a tiny crate the size of a shoe box stacked above several huge boxes. Having that the pile mounted a few inches over Emily's head, she got on her tip-toes, and she flipped the crate on its side to see that there had been tapes and a camcorder from her childhood inside.

Apparently, it was quite dusty, considering it was sitting in the same spot for well over a decade. Emily carefully lifted the whole box and rested it on the floor right beside her. She kneeled down and dusted it off with a couple of quick blows she released through her lips.

When she had glanced over her shoulder a few feet to her right, she spotted a projector sitting on a small cart. It belonged to her father. Back then, Richard would often run slideshows of his trip overseas in the living space of their old home. It was always a good time.

Emily could remember the warm buttery smell from that popcorn that she would often eat when she watched her father's slideshows. She remembered her mother sitting beside her, and they snacked from the same bowl as they all bonded.

Emily didn't take long to set up the cart projector in the center of the attic, although she had to walk through a couple of web colonies to get to an electrical outlet. She soon plugged in that long cord, just before she stepped back. Then, she adjusted the lens to have it point at an open wood panel wall with just enough space to allow her to view them.

With the tapes she'd found inside the box, she connected the camcorder, set a tape in at random, and pulled up an abandoned old folded chair and began the show.

The first photo that appeared on the wall was of the three from a much simpler time. Emily's parents stood behind little Emily while Richard's sixty-three Impala sat behind them, looking crisp and clean as ever.

Unfortunately, Emily knew for a fact her father's old car was history, and she never really knew what happened to the classic Impala. She just knew at that age that she wanted it passed down to her. Her parents seemed happy as they had a hand placed on her shoulder for the lovely photo someone had taken of them.

Emily soon flipped on, and she had come across a clip from her fourth birthday party. The time when her father, Richard had come for a surprise visit. She beamed at the enlarged video.

Then a photo of little Emily hugging her father popped up at the next click. She remembered that day precisely. It was the night she had talked about with Blake at the hospital, and it made her feel quite emotional. She took a quick look off into the floor as she bit her bottom lip while she blinked uncontrollably; fighting back those tears that desperately looked for an escape.

She skipped more ahead, and she came across this photo of when she'd gotten chocolate frosting all over her face from when she'd taken the first huge bite. She chuckled in her seat, not expecting to see a picture such as that to pop up on the wall. Emily hadn't realized the person behind the camcorder had captured that moment, but she could then see she had been distracted by the other kids her age laughing right beside her, and that one impatient kid that desperately wanted a slice of cake.

Most definitely there'd been more photos from her birthday party and plenty of other pictures Dana in the slides, most of which were off guard moments as she had been smiling right at Richard. Those photos made Emily realize she never wanted to be okay with the divorce. Dana had seemed happier with her father in the picture.

She was quick to have gotten misty-eyed. Watching those photos was something little Emily couldn't bear. It was too soon. She skipped, then skipped through some more pictures while most of them kept featuring her mother, but that was the primary reason she pulled out the slides in the first place. She had let the tears drop down from her face, and it was a cry well needed.

About a mile away, Blake stood up front his mirror cabinet while the shower ran steamy hot water. The mirror had begun to fog along the edges, and the heat attacked every cool breeze the room once had. As he stared at his fading reflection, he leaned in a little closer to see that his eyes were bloodshot red. Considering that he hadn't turned himself in yet, Blake compared the look he had to something that was fresh out of hell's gate.

He happened to be running everything in his head from that night again, especially the tears pouring from Emily's eyes, and that moment when the heart monitor hit its flatline.

Soon after, Blake shook his head in disgust and spat out the nasty taste that was sitting in his throat into the solid white sink.

With pounds of guilt bottled up inside, he gripped the glass sink tightly, squeezing as hard as he could from corner to corner. Blake could feel the quick switch of anger hitting him roughly. Every bit of him still tried to convince himself that he was not the killer, but no matter how it panned out, Blake couldn't deny that a partial blame, if not all would dump on him.

He took one look down at his arms as they shook against the sink, and had seen the protruding veins looking as though they were ready to explode.

As soon as Blake glanced back up with teeth visibly clenched, he could sense the potential monster from within'. As much as Blake had tried, he swiftly swept items off the sink, following with repeated punches to the mirror cabinet in front of him. Shot by shot, more glass along with blood and wood scraps flew in separate directions. Multiple cuts appeared on his knuckles, but the adrenaline had brought the physical pain down to a minimum as he continued to plow ahead with his left and right hand.

He grunted through his clenched teeth as soon as he felt the pain in his hands become worse than it did seconds ago. He had witnessed the disturbing image of his hands drenched in all red like he'd dipped his hands in a can of red paint.

Later, he appeared to have settled down a bit from the wild breakdown he had minutes ago. He sat in the tub while the water-head pours, heavy exhaling as blood streamed down the drain, and surely the warm water stung.

Soon enough, he figured he was in desperate need of another bottle of beer in his hand, and to think more about what to do next. He knew that things had to be done the right way, no matter how bad it may seem, but he still just couldn't, yet.

CHAPTER TWENTY

Scope

Richard showed up to the murder scene where he had witnessed several cops searching the area with flashlights in their hands. The man's first instinct was to go around the back and enter the building from there. Even the cops thought ahead enough to collect evidence from the back doorknob, as well as every other one from the first floor. That's where Richard would have started.

Some areas were sectioned off in that dim-lit hallway, and straight down that narrow foyer was a door left wide open as a yellow crime scene strip ran across the doorframe. And that was where all the attention was. Evidently, that's where the murder had taken place.

Richard was able to get through several badged men as they were chit-chatting alongside a wall about something non-work related. Former Marine, Richard Smith ducked under the yellow strip as he had crossed through the doorframe. He observed the little narrow way of which a staircase had been right beside him. Very few men in uniform, standing a few feet high on the midnight blue carpet stair run turned heads in confusion, not familiarized with the man who entered freely.

"Aye, this place is sectioned off!" One of the men called out to Richard from above.

"Yeah, yeah," Richard responded with little to no phase as he continued to walk in, looking corner to corner.

"Walking into a police investigation is a federal crime and will result in punishment!" the same man hollered back at him.

"Yeah, and so will you for your lack of intelligence," Richard called out. "You mean to tell me this is the second day you've scoped this place? It looks to me like you all haven't spent much time looking, but rather it being more like social hour to you lunatics!"

And quickly enough, the entire group of men in uniform listened in on the furious man.

"My ex-wife is the victim in this scene. Now we all gotta hurry up and catch this criminal," Richard projected. "We must not let another sunrise come before the person is off the streets. Track him, find him, take him down or kill him, do whatever it takes, and speed up this process. If someone else is next to die, it'll be on your hands!"

"And who might you be?" said a middle-aged, white-bearded man with a badge and brown overcoat.

"An angry man," Richard turned behind him as he had stared dead ahead at the man's eyes.

Right then, the bearded man smiled. "I like your posture. The way that you give orders, the way that you showed absolutely no fear coming in like this. You served?"

"I was a Marine," Richard stated.

"Well, thank you for your service. I'm Detective Campbell," he introduced himself while expressing a grin on his face. "You want to tell me why a man like you is here? I didn't catch all that you said a couple of seconds ago."

"Someone I loved dearly was murdered in this building recently. I'd like to make sure he gets off the street soon."

"Interesting," detective Campbell quirked. "It takes courage to come up here, bypassing laws to get what you want. But to be honest, I'd do the same."

Right then, Richard kept his lips still, as much as he wanted to smile.

Soon enough, a short, pudgy police officer walked inside and alerted them to some reports of a shooting that had come from the same day of Dana's death from the next block. It wasn't long until the majority of them were in the abandoned diner on the upper level. Agent Johnson was already there examining the several bullet holes engraved through the walls and floors. There were multiple bullet casings Allen was familiar with, and some came from a specific brand of gun that he gave to a very few particular people.

Richard came up from behind Allen. "There's one gun I am familiar with that the bullets could have come from, we used guns like that in the military, so whoever owned that gun would most definitely have got it from either of those departments or some police facility," he informed.

"Which is why it was a good idea to give my recruits a damn perfect traceable gun," Allen devilishly smiled. Richard glanced at Allen as he continued to stare at the bullet holes. It was certain, Allen knew who was involved.

"Alright officers!" Agent Johnson began. "I need you all to check every security camera in and out this block too. I need you all to search this area from the ground up and see what else we can find. Now let's move!"
Then immediately the crowd split.

Hours later [Police Station]

"So, Richards Smith's the name?" Agent Johnson had asked rhetorically, staring at a computer screen of the man himself with listed information, directed to Allen by Officer Campbell who had been tapping into the keyboard on his desk.

"Yup, he just walked in all angry. He's Ex-military, flew in from New York, divorced, and happens to be the father of a twenty-one-year-old woman whose mother had been shot down near Belmont," Officer Campbell stated.

"I am actually glad that this happened," Agent Johnson smiled. "He showed up to the scene, meaning he wants answers. He's motivated. We could use him."

And right then, Officer Campbell appeared shocked. He knew that whatever Allen had up inside his head was something that could be considered downright insane.

CHAPTER TWENTY-ONE

Lurking

In the next nightfall, with hands wrapped in thick bandages, Blake painstakingly got himself dressed in his disastrous bathroom. As unpleasant as it felt to make a precise movement utilizing his palms, he managed to pull through and got his clean clothes on him.

Blake had slipped up a pair of light blue jeans, joining it with a black v-neck t-shirt. He picked up his favorite quarter zipped sweater, although he nearly forgot about Dana's bloody finger smears within' it. He immediately ditched it down the laundry shoot and motioned on over to his room to find a replacement.

He had gotten himself a black, light leather jacket, yanked right off the hanger and timely slipped it on with a face that screamed pain. Even the slightest of pressure in his hands hurt like no pain he has felt before, and he flared his eyes over to his nightstand sitting beside his bed as he recalled the last place he had left his gun.

Later, he pulled the drawer open to load up the weapon again, just before he tucked it away in his pants from behind. Shortly after, he slipped on his shoes and was then ready for another trip through the streets of Chicago, to continue his search for Marco.

Meanwhile, as Blake exited his house, he noticed the weather not being as cold as the previous days. For once, it was not snowing out. Blake stepped down his pathway and made a last minute decision to leave his car behind, and was determined to go for a walk instead. It was the perfect opportunity to get some air and maybe clear his mind even. The number one task for the night was to retrieve his sniper from the rooftop of some building behind Belmont. Finding Marco was just a bonus, something that could wait another day, he figured.

It'd taken him twenty-five minutes to get near the building on foot. From a block away, he'd seen several cop cars parked along the side of Dana's office building. Apparently, they wanted to speak to more guests from that hotel about the things they heard, and the things they might have seen.

Right then, Blake felt discomfort in his chest. It was like someone pressing down on him. There was that sense that at any moment he was going to get caught. Blake Anderson sensed those officers coming to a conclusion, and that's what frightened him to death.

Meantime, he snuck his way up close as he had crossed to the opposite side of the street and hurriedly entered the alley. Blake soon climbed the ladder as fast as his body could let him. Each grip of the handles hurt as each bar touched up on his cuts, which caused him some time, but he had made it to the top, and when he did, he had witnessed something shocking. The sniper was gone. All of it, gone. Everything, including the stand that came with it, and not forgetting to mention his duffle bag.

He took a look beneath his feet as he shuffled around the premise, swiping his feet across the snow patches in all kinds of directions. No luck. It was just gone. Suddenly, he felt a bit light headed. Knowing that if the police had taken his belongings, it would lead them straight to him. Blake presumed he was in a much deeper hole then.

After he had rushed down the ladder, he nearly sprained his ankle when he first reached the ground. The young man grunted in place, but the pain hadn't stopped him from moving. Blake crossed back over to the other side of the street, fast-paced knowing every officer around was inside.

As he made it over, he stood in place looking at the front door of that building, indecisive about whether or not he should check into the crime scene and flash his badge at the officers inside. The man was curious as to what the cops were thinking, but it could be a good idea to try and throw them off on their investigation, he thought.

It was moments later that Blake went with a decision, turned and walked away. Blake must've walked about three miles at least in random directions- no destination. He was in one of the busiest parts of the city. It was getting pretty late, and people scattered like ants around him.

Without expecting it at the time, his cell rang in his pocket. The male picked up his phone to see who it had been. It was Emily. The troubled man didn't bother to pick up the call, so he slipped it back down in his pants and proceeded forward as it kept ringing.

He continued to wander through the city, and Blake happened to remember the time when Emily and his happy self would go out for walks like this. Sadly, he felt they could no longer continue that. With the disturbing image of Emily's mother lying on the floor all bloody and crying, it was hard to pretend everything was okay.

Blake had progressed further down a couple of blocks, and that was when he had encountered some suspicious activity nearby. Immediately he was getting these bad vibes. Something serious was going on, and it all escalated quickly. There'd been at least four cop cars swarming along the curb of a broad sidewalk beside one of the apartment buildings on the right in which Blake froze close beside.

A swat truck even pulled up to the curb across the street. Just about the entire team had hopped out and hastened across as they all headed straight in for the building with police officers hastily following behind them.

For a brief second, Blake thought they were there for him, but something else was happening. Apparently, there was another case going on. *Possibly a hostage situation?* Blake thought.

Pedestrians in the area were curious as to what was going on inside the apartment building. Many people passed by with heads frequently turning back; most of which had their phones out in hopes that they could capture something exciting to share on social media.

"What the hell is going on?" Blake whispered to himself as he took baby steps ahead.

In an instant, flashing lights of red, white, and blue reflected off the building from a police vehicle in front of the other squad cars as a man in uniform stuck behind. Yards up ahead, the officer exited his vehicle and commanded everyone to vacate the area calmly. *That's never usually a good sign,* Blake thought to himself.

"We've got this place surrounded," a loud echo came from the swat truck as a bright light beamed from the top. Blake continued moving forward, slowly, where giggling pedestrians were coming from the opposite direction. It was a group of young women who looked to have been doing a little shopping earlier at a mall nearby. One of the four ladies happened to be taking a few snapshots of the cop cars lined up beside them by cell phone.

Behind the women was a man in a black sweatshirt, following about a foot away from the group, hood up, head facing down, and hands in pocket. Blake hadn't noticed the stranger in black from first looking at the obnoxious women.

The mysterious man tossed his garbage straight from his pocket, then hurriedly cut in between the cop cars and jaywalked his way across the street. From Blake's eyes, he seemed a bit odd and intimidating, like some street troublemaker.

Blake took a look at his feet as he continued straight when suddenly, he heard what sounded like a sonic boom from yards away that instantly startled his eyes closed. It shook everyone in the area; he could listen to the fainted screams as the night skies turned bright orange. One cop car followed after another, and then another burst into a vast gulf of flames.

Blake threw himself back as a surprise caught him off his feet. He'd immediately felt the force wind brush against his clothing as he ended up getting slammed on his back against the concrete. He'd felt the heat press against his face, and could hear more faint screams as his ears weren't functioning well.

Blake was oblivious as to what was going on as his eyes held shut for the majority of the blast, but he could hear windows shattering nearby. Everything had just gotten intensely bright for the moment.

For a second, Blake had thought the building was what had exploded.

When Blake was finally able to see again, he examined the cop cars that had contorted into a huge burning ball of metal. While being all misty-eyed, he breathed heavily from where he sat on the ground as his eyes suddenly widened. The women that had been approaching him were jolted off to the side of the building, bloody and appeared unresponsive.

The shaken up man quickly got up and staggered. Breathing deeply, he took a quick look all around him. He noticed he'd become this confused individual. He wondered "how?" and," who?"

Shortly Blake rushed his way over to check up on the ladies. One by one he examined their pulses. No sign of breathing. He firmly believed that all four were dead.

Taking a swift look about a yard away, the police officer appeared unresponsive with his face half burned to crisp, possibly dead too.

The pouty emotion he had earlier then turned into fury. Very few people around the area stuck around, while others ran a further distance away. Nobody else from the outside seemed to have gotten hurt that he knew about, and he prayed no one from the inside of that apartment building was suffering.

Seconds later, about half the men in uniform had rushed back outside from the apartment. They all appeared clueless. Each of them looked at their burning vehicles in disbelief, listening in to the intense fire crumbling the metal while a crowd of people screamed as they were swarming around the area. The looks on their faces showed they were being timed, that they have tried everything in their power not to let something like it happen, but it was all too late.

A badged Caucasian male with his ripped biceps had stepped out and scanned left and right, looking past the damage in search for something else. He had then paced his way over to Blake. The young male was nervous for a second as he thought he was about to get tackled onto the ground for whatever reason.

"You ok?" the officer asked.

Blake was slow to move his head. "Yeah," Blake answered dryly.

"Have you seen a man in a black hoodie pass by here?" the ripped man asked with tensed eyebrows.

"What!" Blake shouted as his ears rang.

"Have you seen someone come by here wearing a Black hoodie?" the man asked once again.

Blake had to take a moment to think about whether he'd seen the person or not, then it came to him, "Yeah, I saw someone go that way," Blake informed, as he had pointed across the street with a palm resting on his back in total discomfort.

Shaken up and with teeth clenched, Blake waited still in silence as the officer analyzed into Blake's tired eyes.

"Alright, well sit tight," the officer instructed. "Medical help is on their way, buddy."

Not a second more, he whistled in for his crew members as he was already halfway across the street, and they followed him while those who stuck behind helped those who required immediate medical attention.

CHAPTER TWENTY-TWO

The Meeting

Waking up the next morning wasn't any easier for Blake as the same pressure remained in his chest. As he sat up on the side of the bed with his legs hanging, he took a moment to think about that awful night he'd just had.

He didn't consider himself to be lucky. He thought of something opposite. He couldn't help but reflect on the lives that were lost in the explosion. For a moment, Blake felt that it was his fault. He had seen the bomber, but had done nothing to stop him, but then, how could he have known? It sure was a shame Blake wasn't able to catch a good look at the man's face. All that he could make out of him were the freckles of a pale-skinned individual.

Soon, the phone buzzed in his pocket. It was a text. Blake took that moment to see who it was. It was the woman who'd been concerned about him the past week. Except, this time she had texted him the address to a funeral service at 12:30 that afternoon.

Blake shook his head and powered off his phone. He was disappointed with the way he had been coping with his mistake or possible mistake as the man was still trying to shove in his head. He sighed as he tucked away his cell, "I miss you," he muttered.

Hopping out of bed wasn't all that easy. This time around, Blake had lost his balance, his shoulder went crashing against the wall that his headboard shared. That nasty fall from the previous night was more painful than what he had thought.

Blake could feel the tiny scrapes on his back without having to touch it. To describe it, it was like having the chicken pox, except it was only a burning sensation along his back and it felt like a nasty carpet burn.

After a short recuperation, Blake received an unexpected call. The first person that came to mind was Emily, but it wasn't. It was an unknown caller, and that could mean one thing – Agent Johnson.

"Hello?" Blake answered with his hand shaking uncontrollably.

"You have to come in now, we need to talk," Allen responded with a serious tone in his voice. Then he hung up. *What could that possibly mean?* Blake wondered. Whatever it was, it didn't seem quite right. Something was surely up. *Another day, another issue,* he thought.

Not only did he have to show up to this meeting with Allen, but later to Dana's funeral. And with the service being a couple of hours away he became indecisive about whether or not to show up.

How do you look down at a coffin, at the person you've possibly killed? Blake asked himself.

He thought about Emily for a brief second, and right then a pinch of anxiety came in like a thunderstorm. His heart was pumping at a much faster pace, and he could feel the dryness of his mouth; he was getting a bad taste deep down in his throat as his stomach was bubbling.

Blake Anderson sat right back down on the edge of his bed and covered his mouth with a blanket as he began to sob, screaming as loud as he could into the covers.
With the nightstand beside his bed, he jabbed the side of his foot into the drawer, knocking down a little lamp that rested on top.

Blake gave his nightstand another strike, only this time slightly cracking the wooden structure. At that point, he knew he had officially gone insane. He figured there should be something that he could do to settle himself down a bit.

After a soothing, warm shower, Blake dressed with extra precaution as glass and chipped wood remained on the floor from the other night.

Uncomfortably, and with teeth clenched, he placed new bandages on the cuts that ran along his hands, but not soon enough, he was set to go.

He had his dress pants on along with glossy black dress shoes to match. He'd also slipped on a white undershirt along with a black button up, long sleeve shirt. It was all if at last minute he wanted to make an appearance at the funeral after his meeting with Allen.

That gut-wrenching emotion he had about attending the service in the afternoon seemingly invaded his entire soul. He'd been thinking about it more often than the explosion that nearly took his life.

Things might not go all that well if he stepped foot in that church. He was positive about it.

When the time came to be out on the road in his Chrysler, he peered up through his windshield at the clouds that were a solemn gray. He noticed the sun had not been able to peek out. It just added to what was already a dull and saddening day.

Driving across town had not been as disastrous as the last attempt Blake tried to make it to Allen's office. No snowfall, no traffic jams, no morning screams from an ambulance, nothing. It was a smooth ride all the way. Sadly, it may just be the only positive thing to happen that day.

As Blake had thought, Allen was no jolly man that morning. Blake came knocking on his apartment door. "Get in here!" the man called out from the other side.

As Blake had stepped in, he'd seen Agent Johnson sitting in his desk chair, leaning back with arms folded as he stared straight at him from a distance. The expression on the man's face was making Blake feel uneasy. He had a hunch it was about his screw-ups, and he expected his cancellation.

By taking a small glimpse around as he approached the desk, he could see that Allen had done a bit of cleaning since the last time he had been there. Most of the clothes had been picked up, and no dirty socks were lying in a place they shouldn't. For once the TV was turned off. Every time he had visited before, an oldie was playing on the television, which spells that something was just not right.

Taking a seat in front of the desk, Blake looked up at the man, then immediately dropped his eyes down to his knees. "I'm terminated. Is that it? You're going to fire me because I haven't made my decision yet?" Blake's lips quivered.

Allen quickly breathed through his nose. "The Corporation has decided that you get zero income this time around. Instead of voting you off of something you seem to be very good at, we've agreed that it'd be reasonable to suspend your allowance, till next case," Allen said.

"Oh, thank you," Blake sighed in disbelief, with a hint of sarcasm.

"But wait, something else was brought to my attention," Allen addressed.

That line there had a darker tone to it. Seemingly everything that came from Allen's mouth sounded severe. Blake just never knew what to expect.

"Near Belmont Avenue, a woman appeared dead in her office building. And two days later, five more people were killed by an explosion all firmly believed to have been done by Marco."

"Yeah I know," Blake told the man. "I heard."

Getting up from his seat, Allen bent down to reach for something that was beside his desk. Whatever it was it must've been heavy. It was quite long and required Allen to use both hands to pick it up. Then he roughly placed it on his desk.

The object was quite familiar to Blake, and he took only a few seconds to figure out that it was indeed his sniper. With folded arms, Agent Johnson stared straight down at Blake as the young male twisted uncomfortably in his seat. He knew the conversation would lead to something he had never fully prepared himself to do before, which was to lie to a professional.

As Allen stepped a few feet back, he leaned against the covered up windows with arms remained crossed. That's when Blake was getting this nasty taste in his mouth again. That feeling in his throat had also returned with a wildly pumping heart, sweaty palms, and throbbing knees.

"I found this shit out on the rooftop," Allen informed him, tilting his head towards the gun. "This shit was found pointed directly at the front door of the office building. Now, please tell me…please tell me that this wasn't you," he worried as he eyeballed the gun again.

"That's my gun," Blake stated.

"Yeah, I know. You're one of the few I've issued this weapon to, but please tell me you did not kill that woman down in Belmont."

"I didn't," Blake said, with a slight shake in his voice. As he breathed deeply through his nostrils, Blake looked up at the man and said, "I ran into Marco, and he fired at me. I was trying to make the arrest, but then it all turned into a chase that made its way over to her office building. He just kept shooting. And the woman happened to have stumbled into the middle of it. He shot her."

Momentarily, he took a moment to breathe through his nose again to keep his voice steady, then he continued. "Marco shot her. That's when he decided to run. I rushed in to help her, but there was nothing I could do. All I could do was report the incident then ditch the scene before someone else got hurt."

"Umm, okay," Agent Johnson said.

At that point, Allen wasn't so vocal, and from what Blake had picked up, the boss wasn't entirely buying what Blake told him.

Shortly after, Blake could feel his forehead becoming damp and eyes becoming dry. "You see, soon I'll be getting reports back, and in those reports, it will precisely state the brand of the exact bullet that pierced the innocent woman's chest. So if you're thinking lying is going to get you out of trouble, you'd just be delaying what's coming for ya," Allen informed. "If that bullet came from that sniper, boy you are in bigger trouble. I'm talking well over a decade in maximum prison. Maybe life. Now, are you sure you want to stick with that story?"

"I'm sure," Blake stated when he looked straight into Allen's eyes.

At that moment Blake could feel his head spinning. He wondered what would benefit him more; continue speaking or not speaking any further.

To hell with it, Blake thought.

"I'm not worried about anything sir. I know I didn't kill that poor woman," his nose slightly crinkled.

Immediately, Allen laughed right where he stood, "You should be worried."

Blake raised an eyebrow.

"One person dead on your watch, five more within forty-eight hours," Allen explained.

"I'm aware of that," Blake spoke. "But, you assigned me to track down Marco, not some bomber. Our guy is a shooter, occasionally a stabber, but not an explosive expert. Whatever that other guy used, couldn't be purchased from anywhere. It was designed."

"Actually," Allen hurriedly jumped in. "Our guy doesn't have a specific weapon of choice. Marco will kill anyone with anything that he could get his hands on."

"But that doesn't make any sense," Blake interjected. "He goes from killing his family to complete strangers? From guns to throwing bombs?"

"Here's what makes sense," Agent Johnson cut in. "Marco was caught on tape near that area, two blocks further up. That's enough for me to know it was him. There was no need for any further details. I know it was that son of a bitch."

A short pause after, Allen added, "But I wanted to tell you I am truly thankful that you were able to walk away after that. Some of the officers recognized you. They told me you were there."

In a very short time, as he bit his bottom lip, Blake was in utter distraught.

"That's a hell of an investigation you got going on," Blake backtracked. "You guys didn't get a disturbance call and have at least one witness describe the man?"

"And what the hell is that supposed to mean?" Allen snapped. "The woman was passed out in a closet, couldn't get as much from her. We know he was wearing a black hoodie, that's about it."

Bothered. Blake would usually have a lot to say, but he hadn't said much. Especially any mention of seeing the freckled face killer. It would seem Blake was the only one to have gotten the best look of the bomber. He was more sure it wasn't Marco.

Soon Blake lets out a quick opinion. "I just don't think Marco killed half of those people the media is putting on his name," Blake explained.

Staring hard at Blake as Allen realized the young man was unable to look up at him, he had asked him a thought-provoking question. "Are you on his side?"

It was silent for the next three seconds, and Allen seemed to be getting a bit more agitated by each passing one.

"You do understand that Marco is a stone cold killer, and doesn't need a reason to kill? He's a sick individual."

"Yeah, I'm following, sir," Blake answered in a non-convincing tone that he had set in his voice.

"No, you're not!" Allen raised his voice. "I'm not so sure that you get it. How many people have to die before he gets caught? I need you to hurry that shit up because the police have cases on top of cases. They solve one case here, and there's gunfire across the street from another scenario. It's ridiculous. They're backed up enough as it is as I've said before. I want to prove to the government that this program could work. I want my agents to get the credit, not some police officer. So, how many people have to die before you catch that son of a bitch?"

At the peak of his minor meltdown, Allen sunk his teeth into his bottom lip as he was pacing himself back and forth behind his desk to remain calm. He had been trying best of his ability to not flip out and swipe items off his desk like he was known for doing most of his life working in law enforcement.

"None. No one has to die," Blake responded. And he took a huge gulp and corrected himself, "No one else is going to die."

"Good, now get yourself in check boy and hurry the f**k up. Won't be long before another innocent life gets taken," Allen stated.

After a solid nod of his head, Blake hurried off his seat and headed for the door. "I'm on it sir," he called out. "I'm not going to let you down."

And by early afternoon, Blake worriedly drove the short distance to the Church from Allen's office with a solemn look plastered on his face.

CHAPTER TWENTY-THREE

Funeral

Blake waited inside his vehicle as it continued to run in a packed parking lot. He thought of the many ways his entering the building could go down. The idea of people turning in their seats to stare him down invaded his mind. Another thought involved him getting a huge lecture from Emily about disappearing the last couple of days. Then another thought came, the actual huge possibility the others would sense the guilt seeping out of him. It was just too dismaying.

The man had never been a smoker, but for the first time, he had picked up a cigarette from an old pack sitting in the glove compartment that Emily had left behind one night, and lit one. Eventually, his car became foggy and oddly enough, he liked it.

His nerves ratcheted down a notch. It was shortly after his little blow out session that he could feel his anxiety fizzling away, and he could breathe normally again. It was the best breath he'd taken since Dana's incident.

Before he knew it, Blake was ready as he'll ever be to step his foot into that church.

Upon entering, Blake put on a half-smile and gave a bow of his head to those loitering just outside the door.

As he headed inside, he could see the crowd through the framed glass wall up front and of course, the half-open casket that sat in the center. He could hear the sad piano music seeping through the wall that almost triggered a tear.

"This is going to be a hell of an afternoon," Blake muttered as he turned his attention to the huge line forming.

Group by group, they stepped up to peer into the casket. As Blake moved closer, he had witnessed his fair share of tears, tissues, and puppy dog looks on most of the people's faces. "No doubt that I caused this," he muttered under his breath.

As he stared straight ahead at the crowd within, he had scanned all the people that could potentially try to torture him if they knew. But there was no way they could have known, not then at least, he thought. It took a while to locate Emily. He would have recognized her brown hair anywhere, even tied in a bun as it was then. She was seated towards the front, in the second row, next to an older gentleman. Blake did not recognize him. *A relative?* He thought.

Then an odd thought came to mind. Blake was unsure whether it was wise to be seen by Emily inside that church, but out of respect for her mother, it was necessary; he had to.

Meanwhile, Blake moved over to the far left of the glass wall where there was a door, and he stepped into the room. The door closed loudly behind him, and a few people turned their heads to see who had entered. With Emily being all the way up front, she didn't bother to look back. Perhaps that was a good thing for him.

Blake took his place at the end of the huge line that wrapped all the way around the right side of the room. Every few moments, Blake eyeballed the woman he feared to talk to, and the guy that sat next to her. *Could that be her father?* Blake asked himself.

Suddenly, he was feeling more anxious. It never occurred to him that Emily's father would show up. He'd never gotten an opportunity to meet him beforehand. Blake initially thought the day wouldn't come, and right there in that church, was not the way he wanted to meet a relative of Emily's.

The line slowly shifted forward, little by little, and Blake got to the point where he was able to see the side of Emily's head. She soon turned her head near Blake's direction, and he hid behind the broad-shouldered man in front of him. A moment later, he looked past the man's shoulder and saw that Emily had not been looking around anymore. She was looking straight ahead from her spot.

Just then, a family of three entered through the door Blake had come in from; a mother and two children, a little boy and girl. Right away, the family hopped in line behind Blake. He could hear one of the kids in the back asking who it was that lied in the casket. Blake assumed that particular family must have been old friends of Dana's.

The line progressed, and before Blake knew it, he was halfway to the front. He had briefly thought about the night of the family dinner. He remembered the laughs, the energy, Dana's joyful expression when she witnessed her daughter being as happy as she was. It was in that second that Blake glanced over to Emily and realized she had been looking back, near his direction again. She seemed to be scanning the people in the line. There were only seconds before her eyes would reach him.

She rotated her head a little more, then stopped. She looked to be staring right at him. He was momentarily frightened, and his reflexes kicked in. Quickly, he turned his head towards the wall on his right and pretended to observe the details in the wall work.

Blake didn't have to look back over to see that she was still looking. It was one of the most awkward positions Blake had been in for a while, and he could feel his body shaking.

As the line gradually moved forward, he had the urgent need to glance her way. Blake even attempted the neck-crack maneuver. As he tilted his head from left to right, up and around, he discreetly gave her a quick look.

And what a fail that was. Blake could not locate her past the man's broad shoulders, but he had witnessed his old waitress, Kelly sitting in the third row right behind Emily, and a familiar looking male, Trevor Banks in the center row seated next to his grandmother.

It was soon when the young man was up in front of the line. Blake had observed the people that were up on the stage, overlooking the casket with their eyes filled. Blake, himself could feel his cores become full as the intensity of every note of that piano playing in the background absorbed through his ears.

The family on the stage was beginning to leave, and sure enough, it was his turn to go. Blake took a huge gulp as he felt his heart pumping with a little more horsepower. He was sure that Emily had spotted him earlier, and Blake didn't have a clue as to what would happen in the next few moments.

Just as he was approaching the casket, he sensed this massive load building in his chest which had made it hard to breathe. He halted up front, and the young man could see the pale-skinned woman with elbows at her sides, hands overlapping her abdominal area.

Clothed in all black, Dana was fitted correctly in a long-sleeved shirt, buttoned all the way to the top. He had taken a quick glimpse at the broad collar, and he wasn't sure if the garment was chosen randomly by the removal staff, or purposely selected to hide as much of the massive wound as possible. Either way, Blake tried to keep himself together as both hands were clenching onto the casket.

As he looked upon the narrow box, he stared directly at where the bullet had impacted. He tried hard not to think about that night.

Soon after, Blake couldn't help but break. He bawled on the spot. It wasn't a surprise. He knew he'd crack.

"I'm very sorry," Blake choked up. "No matter how the story goes, I'm the reason for this. And although you are in a better place right now, I would do or give anything to have you back here with your daughter."

Instantly after, his eyes flooded. He looked back at Emily where she had remained seated. Her father was quick to have witnessed the eye contact from them as his eyes traveled back and forth between the two, but decided to stay silent.

Blake faced the front, looking back down at the casket with lips that trembled. "Although I've only gotten to see you a few times, it still felt like I've known you for the longest, through Emily. You will forever live in our hearts." Blake murmured.

Shortly after he gave his quick tribute to Dana, Blake felt the rush of oncoming heartburn. He slightly leaned on the casket and got a hold of the edge as the people that were waiting next in line gave him an odd stare, mildly worried about him fainting right there. As Blake held on tightly, he let out deep breaths, looking back again at the remaining people in line.

Right away, he deduced his heartburn was a result of lack of sleep due to stress. He then flashed his attention back at Dana with twitchy eyes as he rested his head on the casket for a second.

As he felt his body settling, Blake took a look out into the crowd. That time, he stared right at Emily as she peered right back into his entirely filled eyes.

Judging by her dilated pupils, he could see that she was concerned about him. Her father had been glancing back and forth between the two again, and he appeared to have picked up on something.

Richard wanted to talk about what he had assumed it meant, but he kept his lips sealed for a little while longer. As for Blake, he ditched the scene as walked straight down the center aisle all the way to the back. Emily kept her eyes glued to him as her head rotated along with his movements until he'd gone out of sight. She saw him exit out the main entrance, letting out a heavy breath powerful enough that her father could sense more pain, without having to hear her speak. "You know that kid?" he asked.

"No, I don't think so," she replied. And Emily was convinced she'd told her father a half lie. The young woman evidently felt she didn't know who Blake was anymore, or why he'd been acting the way he had been lately.

Her father, Richard, glanced down at his pouty-faced daughter and knew the young fellow had meant something to her. "Was he your boyfriend?" Richard asked.

"Yeah, was," she answered softly.
Her father bowed his head. "I see," he responded under his breath.

A while later, a man known as Pastor Josie made an appearance up front and delivered some words of wisdom. "Although times get tough, we must come to a realization that they occur at certain moments in our lives. But with time and laughter, they can be the best medicine ever to be received. I like to perceive that there is light, even in the darkest of times. It's what keeps me sharp, what keeps me going. Sooner than expected, you will come to a point where you'll laugh at the memories nailed into your brain, rather than cry as much as you all have today. We've lost a beautiful soul, but heaven has gained a new angel. And she's out there somewhere, watching."

As the pastor went on, Emily took his words and locked them into her head. She teared up, but she released a closed lip smile.

Time had gone by, and it was that moment for Emily to give her eulogy. She'd spent hours putting her words together as she had practiced them in front of a mirror back at home.

As she stepped up in front of the podium, all eyes were stuck on her. Typically, Emily would feel nervous in a crowd like so, but she wanted to push herself through it, and before she knew it, everyone got quiet and the moment was hers. Emily cleared her throat, then she spoke into the microphone.

"It's tragic to see someone go, someone you love, someone you cherish, and someone you've lived with all your life," her voice shook.

Emily took a huge breath, and she went on to share a memory of hers from back when she was in grade school. "The woman I am speaking of, I remember she would walk me to school, no matter the weather. And she would hold my hand along the way. And I wish that times were still like that, that she could still be here by my side."

As Emily took a brief pause, she could hear sniffling and minor coughs in the crowd. The twenty-one-year-old woman could feel the tears swimming around in her eyes as they were about to plop down onto the podium.

"I remember my sixth-grade camping trip when she came along with me. I was lucky enough to have her as one of the chaperones. And while we were out by the lake, she went with me on my first canoe ride. I remember paddling with her so far out. I was paddling with such force that I kept getting water inside our canoe. She had this bit of panic in her voice, thinking that we were eventually going to sink into the lake," she grinned.

Short laughter sparked in the crowd. At that instant, Emily took a brief look at her father, and he was smiling.

"The woman that I am speaking of shared many laughs with me. We've had multiple fights, but she never switched up on me or left when she had the option to, she stayed," Emily beamed at the ceiling. "She was the one that would usually help me with my homework when I needed it. Even in my college years. She helped me find my first job. She helped me with past boy troubles, and she would always make my days the best they could be. She was very supportive when it came to reaching my goals. She was always there, and that woman happened to be more than just my mother, she was my hero. I love you, mom."

Unexpectedly, loud applause echoed in the room. "Heaven has gained a new angel, and I'll be waiting for the day that I get to see you again," Emily finished strongly.

Just as the crowd continued, she hopped off the stage, wiping her hand across her cheekbones feeling quite surprised of herself.

Emily sat back down beside her father. "I am proud of you, honey," he said happily.

It was then that Emily felt relaxed as she rested her head on his shoulder.

CHAPTER TWENTY-FOUR

Counseling

The following day, Blake made an appointment that he felt he needed at the counselor's office.

"So let me get this straight Mr. Anderson," a woman opened up. "You feel like this recent death has made you believe it was somehow your fault?"

Sitting about a foot from each other, Blake admired the small Purple Heart badge pinned to her suit. It reminded him of his grandpa when he served the Marines. Assuming it had been for her husband, Blake thought it was a unique feature of her clothing.

She was a woman of color, quiet professional, and a sweetheart when she wanted to be. She wore this single button black suit with a white blouse underneath. The neck hole depth of the shirt stretched enough to let the air out through her distracting cleavage. There were moments when Blake caught himself eyeballing a little too long. A few times he had to make it seem like he'd been looking into her name tag pinned just below her Purple Heart badge. The imprinted name read, 'Aaliyah Jones.'

The two sat in a near knee touching distance, no table, no desk in between. Aaliyah wore a matching skirt to go with her suit, pressed and clean as if store bought. She had her legs crossed with a red clipboard above the knee as she's determined to get to the bottom of Blake's situation.

"So you're telling me; you feel like you're the one to blame?" the woman rephrased.

Blinking uncontrollably after catching himself being distracted again, he answered, "That's exactly how I feel."

"Why do you think like that?" Aaliyah asked.

"Because," Blake answered tediously.

"Because of what? Elaborate."

Blake dropped his head down as he stared at his own feet. Mrs. Jones could see the thought process in his eyes; he looked worried, uncertain, and fearful.

"Mr. Anderson?" Aaliyah snapped him out of his thinking.

"I just feel guilty, and I just don't know why I feel this way," Blake muttered.

With not much to go on, Mrs. Jones had to take a second to think. "So in a way, do you feel like there was something that you could have done, something that would prevent the unfortunate occurrence?"

"Yes, that's exactly it," Blake replied.

With the pen in her hand, she jotted down some notes onto a paper attached to her clipboard. Blake watched as the pen shifted across the sheet. "How is your relationship with your parents, and other members of your home?"

"I'm an only child, and I live on my own. My mother and I ain't that closely connected, but we're on good terms," Blake informed.

"So your parents are together then? Is that correct?"

"My father died years ago, but my parents had always gone on and off."

After quickly jotting down some more notes onto her paper, she clipped the back end of her pen closed. "Using any medications?"

He took up a moment to think. Blake believed she spiraled up a thought that he may be on a prescription or something. "No, nothing at all," he said.

"What about a girlfriend? What's that like?" Aaliyah asked.

"I haven't spoken to her in days," Blake said, dolefully.

Blake looked over at the window on the right. He knew what her next question would be.

"Why is that?" the woman wondered.

Blake took a look down at his feet again, then sighed with a great big shrug of his shoulders. "I don't know," he answered cautiously.

"And whose fault might that be?" Aaliyah asked in a delicate voice.

Blake then sealed his lips shut as he had twisted uncomfortably in his seat. He began to look all around the room. His eyes wandered anywhere but the person that was sitting across.

"Would you say that you love this girl?" The woman asked.

Blake cleared his throat before opening up. It was not the type of discussion he wanted to get into; he knew it would be a sensitive topic. He blinked uncontrollably, but he answered, "Yes."

"Then why stop talking to her? You must let that pride go, and speak to her. Show her you'll be there for her."

"I know," Blake muttered.

And she then clicked her pen open and scribbled onto her paper. "Some signs are there," Aaliyah stated. Blake somehow knew of the next word she was about to project, and she said it. "Depression."

She briefly explained her theory. "With the loss of your father and parents constantly going on and off throughout your life. The route you and your girlfriend may be heading is eating you up inside. Going through these changes may be why you are feeling some guilt. You want to make these changes because you feel like you're the only one that has to. Therefore, this recent death may make you feel guilty because you feel like you have to be the one to take action. Perhaps because someone needs closure with something and this fixture with the people you hold close to your heart. You may not have depression, but through time I'm going to have to see where your mind's headed before it turns into something serious."

Then it was sudden when Blake was able to look back into the woman's eyes again. He gave her a slight nod of his head, showing Aaliyah a bit of understanding. Right then and there, Blake knew what he wanted to do next, and that's paying Emily a little visit. "I hope that I have helped you open up your eyes to understand where the guilt may be coming from," Aaliyah said. "It happens to people."

Minutes later, the woman got up from her seat as she informed Blake about his next due date back at the counselor's office. "How does the following Monday sound for you?" She projected as she had just made it to her desk.

"Yeah, that's fine."

Aaliyah ran her pen across a business card she had on the edge of the surface. Blake had slowly raised from his seat and began to walk up to her desk where she had then notified Blake about his next arranged appointment. After another quick clip of her pen, she replied, "All set. I'll be seeing you next week."

Blake bowed his head with a blank expression on his face. Then he gave her a firm handshake, where he was received the business card.

From yards away as he stood in front of the door, Aaliyah called out to say, "I'm truly sorry for your loss. I know that she's watching you from above."

After that statement, he didn't bother to turn back. The young male blinked uncontrollably right where he stood as if someone was throwing several fake punches to make their peer's flinch. It was evident her last comment did something to him. Blake reached for the knob and opened up slowly. He wanted to say something without knowing what he wanted to say. At that time, he remained calm and proceeded forward.

Over at the Stoner's residents, Richard walked in through the front door where Emily stood by with folded arms, seemingly concerned about something. "How you holding up, honey?" her father first asked as was placing his red and black checkerboard coat on a hook beside him.

Richard could quickly tell by the wrinkling of her forehead and the dilated pupils that she had a ton on her mind.

Emily's father extended his arms out for a hug. "Everything will be ok," he told her.

Emily managed to control the tears that had almost made contact with his flannel shirt as her head rested on his chest. She'd done this quick hard sniff before she finally said something. "I want you to do what you can to find the man that killed mom, and give him what he deserves."

"Look, honey, the cops are gonna catch the guy soon, I promise."

"But I don't want them to find him. I want you to find him. I want to see him shatter. I want him to die in the worst of ways."

"Don't worry," Richard said calmly. "Whatever happens, I will have the rookies make sure that he's not gonna have it easy. If blood falls, we can hope that it all drains from his body. I am with you, Emily."

CHAPTER TWENTY-FIVE

The Gift

It was approximately five-thirty in the evening when Blake arrived on Emily's doorstep. It was chilly out with temperatures only reaching its mid-thirties. The dark skies were clear, and for what it felt like the first time in forever, there was no snow drifting downward.

It had taken several knocks before Emily opened the door. When she did, she had this look of shock on her face. She threw her head back, and her eyes bulged. Blake couldn't help but grin this awkward grin. It was a moment that became all too discomforting for him in a matter of seconds. He looked down at his feet to avoid as much awkward eye contact as possible.

What do you say to the woman you've been avoiding?

The look he received made him fear her more than ever. He shook as he stood in the wind as he cleared his throat. "What are you doing here?" Emily asked.

Blake glanced into her eyes as his closed-lip smile became visible again. It was his way of convincing her that there was nothing wrong in the first place. "May I come in?" Blake asked softly.

There was a short, uncomfortable silence. Emily was evidently debating on it. "I don't know," she said. "I don't let strangers into my home."

And her words were like a punch to the chest. He sighed while he took the next few seconds to process his transition with Emily. While his mind went blank, he stared off into the snowy ground, and the painful silence was creeping back in. "Please," he begged softly. "Just let me in?"

Emily rolled her eyes and eventually opened the door wide. With caution, Blake entered. His shoes were drenched and squeaky on the hardwood, and he quickly rubbed off his feet on the floor mat nearby before anything began.

The aggravated woman closed the door behind him and turned her attention to the troubled man as she leaned against the door in silence. Blake slowly rotated, then stared straight ahead at Emily as she gave him a glowering look. He was ready for whatever type of hell was about to come his way.

She folded her arms together, and Blake felt his head beginning to spin. The silence continued until Emily finally spoke. "What are you doing here?" she asked. Throwing her arms up in frustration, she added, "Better question, where were you?"

Blake glanced at the floor. "I am sorry about everything," he muttered to his feet.

"You disappeared for days, showed up at my mother's funeral, and didn't even bother to speak to me or check up on me, then you disappear again? You haven't been picking up the phone. This whole time I've been wondering where you were!" She progressively raised her voice.

Clenching his teeth behind his tightly locked lips, Blake realized he hated himself much more than ever before. Interesting enough though, he didn't think there was any room left for more hatred towards himself.

Blake tucked his upper lip in his mouth when he felt it dry up. He bowed his head in sorrow. "I am truly sorry, Emily."

Gently, she pushed herself off the door and slowly motioned on near the family room. "Is that all you can say?"

Emily wondered. "You're lucky my dad is upstairs taking a nap right now. Otherwise, I'd be screaming at you," her voice shook.

Slowly, his eyebrows rose. He then thought it might not have been a bright idea to come to talk at the moment. There were much better settings for that type of discussion.

"You couldn't stick around for my mother's funeral? What makes you think you can stick around for anything else?"

"Don't say that," Blake begged.

"When I needed you most, you just ran off on me."

"I know, I know and I apologize for that. It's just..."

"Just what?" Emily demanded quickly for a reasonable answer. "What the hell is wrong with you? You're acting strange, Blake. I'm stressing so much. I even failed my final."

When he let the last thing she said scramble in his head, the young male himself couldn't help but look over to his right into the living room. That's when something resting on the coffee table caught his eye. It was a big yellow shopping bag, and it looked to be the exact bag her mother had been carrying that night of the incident.

Emily noticed he was staring straight at it. As Blake gawked at the bag, images flashed through his head of the murder scene.

Blake had retained every detail from that night. He envisioned the raw image of Emily's mother lying helplessly on the greenish tiled floor. He remembered his hands getting drenched in Dana's blood, and he could hear the last few words that came from her. "Watch after Emily for me."

There was no way that bag could be from the murder scene, could it? Blake wondered.

What is it?" Emily stared aggressively at him.

Blake flinched where he stood as Emily rolled her eyes once again; she then walked over to the coffee table.

"There's something in here for you," she told him as she opened the bag.

Right then, the shivering male appeared confused as his eyebrows tensed up in an instant. He wasn't exactly sure if he had heard Emily correctly. "What?" he replied, leaving an open mouth with lowered eyelids.

Emily dug through the bag and pulled out a twelve by nine and a half gift box, wrapped in a bright silver paper with a tiny red bow taped to the corner. "My mom got you something for Christmas," she sniffled.

When she nearly broke down, Blake's only solution for the moment was to step closer and give her a comforting hug. As Blake sheltered her with his arms, she became a bit hesitant. A part of her wanted him to stop, but she knew she needed some type of relief. A temporary fix.
Blake had done his best to hide his teary-eyed self. He blinked them tears back into his system without letting a single drop, fall. Seconds later, Emily pulled away, but Blake had pulled her back in for just a moment longer, in just enough time to let his eyes clear up.

When he soon released her, she handed him the gift, and as he had held it in his hands, he stepped away slowly, staring at the neatly wrapped package that looked way too precious to rip apart. A good five feet distance away from Emily, he tore through the tape and wrapping paper with trembling hands, slow paced. He then lifted the lid of the box like taking the top part off a sandwich cookie and holding it side by side.

He smiled, and his eyes puddled up again. He sniffed his nose clear and took a long look at his present.

"You ok?" Emily asked.

"Yeah, I'm all right," Blake replied, delicately.

He lifted the clothing to examine the length for proper fitting. It wasn't just any bodywear; it was a brown version of Blake's favorite gray quarter zip sweater.

It was then when Blake had wished for a way to show his appreciation to Dana. It was a beautiful gesture, he thought.

Emily came up and stood in front of Blake, looking into his bloodshot eyes. "Please tell me what's wrong," she asked softly.

"I can't," he shook his head.

For a moment, silence filled the room as she analyzed the puzzled looking individual.

"I have to go," Blake spoke.

The perplexed male took a step forward, attempting to pass by Emily, but she pressed Blake a few feet back. "I need an explanation now!" she screamed.

"Shhh, you'll wake your dad up," he muttered.

"I don't care!"

Blake's lip quivered, and he refused to make any eye contact. He wanted to tell her what had happened that night, but he couldn't. His anxiety had gotten worse, and his heart pounded irregularly loud as he could feel the thumps in his ears. He could perceive his knees were getting weak and all that he wanted to do at the moment was to drop to the floor and hopefully, sleep through what he wished was just a long and terrible nightmare.

"Look, Emily, I wish I could tell you something, but I just can't."

"Tell me."

"I can't!"

"Is there a new girl?"

"What? No, there's no other girl," he quickly shook his head.

"Fine. If you want to act single, then get the f**k out of my house!"

"What the hell is going on down there!" Father Richard called out from near the upstairs balcony.

Instantly, Blake was stunned. It was time to make himself scarce. Blake brushed through Emily, and no more than a second later, Blake made his way out the front door without another word said, leaving Emily in tears.

Later that night, Blake had found himself to be seated dolefully in the middle row of a church building all alone. It's been years since he's been in one, willingly. "Please forgive me," he muttered to the floor with both hands joined, elbows planted on his knees. "I will do right in this world. I promise"

While doing the best he could do to hold himself together, Blake had still been processing images in his head of that night, wondering if he'd done what he thought he had done. The young male tried making sense of another possible scenario that would lead him to believe the bullet wasn't his.

He eventually caught himself looking up at the huge rounded ceiling, asking again for forgiveness. He peered straight ahead at the wall hanging of a cross. "I'm going to set things right, heavenly Father," his lips shook. "I think I know what I have to do."

And right after, Blake left.

Once he had gotten home, Blake received a phone call from his old buddy Terrance Patterson.

"Hey, what's up?" Blake answered with no hesitation to pick up the call.

"Bro, how you holding up?" Terrance worried.

"Wait, what are you talking about?" Blake asked confusedly.

"Emily's statuses. They are looking like you guys broke up, or some shit," he informed Blake as he scrolled through his newsfeed from a desktop monitor in his apartment.

"I don't know man. I just don't know anymore," Blake replied.

"Look, she's probably just on her period or something. It gets me every time. Just stare right at her belly and be like, 'forget you, hormones!'"

Right away, Blake let out a little laugh. It was odd; Blake never thought he'd have a genuine laugh again.

"Yeah, sorry to call you this late in the night. Just needed to check up on the homie, you know what I mean?"

"Yeah, I understand," Blake responded.

"All right boy, let me know if you need help. I still got to pay my respects to the man that helped me get that nice ass little diploma hanging on my wall. We all knew my grandma had her worries," Terrance smiled.

Blake grinned from where he sat. "Glad things worked out well for you, and if I ever need something, I'll let you know."

Then shortly, Blake hung up the phone.

Terrance had to hold his cell up front to be sure Blake was the one to have closed the call. Terrance sat there worriedly as he stared down blankly at his desk. "I think my boy needs some help," he muttered.

Remaining where he was, Blake was thinking of everything; Emily, the argument between him and her, the murder scene, the cops coming closer to finding out the truth, his high school days with his best friend Terrance, all of it. He just knew he needed an escape, from everything.

But then Blake soon realized something as he kept thinking about the moment he pressed the trigger. The bullet size, the speed. Blake didn't recall hearing about the bullet coming straight out of her back in which with his sniper, it should have.

Later that same night, Blake knocked on Terrance's front door.

"Blake?"

"I need to use your laptop for a minute," Blake immediately stepped in

"Ok, but can I clear my history browser first?" Terrance asked.

Before Blake could even touch the laptop, he glanced at his best friend in disgust, nearly giggling.

"It was just a joke," Terrance said. "Just don't go on my google to type in the letter 'p'" Terrance went on.

Meanwhile, Blake slipped on some latex gloves, not because of what his friend had been saying, but because he didn't want to leave any fingerprints behind. It was risky enough to have a suspicious search history. That's why he'd been at Terrance's house. Law enforcement wouldn't think about tracking Blake there.

"What's with the gloves?" Terrance asked.

Blake ignored. He had searched up the exact brand of a sniper he had used up on that rooftop. He studied it. The bullet size, where it came from, how it was built, what places had it, and how fast a single bullet could travel.

As it stated on one of the websites, a single shot would have gone straight through the person whole.

"Why you searching up guns?" Terrance asked.

"Boy you got a big ass mouth," Blake laughed.

Shortly, Blake had clicked out of the site and got up from the desk chair. He was a little relieved. The man soon figured the bullet might not have been from him, but he still wasn't convinced enough. He needed to know more, but it was all for one night. He swiftly left the apartment leaving his friend confused. "I need more Black friends," Terrance complained.

CHAPTER TWENTY-SIX

The Call

It was a bright morning the following day. Christmas was right around the corner with only three days left to go, and Blake had never felt the holiday spirit any less than he had then.

It was an odd morning. For once after the whole incident, Blake was able to sleep the entire night through. That was until he was woken up from a dream which felt so genuine. Surprisingly for the troubled individual, it had felt like a positive one.

Blake dreamt about being in a huge family cookout down at a local park on a warm summer's day, hosted by Dana. The gathering had loads of food. There was everything from hot dogs to cheeseburgers, and many traditional multicultural foods.

The great smoky smell filled the air from a mini grill and shockingly, Dana was the cook. As Blake remembered, Dana's been enjoying every minute of it as relatives worshiped her.

Over at a picnic table that Blake shared with two strangers, they all sat on opposite corners from each other. Being the goofball Emily was, she snuck up behind Blake, single-handedly hugging him around his neck while setting full plates she'd prepared for the two, flat out in front. He was quite impressed with her waitress balancing skills. Ironically he says to her, "I think you've found your new job," referring to her as a future server when indeed she had been one.

Also, in his dream, Emily planted herself next to Blake, and although she had her food sitting in front of her, she, however, scooped up a spoonful from his foam plate. Blake remembered chuckling in his seat as he glanced over at Emily, admiring her facial features and her unique way of joking around.

Meanwhile, Dana stared directly at the two. She seemed satisfied. Perhaps she thought Emily had finally snatched up a keeper. The woman smiled from a distance, and it wasn't long before Blake caught Dana's eyes aiming their way.

Shortly Emily noticed Blake peeking over her shoulder, so she swung her head back to capture where the young male's eyes had gone. The delightful couple smiled back at Dana. The expression on Emily's eyes revealed to the mother that she'd been enjoying Blake's company and that she'd cherished him adequately.

The young male's eyes settled in the same direction awhile longer, holding a closed lip smile as Emily began chowing down on her food. It appeared to Blake that Dana had mouthed the words, "thank you" then she disappeared off into the smoke, and that was the end of it, Blake was woken up. He sat up on his bed with his back pressed against the headboard wondering what she intended by it. It had to have meant something.

Blake was aware that dreams could be meaningless, and not have any sense to them, but this was different, he knew it meant something. Those two words Dana mouthed brought him to the murder scene when Emily's mother requested Blake, a promise from him regarding her daughter. The dream felt as if she was leaving a message after keeping an eye out from the sky.

"Please take care of my baby," he remembered Dana telling him.

Gawking where he sat as he zoned straight ahead at the wall of his bedroom, it didn't take long before the man started looking doleful again. This time, he wasn't entirely sure for what reason. It wasn't the unintentional, yet possible murder, but he had been thinking about Emily. At that point, he wasn't quite sure if they were still together.

Soon, he had gotten sidetracked as his phone rang somewhere in his bed. Immediately, Blake scattered his hands all across the blankets and under the bed skirt. His hands and eyes followed the sound as he begun to get a little impatient.

The young man had forcefully whipped up the covers from the bed; then he'd heard his phone drop near the bottom edge of his mattress. Blake hurried in and dived for his phone, and he answered, quickly, "Hello?"

"He's here, the man is here," a male's voice shook in a near-breathless voice.

Blake was utterly confused for a second. He knew for a fact the person was not on his contact list, but the voice sounded familiar, and it seemed foreign. It took him another moment to understand what the man on the other line meant before it came to him.

The family in the cabin in the woods, Blake thought.

He'd forgotten he handed out a private number linked to a downloaded web application he had on his phone. Instantly, his eyes widened. "Ok, I'll be right there!"

As Blake stripped down to his socks and boxers, he immediately scattered the drawers for a clean pair of clothes. "Lock your doors and windows and remain hidden," Blake instructed while his shoulder held his phone against his cheek.

"No!" the man repeated like a broken record. "I-I see him. Please hurry. Just please get here fast " he added.

"What do you mean you see him? He's inside?" Blake asked in a foreboding tone as he slipped on a black v-neck.

"No, I see him walking outside. He just walked passed my house. Hurry," the male instructed.

From the sound of his voice, Blake could sense the eagerness. Whatever the cabin owner was seeing, Blake knew he had to act quickly. Blake then squeezed himself in a pair of black running shoes and slipped into his freshly cleaned gray quarter zip sweater as fast as he could.

"Ok, I'm coming," Blake muttered to the man on the line.

Blake hung up, nearly tripping beside his bed after stubbing his big toe on one of the metal legs. He grunted on the spot, but that didn't stop him from hurrying in for his pistol resting on top of a drawer. He quickly stuffed it in his pants then races to his vehicle. Blake fired that four-wheeler up and zipped through the neighborhood, doing a dangerous U-turn at the intersection, then floored it down the street with the face of determination.

Later, Emily's house phone rang. She usually wouldn't pick up a calling number she didn't recognize, but considering everything that had happened recently, she answered.

"You must be Emily," a mysterious male voice had spoken.

"Yes, this is me," she said nervously.

"This is Agent Johnson speaking. I've tried calling your father, but let him know that I will be expecting him shortly. That's if he wants to catch the guy."

And right away she seemed interested. "Go on. I'm listening," She told Allen.

CHAPTER TWENTY-SEVEN

Woods Chase

As Blake zipped down the wet streets of Chicago in his Chrysler, Blake repeatedly swerved from one lane to the other, passing up multiple vehicles in proximity.

Undoubtedly, many angry drivers honked at him as he did to them. At one point the young male had almost smashed into the rear end of a brown sixty-four Mustang that purposely stopped in the middle of the road. Blake lurched into his steering wheel, and immediately expressed this angry look on his face.

He was able to see a senior man staring directly at him through his rearview mirror, and the two were too stubborn to move. It was an apparent contact, and Blake decided to whip up and brandish his weapon in mid-air.

The gray-bearded man became stunned as he immediately pressed on the gas. Sure it might have been harsh, unlawful, but it worked, and Blake laughed it off. The path was then clearing, and he moved onward, reaching the speed of eighty in less than four seconds.

Blake managed to minimize a twenty-minute ride, to nearly half of that. He had parked in the same spot as before when came for those footprints.

He had briskly shut off his vehicle and ditched it. It was time for business. Blake made his way down the slight hill with fast moving feet, heading straight for the woods.

As he walked with extensively stretched leg movements, Blake had been keeping aware of his surroundings. Compared to his last visit, he noticed there'd been a lot less snow which made it a much easier get by. As he was motioning by, it suddenly came to him that it could all be a trap. After being spotted a few times in the same area, why would Marco come back? It's not like Marco intended to make the police or even Blake to get a smooth capture.

Faster than the last time, it hadn't been long before he made it to the cabins. Apparently, the couple living inside had been peeping through the window as they quickly opened up as Blake was passing by. Blake's attention immediately switched over to them as he heard the door creaked open beside him. The cabin owners poked their heads out through the slight opening, and with trembling fingers, they each pointed the direction they'd seen Marco headed earlier.

"He's over there, he went that way!" they said, eagerly.

Promptly, Blake ran that direction. He became more alert and slipped up his weapon almost immediately. A couple yards up ahead Blake was able to spot a few footprints that trailed off quite a distance. He knew it was Marco's. It was the same prints that Allen had shown him, the same ones that he'd seen at the abandoned diner. The hunt was almost over; this could be it, Blake felt.

Blake ran further down, through the woods till eventually, the cabins were out of sight. Soon enough the traces were hard to follow as there came the point when the footprints lead to three different directions. It appeared as if Marco tried to throw the young male off on his hunt.

Blake laughed in place as he looked around like an airport wave scanner with a finger lying delicately on the trigger. He hadn't noticed anything else that appeared strange to him, although there was a bit of chance Marco was camouflaging within the dirt and trees.

At that instant, the whole search with no doubt was a setup for something.

With his background in training, it was time to put his intelligence to the test. He observed those footprints to decide which pathway had the more likelihood of leading him to some evidence, or better yet, the criminal himself. As he glanced at the trail headed diagonally to the left, it continued till it reached a tree. There was no possible way he could have climbed it. The tree was thick, no branches below that he could have used to make it up, and there had been no tracks moving around the trunk.

After being assured Marco wasn't hiding up in the tree, he canceled off the first path. While he was making sense of it, it appeared to Blake that the person must've stepped back to align his feet precisely to his previous footing. Taking a closer look, if anyone were to be analyzing midway of the first trail, they would be able to notice that Marco had lost steadiness, and that's for sure when he changed position. It was evident at that point that Marco shifted to the right to start another trail.

Right, where Blake stood, he couldn't see where the second set tracks had ended, but it ran quite a distance until it curled off behind a tree. Blake assumed the path ended there.

After he had looked at the third set of tracks, it was the only one that made sense. The pathway ran as far as the eye could see with no interruptions. At that moment he felt confident about which direction to follow through with, so he went along with it and tracked off there. The further down he went, Blake was believed to be correct, and all Marco had been doing was delaying his arrest.

Strangely, up ahead were no exceeding footprints. A great deal of dead rotten brown leaves scattered around the ground near him. For that reason, it made it quite challenging to look for any traces.

He soon noticed the leaves were scattered along in just one section like they were purposely grouped up to form a huge pile in the shape of a circle. Blake didn't dare step through it. It looked as though this whole time Marco rigged the woods for his benefit.

The muddy, damp, discolored leaves could be a form of technique Marco used to disguise his own footprints, considering that in that precise moment, Blake had witnessed several trials from a distance, all leading in a variety of directions, in and out of the great big pile. It was confusing to read, to determine where to go next based off of all the trials Marco had left behind. But that's when Blake went with his gut instincts and curved around the huge leaf patch and went straight onward.

About a quarter mile out, Blake came by the edge of a small yet steep hill that stretched horizontally all the way across the woods. And it was the first that Blake had seen it. Never once had he gone this far into the woods. The young male had stopped to think for a moment if it was necessary to proceed to the bottom. Chances were up in the air that Marco could have changed his course a mile behind him.

With not much time of considering, he decided to hike down the hill carefully. Blake reached the level ground and moved roughly ten yards out, then stopped. He took a quick scan of the area and nothing. Pure silence. It was too quiet for comfort. Not even the sounds of the wind were whirling in and shaking up the branches above. The mind-boggling possibility of a weapon going off was something he had hoped he wouldn't experience within' the next few seconds.

He took another look, eyes moving left to right, forward and what not, and he noticed something behind him that struck out as weird to him. It was from within the wall of the hill, buried.

Blake immediately walked up closer, and it seemed to be a thin bike tire. He rummaged through the dirt for a bit. After a few good tugs as he had gripped onto the bent tire with both hands, he got it halfway exposed, but it was still hung, revealed enough to know for sure it was the pink bike that belonged to the people in the cabin.

Blake never thought he'd come across the bicycle. He figured it was long gone when he first heard about it. If only Marco could get captured just as simple as the bike, Blake was thinking.

Walking miles and miles deep in the woods for the second time and not being able to find what he'd been looking for made Blake's blood boil. His eyebrows shortly pinched together as the man stepped about ten yards away from the hill again, and looked onward through the quarter mile left of the woods.

At that point, he felt he could find something else soon. There was something else there, he could feel it. With the pistol that was shaking in his hand, Blake heard a loud plop, as if something had fallen. Then he had detected a creaking sound that came from the top of the hill. It was indeed him, Marco. The criminal was on the move, dashing straight off the edge of the slope to only change his course, disappearing behind it.

It would appear that Marco had come from behind a tree, falling onto the ground somehow, and stepped on a small twig when he'd started to make a run for it which caused that loud creak sound Blake heard from the bottom. That's what quickly caught the young male's attention as he whipped his head behind him. In an instant, his pupils dilated, and that was when Blake had done an angry low pitched growl through his clenched teeth.

Blake sprinted his way up the hill, keeping his eyes glued up ahead on Marco with every step he took. The furious male could feel the adrenaline building inside as soon as he'd reached the top. Blake Anderson dashed through the woods while Marco ran as fast as he could while he held onto his baggy pants with one hand. Having been that his pants were oversized, it made Blake accelerate much closer to his target.

As he zipped through, Marco turned his head back and noticed Blake being at an uncomfortable distance. That's when Marco began zigzagging around one tree to the other, and whenever Marco got the opportunity, he would push and kick himself off from a tree trunk to accelerate his speed.

Blake furiously took wider steps, having it reach up to their full potential as he had no intention of stopping anytime soon, even if he were to become breathless. Not even clashing through numerous tiny tree branches, scratching up on Blake as he was passing through was going to make him stop.

Blake had soon raised his pistol. He aimed his best at the moving target. Being behind the weapon as they were fleeing was not making the shot any easier on Blake, especially with Marco running behind one tree after another every few seconds.

To hell with it, Blake thought.

He simultaneously pressed the trigger and fired three rounds. Two bullets hit the unleveled ground while the last one ricocheted off a tree trunk that nearly hit Marco's head. The wanted man had stopped for a moment to look behind and give Blake the deadliest stare. Marco stood there as he waited for the young male to catch up but then decided at the last few seconds to keep on running.

A few yards out, Marco ran up this enormous dead tree branch lying on the ground and made a daring jump off of it. Marco landed back on the mud as Blake hunches under the branch arch.

Marco was only a few yards ahead. When Blake felt bolder, he made a complete stop, locked his feet in place with eyes straight ahead at Marco with shoulders back, aiming, then he discharged.

"Bam!" Blake yelled as the metal round zipped off the side of Marco's calf. The shot roughly threw him from his feet as he went tumbling to the ground with immediate blood gush raining off from his leg. Marco screamed at the top of his lungs while dirt bits got smudged onto his forehead as he skidded on his front.

As fast as he could, Marco got on his feet and began limping his way up a small hill, but he had collapsed back onto the ground.

For his second attempt, he lifted himself up and staggered. That's when Blake paced his way to the runner. "Get on the ground! Get on the ground before I put another bullet in you!" Blake commanded from just a few feet away.

Marco proceeded to disobey direct orders from Blake by standing tall, facing away from him. That was when the twenty-year-old man began to charge towards his target with a gun that had been aiming towards Marco's head.

As soon as Blake was in arm's reach, he pressed the tip against Marco's skull. A quick, unexpected reaction occurred when the wanted man swiped Blake's arm off to the side, knocking the gun right out of his hand.

Rapidly, Blake tucked down and tackled Marco from the side, and the two went crashing into a tree. With Marco's quick reflexes, he tightly wrapped his arm around the young male's neck then jolted his body to the side, causing them to lose their balance and come smacking against the soggy ground.

Marco crawled off the dirt first and had pulled out a pocket knife he had stashed in his front pocket. Blake scarcely got back up on his feet as his attention switched over towards the sharp steel in the hands of a said 'killer.'

Marco began to charge in closer and swung his blade, but luckily for Blake, he threw his body back, then he had charged in for Marco's stomach like a football tackler. The older male was lifted about a foot off the ground and was then forcefully thrown onto a tree up ahead. It was a disgusting hit. Blake could hear the sound of the fugitive's spinal cord crack as it made an impact. Marco's head bounced off the trunk, and for a second, Blake thought it was the end of it all. He took that moment to catch a breather as he stared at him lying on the ground as he kept his distance.

Marco hurriedly staggered back on his feet while he shook off the pain. As he had looked down at the dirt smeared all throughout his clothing including the gunshot wound as he continued to bleed, Marco was feeling hesitant about resuming the fight, but the aggression seemed high on Blake. Marco didn't want to give up on running.

Marco gripped his knife horizontally with a firm grip. He was breathing hard when he had said, "The thing I hate most about cops... they don't know what the hell they're getting into most of the time."

At that point, Blake had become tired of interacting any further with that deranged human being. The knife in Marco's hand was making him uncomfortable enough. Blake's only solution was to come rushing in, and when he did, the wanted man had released a right cross and Blake was able to leap his body backwards in time. Marco then immediately swiped it back up, nearly slicing through Blake's skin. The blade ended up leaving behind a sizeable diagonal cut across his sweatshirt. Right then, Blake had been taken by a surprise as he took a quick glance down below. He was unsure whether or not he'd been cut.

Scarcely, Marco proceeded to go at it. He took a step forward and threw left and right hooks near Blake's head. With each arm thrown at him, Marco seemed to become more precise.

Blake was in fear for his life. He moved his torso like never before when avoiding the rapid-fire blade that kept swinging at his direction. Blake Anderson used his forearms to prevent his stomach from being sliced open. The thickness of his sweatshirt sleeve saved him from being brutally cut. He witnessed the snip bits of his clothing snipping away. He felt

the wind force smack against his face from each motion
Marco released.

Quickly, Marco switched the direction of his wrist
and began jabbing his knife towards Blake's chest. With the
adrenaline running through his body, Blake's quick reflexes
had him ducking out, bending, twisting and jolting out in
unexplainable ways.

There was a point when Blake finally built up the
courage to swiftly take a step closer and jab his foot into
Marco's calf wound. The impact made him lose his balance,
having him fall right on top of Blake.

In an instant, the discomfort could be read all over
Marcos' eyes as it dilated. He remained on top with all of his
weight pinning Blake's arms beneath him. Marco got up
halfway, and wildly threw a punch. Then it was one more
after another, that it went on in a continuous motion with the
blade still at hand.

Blake tried so desperately to block each and every one
of his throws as soon as he was able to shake his hands-free.

Relentlessly, Blake was feeling both sides of his
cheekbones becoming swollen.

Still trapped, Blake continued to shake his way free,
but couldn't.

Young man, Blake was blinded for most of the time
being, and although he was unable to see with both eyes, one
thing was certain with him, Blake knew his blood spilled near
his eyes from his nose. Next thing he grasped, Blake was hit
in the eye socket even harder.

Immediately, Blake felt that stingy sensation growing,
and he could feel it spreading like waves washing up on a
shore.

As there were more hits to the face, Blake was feeling
weaker and weaker with a growing migraine.

Abruptly, it became quiet. Blake had kept his eyes
squinted as he was waiting for another blow to the face. Since
being that three seconds had gone by without receiving any

further hits, Blake slowly opened up his twitchy eyes with palms pointed straight out to the sky.

As the man remained kneeled on top of the bloody-faced, twenty-year-old, Marco glared down at him as if he was this pathetic, worthless meat suit to the world. Who knew what his next move was going to be?

Marco stood up tall as he let out a heavy breath of frustration. He'd taken a second to lower his eyes right back down as the young male was lying on the ground, helpless and spitting out blood beside him.

Marco kicked once at Blake's shin, nearly losing his balance. "You should leave shit alone that you know nothing about!" Marco yelled. "I'm doing this for my daughter, for my sons, my family."

Hearing Marco's last statement, he was unsure of what he truly meant by that. Things weren't making sense to him. "If I ever catch your ass again, I swear, swear on everything, I'll kill you," Marco warned as he then began limping away from the scene.

Blake remained on the ground as he rolled on his side to spit out the blood which dripped onto his lips. Marco was out of sight, and Blake soon lifted himself on his feet, hunched over. He didn't bother to chase him down. He stood there in place with confusion.

He couldn't help but feel saddened that an individual beat him. It was unlikely; Blake was never this easy to take down, especially when the suspect himself was injured.

It was a strange feeling. In a way, Blake thought he had deserved it all for everything that has happened with the Stoner family, but also believed that it was still not enough. Blake limped his way to retrieve his gun and then proceeded to his car with shame and dropped shoulders.

CHAPTER TWENTY-EIGHT

Hospital Visit

Blake took a seat in his car. As he leaned back breathlessly, he began to wonder why Marco hadn't killed him then. He had the advantage; why not take the opportunity? After all, Blake had been the one to be persistent with Marco. Swinging at him, chasing after him, even shooting at him. Blake didn't wish for Marco to finish the job, but it was strange for a murderer not to kill the man who's been hunting him down this whole time.

Although Marco had vanished without murdering him, Blake realized he hadn't put in a hundred percent during the fight either, but why? It was very unusual for him. Why does he go easy on said psychopath?

Later in the day at the nearest gas station, he parked his vehicle off to the side of the building. He wanted to get cleaned up inside the restroom, although he managed to wipe most of the blood off his face beforehand. It still raised suspicion as the cashier noticed a man with cuts and blood smears all over his sweatshirt, tiredly entering the shop.

Blake hadn't really bothered to hide it, but luckily, the clerk hadn't acted upon it. Cops were no good at a time like that, and the young male wanted to spare his moments at the hospital nearby for more information.

Meanwhile, as Blake soaked his face with cold water pouring down at full speed from the bathroom sink, he took one look at the mirror and noticed a small bruise on his cheekbone. Blake leaned in closer towards the mirror for a better view of the yellow-green puncture. Being the man that he was, he lightly tapped on it to get a better understanding of his discolored skin.

Coming about it again, Blake was still unsure of why he hadn't put a hundred percent effort into this mission. He had the authority but did not take it when he had the perfect chance back in the woods. The young man knew a single bullet could have ended it all then but decided against it. Now his only question was, why?

Without a clue where the wanted man had gone off to, the only thing left on his mind was to look in on Veronica once again, for anything he could get out of her. It's been days since his last stop. Chances were mild that her condition could be much better by then, he thought.

Shortly, after getting cleaned up, Blake took off his favorite sweatshirt and disposed of it inside the trash can below the sink.

He'd taken a moment to look down at his shirt with the tiny incisions on it. He ran his fingers straight down and must've felt at least twenty tears in his clothing. He had this sigh of relief when he realized just how close he was from having his intestines disgorge from its natural place. He hadn't been entirely thankful; more like surprised he was able to walk away from a knife attack by bare hands.

Soon enough, Blake had come out of the bathroom, and he made a quick exit out the door just before the cashier was able to turn around and watch him leave as he'd been restocking lottery tickets on a rack on the back wall.

Meanwhile. As minutes passed by like seconds, Blake entered in through the same entryway of the hospital's lot as before. The young male was quick in dressing himself up in his car, and never once had he worn the agent wardrobe while working a case until then. Blake slipped himself into the white button-down, a red tie and a pair of black dress pants, then a top hat to match.

It was the only spare clothing he had nearby; tucked in a brown briefcase he had always kept in the backseat. Then, lastly, the overcoat of which became a nice touch for the weather being so cold.

Compared to his last visit, there had been fewer parked cars around, although he still hadn't parked till halfway down the lot. It was quite a fair distance walk before entering the building with fast moving feet. The first thing he did was checked in at the front desk. Luckily, there was a nicer woman behind the counter. Not shocking to him, Veronica hadn't signed out. It was double the luck within a minute.

After he was allowed into the halls, he took off. Up the elevator, and through the halls, Blake was pacing himself by memory, and he made it there in a jiffy.

Blake moved near the halfway sealed door and poked his head out to see if she'd been asleep. The woman sitting up on the bed seemed occupied with a load of fashion magazines resting on her lap. Blake gave the wall a couple of knocks to let his arrival be known, then walked right inside with a slight push of the door.

She delicately sets her magazine flat on her stomach, almost didn't recognize the man at first, and the first thing she said in the lightest voice was, "you're back?"

She appeared better, and by the sound of her voice, she was surprised. The expression on her face looked as though her mind was made up of questions about Blake's green eye socket, and his agent suit. "You look to be doing much better from the last time I've seen you," Blake told her just as he expressed the friendliest grin he could ever give as he stopped in the middle.

The woman smiled as she was taking a look down at herself. "Whatever I've recovered, you've found," Veronica laughed softly. "You look like hell. Now, what brings you back here? Isn't one Agent enough?"

"Wait," Blake responded confusedly. "What are you talking about?"

Veronica kept her mouth shut for a moment as she stared ahead at the puzzled man.

"Some guy came in yesterday, wearing the same exact suit, asking for Marco. I assumed he was a friend of yours," she explained.

"You remember his name?" Blake wanted to know so desperately, without making it seem like he did.

"Agent Dack, I believe."

And right then Blake tucked his bottom lip into his mouth as he bit down. It would appear that Agent Johnson assigned Matthew the same case, which was slightly unusual to Blake. Usually, Agent Johnson would trust Blake enough to handle tracking down someone without the help of another agent, but it was more apparent at that moment Allen has had his doubts all along, which would probably explain how they came across each other outside Allen's door days ago.

He then slowly stepped in beside her bed and quickly switches discussion. "Well, I've run into Marco," he mentioned.

"Oh really?" She said, seemingly fascinated. "And what, is that asshole behind bars now?"

Blake dropped his head down with a soft laugh that followed. One look at him, she figured the next thing to come out of his mouth was something she would not want to hear. "He's been a real pain in my ass lately," Blake began. "He managed to get away from me twice. But next time I assure you he won't be able to get away from me again. I just need to know where he's headed now."

Veronica took a heavy breath, and the room became silent for a moment. Blake took a seat in a chair beside her bed and examined her facial expressions, hoping that she would reply with something, anything.

"What are you thinking about?" he asked her.

"Nothing. It's just-"

"Just what?" Blake asked concernedly.

"Marco hadn't always been this way."

In an instant, Blake cringed at Veronica's last statement. His eyes zoned in at the floor, trying to fathom the last few words that spilled from her mouth. For that moment as the room went quiet, Blake thought to himself. "Impossible," he muttered.

He thought about what he'd read about the wanted fugitive; Marco was a member of a gang for many years, nearly two decades. Was Marco once an innocent human being? Blake questioned himself.

Blake glanced back up and leaned forward from his seat with undivided attention and said, "What can you tell me about the man you once knew?"

Scooting up to make herself comfortable on the not-so-comfy bed, she appeared to be preparing herself to pour out what she had in mind. Right away, she seemed to have no trouble opening up to Blake. She cleared her throat as she was about to speak. "I know this is going to be hard to believe, but trust me, he was a sweetheart in high school. That's where we met. With all the gang-related activities he and his friends were getting into, Marco never failed to show me love, honesty, and respect."

Once again Blake cringed, and Veronica continued to elaborate. "He protected me in high school, and he would always stop by my house after school to chill. We would smoke, drink, do homework or whatever, and just play dumb with each other. Back then you would never have guessed he would end up being a killer."

"Hold up," Blake interrupted. "What makes you know for sure that he was faithful, or even honest with you from the beginning?"

"Because he was pretty much with me every minute, and it's just something you know about a person," she explained.

To hear where she'd been coming from, Blake had to seal his lips a moment longer as he was feeling a series of questions sitting on the tip of his tongue. Positively, she answered some of what he had wanted, but he urgently needed to know why she felt Marco hadn't murdered anyone else throughout the relationship.

Veronica continued to share her thoughts. "Years later, things were starting to become more real with each other. He suggested leaving behind the thug life. It was him who had suggested it, not me. And at that point I remember how special it made me feel, to have someone change from their wicked ways to better themselves."

"Wow," Blake said in amazement.

"It's just sad to see him turn out that way," Veronica sighed. And she instantly became teary-eyed.

"It's just horrible that my kids were taken from me before they were able to understand the true meaning of life; Before they were able to experience school."

With eyes that welled up, she turned towards Blake. "I missed my kids' funeral," Veronica choked. "Just yesterday I was told that my kids had gotten cremated."

Immediately, Blake dropped his head down. Disturbed. He took a look up at her to only get a sense of what it was like to have lost someone close again. "I just wish that I was able to see my kids. One last time at least," the woman cried.

"I'm sorry," he told Veronica in a light voice.

As the young man stared at the tiled floor, he began to imagine Marco's younger self the way the woman had described him. Coming across him recently made it difficult to picture him in such a way. Strangely, he pulled through and imagined Marco being a decent human being. It was nearly believable, but everything she stated, he took her word for it.

Blake's alive. Marco practically set him free in the woods, and something about that just didn't add up to the young man, but that very thing is what made him believe her.

"The only thing that makes sense to me is to give him what he deserves, for my children," Veronica declared.

"I understand that, and If I were a father, I'd be saying the exact same thing," Blake muttered.

"What will you do when you catch him?" she added.

"He won't get away this time, that's for sure," Blake promised, just as he stared blankly at the floor.

"Alright, be sure to recheck the diner. Marco might be running a reverse psychology effect since he was spotted there, thinking cops won't check again."

"Most certainly. I knew I needed to revisit you for something. Thank you, Torres," Blake smiled. "I'm going to get on it right now."

Promptly after, Blake jumped out of his seat and began walking backwards towards the door as he kept his eyes on Veronica. "I am on it," he beamed at her.

And just when Blake had quickly spun all the way around to exit the room, he'd bumped into a man whose body felt like a wall of sandbags. The impact set Blake about a foot back, and that's when he had a clear view of the well-built man in a red and black checkerboard coat.

Blake recognized him from the funeral. Emily's father. Richard Smith stood before him with darting eyes.

"You seem startled kid," Richard grinned at Blake, letting out an evil-like laugh. "Didn't mean to scare you, but oh, that's a nasty bruise you got there on your eye," he pinpointed so briskly.

Without a word said, Blake tucked his upper lip into his mouth and zoned into the man's chest.

"You look so damn familiar," Richard again, speaking with a smirk on his face.

"Do I, really?" Blake asked softly, attempting to throw Richard off.

"Yeah. In fact, you look so damn familiar I am going to have to ask you for your name," Richard suggested just as he stepped in closer.

Blake took a quick look down at his feet as he discreetly gulped. He then glanced over at Veronica, and she sensed something odd from it. "You ain't a fraud right?" she spoke over the blankets.

"A fraud?" Richard glared at Blake with a broad smirk. "A fraud of what? a cop? an undercover agent?"

"I actually am working for the police," Blake responded, clearing it up for the two.

"Ah, so you must be Agent Anderson then? The man who was chasing down Marco the night a woman died in Belmont?" Richard spoke as he was more than likely sure.

"No, I'm Agent Dack," Blake's lips quivered.

"Really? well, your buddy, Agent Johnson told me that you might just be here. I too, am looking for the man that killed Dana Stoner."

In a flash, Blake's instincts were telling him to bail, but that wasn't the brightest of ideas. He knew he needed to lessen the possibility of having Emily's father finding out about everything Blake saw that night; everything Blake wasn't saying.

"We'll all get our wish soon. We just have to keep both eyes opened," the young man said.

"You're right about that," Richard smirked. "So, where you headed now?"

"Oh, I'm not really allowed to have unauthorized people joining with me," Blake informed.

"Oh, that's not why I am asking," Richard laughed. "My ex-wife was the woman that died in her office building, and I demand as many answers as possible. And I think I deserve a little more flippin' respect than I am getting from people. Now, please boy, I know you're working this case as well, and you know much more than anybody out there. So tell me, where you are headed?"

Blake took a minor gulp. "I'm thinking about checking the local stores, Marco might be snooping around for food soon," he lied again.

Blake glanced over his shoulder to see that Veronica had been staring confusedly at him and the intimidating man standing in front of him. Richard was getting a strong sense of some dishonesty happening before his eyes.

"Ok good," Richard smirked as he peered into Blake's eyes.

"Listen, I'd love to sit and chat, but I really gotta hurry up and do this," Blake mentioned.

"Alright," Richard grinned oddly.

As Blake was about to walk out, Richard added something. "This is weird," he said. "Earlier, I could have sworn you were that wuss boy I've seen at the funeral. My daughter's ex-boyfriend, Blake Anderson."

"Oh yeah? I get that a lot. Everybody says I look like somebody," Blake chuckled as Richard mocked along.

"I guess I have a twin brother I've never met before," he joked. "Believe me, I am not dating your daughter" he laughed some more.

Blake then slowly motioned to the door, and bounded out. Then just as he became out of sight, he sped walked all the way down the hallway.

Richard stuck behind and whipped his head back at Veronica. "Tell me everything he's shared with you," he firmly demanded.

"He's going to the abandoned diner by Belmont," Veronica spilled out.

"Ah, and his name?"

"Agent Anderson," Veronica stated.

"Great."

Right then, Richard had let out a malicious grin just before he rushed out. He pulled out a walkie-talkie straight from the inside of his checkerboard coat as he had witnessed the doors to the stairwell down the hall coming to a close.

"It's confirmed! Blake Anderson is in the building! I repeat! Blake Anderson is in the building!"

Richard hurriedly strode through the hall as he set his radio back in his coat, then he took out an empty-handed gun. He quickly reached back into his jacket for a pistol clip and loaded himself up.

"Watch out! He's got a gun!" a nurse warned out to all her co-workers in plain sight, then she immediately hid in a room nearby.

"Get out the way! Get out the hell out the way!" Richard screamed at those who didn't merge off to the side quick enough.

A split second later, the hall was full of commotion as panicked nurses were rushing out the area.

Soon enough, Richard decided to pick up his pace by running his way through the hall with both hands on the gun, keeping it pointed to the floor. He could sense dryness in his mouth, and his forehead was becoming a tad damped, knowing that he could get shot at any moment if the police were on the floor.

CHAPTER TWENTY-NINE

Runner

Traveling quickly down the hall, Blake had thought Richard must've stuck behind with Veronica, but he still had this non-stop, uncomfortable, sickening feeling that he felt in the atmosphere.

It began with Richard, but then the number of police officers he had seen scattered out in the main floor increased that pressure building up inside his chest. They were all talking to bystanders, appearing to be looking for somebody. He just felt they were on to him. Blake knew he had to get out of there quick with no association by any means. He lowered his head and continued to move down the hall at half-speed, hoping it would minimize attention, and Blake had no intention of making eye contact with anyone along the way.

As Blake entered the waiting area, three sheriffs stood near the front desk. Blake flashed his head away as he headed for the door hoping he hadn't drawn so much attention with his eye-catching overcoat and red tie. Shockingly, Blake heard a voice from behind that felt similar to a clench of his airway tubes. "There he is!" a man's voice quickly called out. It was those three words that made Blake zip towards the door without taking a look back. That was when he heard multiplied footsteps slapping against the white tiled floors from behind, seemingly becoming louder.

The sounds of keys clinking followed, and Blake's level of fear skyrockets through the roof as he could feel his eyelids stretch further apart from each other.

As soon as Blake made it outside, he took a right in the parking lot and continued running. Three men in uniform barged out through the doors. "Suspect is getting away!" one of the men called out, and that line was as bad as someone choking him. He was losing his breath quickly, but that didn't stop Blake from running.

"Stop right there!" another officer called out.

Inside the hospital's central floor area,

Richard was charging through, but the officers inbound tackled him to a wall. There were at least three of them trying to force Richard to the floor. "Drop the gun!" one of the officer's called out. "Drop it!"

"I have a gun permit!" Richard yelled at the top of his lungs.

"Doesn't give you the green light to go out and kill!" one of the officer's responded back.

Meanwhile, during Blake's situation, outrunning them was not the only challenge, but keeping himself from looking back was one too.

Blake crossed a busy street, nearly smacking into two rolling vehicles in the process, and the driver's horns blared near the man's ear. It didn't take a second after he'd gotten out of the way before the operators pressed on the gas. Blake could practically feel one of the cars brushing against his over-coat as they zipped past him.

Barely making it safely across the street, the men with the badges proceeded to follow on foot, but a considerably big garbage truck cut them off, having them lose sight on the runner for a dragged moment.

Blake immediately hurried into an alley straight ahead in between two buildings with multiple passageways.

By the time the officers made it across, their assumption had directed them to believe they had lost Blake. The group was too small for a hunting party. They figured they were going to need more help.

A long moment after, Richard was being escorted out the hospital with two police officers standing alongside him, and just one more following behind. They halted up front where Richard was getting his uncomfortably clipped handcuffs removed from his wrist that he had placed behind him. Richard had served the country, and the badged men were feeling lenient. They figured letting Richard off with a firm warning was a way to sort of give back to him.

And just as one of the guys inserted the key in the handcuffs, Richard's attention switched over his shoulder where could hear hollering from across the street. It was evident the police officers had lost the young man somewhere near those buildings as they were speedily scanning all along the area.

As soon as Richard felt the release of those tight locking handcuffs, he jerked his body to the side and began running towards the street. "Hey!" One of the officers called out to him as they promptly went after him.

Richard swiveled and hopped all around as he was crossing the street with cars reaching in dangerously close. He made it across safe and sound, but he didn't stop there. He continued running while the three cops stuck back in the hospital's lot, hoping those across would get him.

A semi-truck that was passing by blocked their point of view, but it didn't trap the sound of one of the guys that screamed, "Hey, get that guy!"

Immediately, an officer blaring his flashlight at a basement window turned around just as Richard was zipping through, and he reached out for him, but Richard was quick to grasp the officer's arm to twist it. The policeman groaned in pain just as Richard swung him around like a rag doll and released him, sending the badged man crashing into the brick wall to the side.

Meanwhile, he noticed an officer had been looking up at a half-open window on the fourth floor before his attention had switched over to Richard. Richard started to run, traveling up the staircase that was adjacent to him before he even knew there were other cops, yards ahead on the ground that had been running towards him.

Richard was at least ten seconds ahead of them, and he immediately carved him up an excellent twenty-second window by jumping off a rail, four stories high and land into another set of a staircase. He was able to get both hands on those sturdy steel bars with no surface beneath his feet until he effortlessly leaped over the railing.

There that cracked window was, just a few feet over the railing up ahead. Richard had no problem climbing over again. He placed himself on the rail with a firm grip on those bars with very little foot space as he'd been staring down at a fifteen-yard drop.

Richard quickly extended his foot out onto the concrete window ledge, making it appear quite easy at first. When he had first planted his foot on the frame, it soon slipped, nearly losing his shoe.

Richard went for a second attempt and slapped his foot back on the ledge, with as much grip he could get with a sweaty hand on the window frame. Appearing like a human X, he looked below but hadn't become phased at such depth of the space between him and the ground.

Soon enough, Richard pushed off the railing, and for a moment his right foot had nothing beneath it. He managed to get both feet on the concrete window ledge, to slide that window all the way up, and hop right inside.

Oddly, and coincidentally, Blake had been standing across the seemingly vacant room. All drawers of every furniture piece in sight of the apartment were left open, which lead Richard to believe Blake was looking for a weapon, but he appeared to be bare handed.

"Don't do this," Blake implored.

But it seemed as though his words were quick to have gone in one ear and out the other. Richard briskly charged in at him.

Lightheaded, Blake was jolted straight into the front door. Blake then dropped while his hat flew off to the side. He had sensed Richards hurried footsteps approaching him, so he quickly lied on his back and placed his legs in the air to block the hostile man that reached for him.

Violently, Richard swung as Blake begged the man to stop. "Wait!" the young male screamed as he reached out with both hands to shield those massive power-force fist thrown in his direction.

"You killed that woman, you piece of shit!"

"I can explain!" Blake shouted.

Abruptly, Blake's left ankle was clasped with both hands as Richard skidded him across the floor to the point he was elevated a few feet high. Richard released, and Blake was then flown into a wall where his head's flung against a hanging picture frame.

Glass shattered, and it rained down on him.

While his head spun, Blake sat up quickly against the wall, although he had trouble seeing for those couple of seconds.

"You shot her in cold blood!"

"You don't understand," Blake groaned.

Richard had rapidly grasped onto Blake's red tie, yanked him closer, and threw him off to the side. Blake landed on his shoulder again, and Richard had stormed up closer, bent down to plow more punches at his face.

Luckily, Blake jerked his foot just below Richard's knee so quickly, that Richard himself thought his leg had gotten broken. He had been looking down at his oddly bent leg, and Blake directly soccer-kicked Richard in the ribcage that sent him staggering to the other side of the room.

Blake got up and removed his overcoat and tossed it to the side with his fist up and ready. Richard quickly stood up from the floor and gave the youngster a piercing look.

"I made a mistake!" Blake screamed. "I will pay for what I've done."

Tiring enough, Richard kept his fist in the air, just as Blake slowly raises his own. Blake rolled his eyes as he dropped his arms down and let out a heavy sigh, then brought them back up as they were.

"My daughter means a lot to me. Didn't you think about what you were doing before you killed her mother?"

"We don't know who did it yet, but I swear I will pay. Just buy me some time. Let me set things right," Blake nearly broke.

Richards' teeth visibly clenched. He wasn't much of a talker, just a straight to business kind of guy. He came charging in again while Blake took a step forward. Surprisingly, Blake was able to dodge most of Richard's rapid-fire swings, and Blake didn't dare to swing back at the man. It was difficult to even think about harming Richard. Those eyes appeared quite familiar to him, by a certain somebody with a whole lot more hair on their head than him.

At one point, Blake was nearly hit dead in the center of his mouth. The young man had stepped back a few feet to brush his hand across his lip to ensure he hadn't been bleeding. "I had enough!" Blake shouted.

Blake drove up a stream of anger that made him karate kick Richard into a flat screen sitting on a large wooden entertainment center. Evidently, the older man was caught off guard, appearing a little winded while he rested on the floor. Blake then managed to creep up closely to clip a pair of handcuffs on Richard's left wrist and attach it to one of the legs of that furniture piece.

"There's something I have to do," Blake dolefully mentioned.

Blake strode near the window and noticed a shadow on the concrete ledge. Apparently, someone had been waiting by the railing.

Seconds later, some fidgeting of the knob of the front door was in play. Blake had to act quickly by stepping away from the window to get a running start because, for him, it was the only way.

Firstly, Blake looked all around for something small, but with some weight to it. He grabbed onto a desk chair that was in arms reach, and swung it across the room, straight in the center of the window which completely tore off the whole frame. And down it goes with one clean swipe.

Right after, Blake ran as fast as he could and made that huge leap off the concrete ledge. Those very few officers on the ground watched as they were shocked by the eight-yard spring Blake made into the railing of the building across like some superhero. Blake held on for dear life. He didn't dare to give up then.

Blake pulled himself up to a stand and glanced behind him at the puzzled looking officer before he had climbed onto the stairwell. No cops even considered jumping across.

Richard was quick to have freed himself after lifting the massive entertainment center enough to release the clipped end from underneath. He then went on to look straight out the window, and was quite impressed with Blake's brave actions.

And there those police officers were, barging into the room and quickly got a hold of him.

Blake witnessed an officer down below quickly drawing out his weapon before he opened fire. Blake swiftly pressed his back against the brick wall as the bullets chipped debris down on him. Right there at that moment was a moment of too many close calls. The sounds of bolts piercing the steel stairway were aggressively loud in his ears.

"Hey, hold your fire!" Officer Campbell screamed at the officer whose gun remained pointed upward. "What the hell you think you're doing?"

"I'm trying to shoot him. The hell you think I'm doing?" the man responded.

"He's not a killer, idiot. He's still a kid. He made a mistake," Campbell clarified.

Another lookup, Blake was gone. He abandoned the scene through a nearby window.

Meanwhile, handcuffed Richard was escorted up to Officer Campbell with four police officers behind him.

"What the hell?" Campbell raised his arms in the air with fury.

"Who fricking taught this guy?" Richard asked just as he took a squint upward, imaging Blake's jump in his head.

"Listen. Now I can't trust you to be out and about. Your jail sentence will run until Blake gets captured."

"Well, he's going to be at that diner again tonight," Richard grinned.

"Tonight?" Officer Campbell asked. "Alright well, we're going to capture him earlier than that. At his house."

A long hour later, Blake had been hiding in a different building nearby. He snuck into an apartment room through a window on the third level. He buried himself deep inside a coat closet as he waited for the area to be free from those officers, including Richard.

Indeed, there were residences inside; behind the shared wall Blake rested his head on. For a known fact, they were teenagers all in a single bedroom, fooling around and causing the old walls to shake.

As Blake curled up inside the dark, he waited until his heart settled from pounding like a speeding pad drummer. He must've hesitated in his escape four times, firmly believing one of the loudly spoken teens would come out of the room at any given time.

With the amount of laughter and tumbling from the bedroom, Blake assumed no one planned on getting out so soon. Blake eventually opened up the closet door with caution, then gently advanced out into the living room. Instantly, he sprinted to the door and entered into a narrow hall. Blake silently shuts the door from behind, and finally, Blake was able to exhale deeply.

He sure was lucky the hall floor was vacant. Blake wasn't sure of how long he could outrun, let alone outsmart those trained professionals.

Blake continued. He ran all the way through with only a hunch that no police officers were in the building. When he reached the end of the hallway, he found himself a staircase. The man progressed downward with his right-hand gliding on a rusty metal railing all the way through.

As soon as he reached the bottom, he saw a back exit door and barged out. Back outside he was again. Without looking anywhere else, he only focused in on what's up ahead, and he kept it moving.

At that point, he wasn't sure whether he lost them or not. All that mattered then was for Blake to keep on running. He passed various allies and busy streets. Not having a single clue where the officers held back, his anxiety steadily increased. He felt he was being watched again from an area he couldn't see. Blake had to assume that nowhere was safe.

Soon it made sense to him to climb a staircase of a five-story building. As he advanced all the way to the roof, he crouched down and began to kneel his way to the perimeter ledge where Blake then decided to lean against with agony.

He rotated off his back once to take a look down below. He hadn't spotted any squad cars around. That may just be a good sign to him. The troubled man could only make out multiple taxi cars in traffic this hour.

Blake twisted his body back around and kept his head low, breathing amply as he faced up to the sky.

As he lied on the snow-filled roof, Blake slipped out his phone from his dress pants. He stared at his screensaver for a moment with a solemn face. It had been a photo of Emily and him. Her arm was wrapped around his neck as her nose pressed against his cheek with glee, exposing her fresh snow colored teeth.

That time he realized he'd paid more attention to his screensaver than ever, and it bothered him, but at the same time, it made him smile.

A short time later, he sensed his heart slightly increasing its speed, enough that Blake could practically feel the thumps hit his head. It appeared to Blake that his anxiety wasn't going to fade away for a while.

In what seemed like such a short amount of time left, the young man knew what he had to do. Since things were clearly on display that he was in more trouble with the law; it was time to let the truth be known. Blake decided to give Emily a quick call. It was a wild idea, a very frightening one, but he figured it had to be done at that precise moment.

As he waited while his phone operated, he took a deep breath. He hadn't spoken a word to Emily yet, but he was prepared to spew his brains out. It was by each ring that he felt his heart go faster. He hadn't even decided on what to say, how to say it, how to explain, but there was no turning back.

Blake squinted his eyes to keep the tears back and in control. Nothing good was going to come from this, he knew it for a fact. Several rings later, Emily picked up. "Hello?" she answered, in a not so welcoming tone.

Blake clenched his teeth tightly together, then went straight to an apology. "I'm sorry," he began. "I'm sorry for everything that has happened to you, and to us. And if you don't hear from me the next four hours, I'll probably be locked away, or dead."

"What are you talking about?" She sounded panicked.

Blake took a deep breath before briefly explaining what he had in mind. "That night your mother died... it was my fault," he sniffled.

"What are you talking about?" She raised her voice.

"Your mother is dead because of me! I pulled the trigger," he shouted with a shaken voice. "It made a mistake, Emily."

For the time being, the panicked male pounded the back of his head against the brick ledge.

From the other side, he could hear her taking a deep breath as Blake held quiet as he waited for her response. "I still do not understand," Emily replied. "There's no room to be joking. I don't have the time for jokes, especially about my mother."

"Listen to me!" Blake had cut his way in. "I got into some shit, and I ended up running into your mom by mistake. I know apologies don't mean shit to you, but I just wanted you to know I screwed up, and am going to pay for what I've done."

Then a long pause came to be. Blake figured she must've ditched her phone out somewhere.

"Hello? are you still there?" Blake asked nervously.

With a projected voice, Emily spoke clearly into the phone. "You're the worst person I've ever let into my life. I hope you die!" Then she ended the call right there.

At that point, Blake had been left hanging. Those last few words Emily had spoken to him hurt like a puncture to the chest. But the conversation didn't go as bad as he thought. It was sure one less thing he had to do, and there was a little sense of relief from that, even though Emily's last words were unforgettable.

Blake was unsure whether Emily believed him, but worst of it all, he knew he wasn't joking.

Blake suddenly felt this rage his body could no longer seal inside. A moment passed by, and he stood up on the roof with squinted his eyes, and not because of the sun peeking through the light clouds, but because Blake knew things were about to get serious again soon. He panted as his head spun. Another life was about to be in danger.

CHAPTER THIRTY

Prepare For War

It wasn't until mid-afternoon when Blake retrieved his vehicle from the parking lot. Beforehand, he had been staking out at an apartment building across the street from the hospital, peeking out through a small window in the hallway.

The area had seemed clear from law enforcement officers, and that's when Blake had taken the opportunity to sneak his way back to the hospital's lot. He knew it was a difficult task to proceed, but he had no intentions of leaving his beauty behind, even if it meant his car was being watched the whole time from a distance. After all, it may be the last few moments behind the wheel of his Chrysler.

It was a short ride home. The sun was weakening quickly as the blue skies were fading away while the moon was making itself more visible. In the time that Blake spent navigating through the streets, everything had suddenly seemed quite odd to him. Everything was uncomfortably dull, and the streets were silent like never before.

Blake sat there in his vehicle as he was parked alongside a curb out front his house while the motor was still running. It was then when it dawned on him; the feeling that he had no one he can get down with on a personal level about his problems, not even Terrence, at least not with that issue. But being alone was just another predicament added to his stress bank.

By then, it was definite he had been eliminated from the police program, possibly even his spot at the donut shop. It was all just so heartrending, and everything seemed to be hitting him all at once.

Woefully, he ditched his vehicle for a moment as he rushed inside his house. Whatever Blake had planned, he had to move fleetly. It wouldn't be long before the police would arrive at his location.

He hurried up the stairs and into his room where he switched out his dress shirt for a solid black t-shirt, a bulletproof vest and his new brown quarter zipped sweater. It wasn't long before it had become his new favorite clothing piece. What made it so special was that it came from Dana. It was the last thing he figured he'd wear.

As Blake was about to head out his room, his cell abruptly rang in his pocket.

Startled. For a second, Blake felt some sense of relief. He thought it was Emily that dialed him up. Sadly, it wasn't. It was an unknown caller. By then he knew who it was; Agent, Johnson.

"Hello," Blake answered with a dry mouth.

Indeed, it was Allen. Blake's heart had pumped with excessive force before the middle-aged man even said a word. *Nothing good would come from this,* the young male processed.

Being accurate most of the time was starting to have its downfall, and this time, he wished he was wrong. Allen cut straight to the point, projecting his voice. The tone made it sure he was ticked off. "How long did you think you could hide the truth? Have you not heard the saying, 'the truth always comes out?'"

Speechless, Blake remained still as Allen laughed from the other side. "Cops are getting hot, you're terminated boy," Allen chuckled.

Suddenly, a loud boom came from downstairs, startling Blake. It appeared as though someone had barged in through the front door, knocking it completely off its hinges.

Next thing he noticed, the sound of footsteps began swarming inside the house.

Blake quickly gathered his spare pistol and keys, and then rushed out into the narrow hall outside his bedroom. From the peak of the stairs, he saw the shadows painted on the wall down below of several men with heavy weaponry, moving fast like snakes. "Freeze! Hold it right there!" an officer commanded.

Blake immediately stepped into the room across from his and shut the door, locking it behind him. "We got him!" another police officer called out from the other side.

The adrenaline was intense in Blake. He headed towards the window and unlatched the hook while the men behind the door were roughly shaking the door handle. "Open up!" a voice commanded. "You don't want to make this any harder on yourself!"

One by one, he heard nearly every officer speak from the other side of the door, including the one with an old familiar voice.

"We got this place surrounded!" an officer spoke.

Then the other. "We are coming in!"

And then the one that he recognized. "Blake, just open up," the guy spoke on the softer side.

Blake paused with a leg raised on the window frame as he was about to climb over when he heard that voice. "Matthew?" he uttered to himself.

Why would Matthew Dack be at his house? An old friend of his.

Why is he here with the police? Blake wondered.

With each pound on the door, Blake nearly jumped out of his shoes. They all were loud and aggressive. He slipped the bedroom window up all the way and sat on the frame while he took a quick glance down at the ground. No human could make that jump without dislocating something.

He let his foot hang off the ledge, knowing there was no turning back. It was the only way.

Perhaps, Blake may have a bit of luck. There was a trampoline right below him that had been left behind by the previous house owner, but even then it was a risky move. The mixture of the winter freeze and several inches of snow resting on the mat increased the likelihood of him going right through.

The men who continued to bang against the door were just seconds away from getting in. They tore one of the hinges completely off and chipped the wooden top frame of the door.

"You can't keep running! This is your last warning!" one of the men aggressively called out.

There was no time to think, only to act on his escape. He took another look down below as his heel bones touched the house siding. He gulped hard when suddenly a loud crash came from behind him. They were in, and It was evident they had busted the door right onto the beige rug. He could hear them swarming in. "Freeze!" one of the men called out.

Blake instantly took the pulse-pounding, breathtaking jump. As he let himself loose from the ledge, one of the men rushed to the window to catch him, but it was too late. From above, that same officer watched as Blake went crashing dead in the center of the trampoline. The impact looked rough as Blake the courageous man was engulfed in snow. The officer up above had completely lost sight of him.

For the stunt Blake just pulled, he was lucky. The trampoline had torn, but not enough for the fabric to swallow him whole. The twenty-year-old had his spine on the ground against the ice as his feet were tangled in the rips and tears of the mat while the snow was beginning to smear on his face.

He yanked his leg back and was let loose while an avalanche of snow began pouring in, quickly.

Blake immediately crawled across the thick layer of ice that circled underneath, and then promptly dug through the wall of snow that barricaded him in. He used his fingers like claws, running them up and down the wall as fast as he could, like rummaging through papers in a desk drawer.

Eventually, he had dug himself just enough room to fit through it. Blake squeezed in so quickly and rolled himself out of the snow barrier and climbed to his feet.

Breathlessly, he hurried straight for his car as the men inside were most likely running down the stairs to catch him. Blake hopped in his vehicle, desperately trying to catch some air while struggling to insert his car keys in the ignition. For that second, he peered through his window up front and saw three cop cars parked in his driveway. "Oh shit," he mumbled under his breath.

At least six men in uniform swarmed from the house. In an instant, Blake threw his car into reverse. He put more force on the gas as he spun the wheel a hundred and eighty degrees, then rapidly shifted into drive and pressed on the gas again and sped out.

Blake had made himself lurch forward, even the bag in which he'd kept the proposal ring. It slipped out from under the passenger seat. He flashed his eyes down on the foot mat beside him. Right away he had thought of Emily when he witnessed the bag lying helplessly. His face was quick to express a pouty look, and with a quick hand, Blake reached in to tuck the purchased item back in under the seat, making sure that it was secure, then increased his speed down the streets.

CHAPTER THIRTY-ONE

End To It All

He'd driven himself a block from Belmont Avenue to pull up at the same spot as before. The sun was completely gone, and the skies were a dark blue glow. He had been staring straight ahead through his windshield at the office building across the street when he noticed how still everything seemed to be. "What I'm about to do next, is for you," he mumbled.

After Blake had hopped out, he shut his door gently, hoping that he would make as little noise as possible. There was still chance a group of men with badges were around the area, specifically waiting for him.

Whatever he had in store in that crazy head of his had to be done fast. Blake crossed the familiar alley between the two buildings and set foot onto Belmont; proceeding left down the sidewalk.

As Blake closes in on that diner, the young male had seen a rusty old blue vehicle parked just across the street. It was odd, but Blake hadn't been sure if it was 'thee rusty blue vehicle,' as Allen had mentioned to him about.

Right there he stood out front, exhaling deeply through his nostrils. For a man like Marco, it was wise of Blake to pull out his weapon that very instant, before entering.

Blake placed both palms on the grip and pointed his gun down just a few feet away from his toes, then whipped the entrance door wide open with a powerful kick. Blake rushed inside before it bounced back shut.

Right away, he rotated his body in every direction with his pistol pointing ahead. All clear, it seemed. Blake was confident that the wanted man wasn't hiding behind the counter straight ahead. A hunch was telling him Marco was on the upper level, and it wasn't long before Blake had his back against the wall as he glided up the stairs with uncertainty and slow-moving feet.

At the top, he'd seen that a torn off crime scene strip partially hung on the doorframe.

When Blake entered the room where the shredded mess of wood and bullet holes remained, there was Marco, standing in front of that same window.

Blake glanced downward and noticed something tied to Marco's calf. It appeared to be a white blood-stained tee shirt.

That time around, Blake kept his guard a few yards away as he pointed his weapon directly at the back of Marco's skull. Marco heard the footsteps, and he'd seen the fainted reflection of Blake being behind him. At that moment, Marco dropped his head, he shook it in disappointment and said, "You should have stayed yo ass home, boy."

Blake didn't know whether to take it as a threat or a helpful tip. "Why is that huh? You're going to try and kill me too?" Blake spoke intimidatingly.

"Shut yo ugly ass up!" Marco blurted. "You don't know shit. I ain't gotta tell you nothing… There's no point." It hadn't been a minute on the upper level, and Blake could feel the tension rising through the roof at a great rate.

As seconds passed, Blake began to feel more eager to put Marco down like a deer during hunting season. He was just waiting for that 'perfect moment'.

As he stared blankly straight ahead, Blake hadn't understood why at that moment, and in that very case, it was hard to take Fuentes down. It was like he was being pinned against a wall, unable to perform well as he had done in other cases.

Either way, it was the night for all odds. The two felt in a matter of seconds that they would go at it. It was destined to happen. After a long pause, Blake continued. "The point is, you killed your two sons, your mother, you've beaten your girlfriend half to death, and you murdered your one and only daughter!"

After a quick deep breath, Blake then asked, "How can you live with yourself?"

Marco snarled at the end of Blake's statement. At that instant, he turned his back away from the window and then stared straight ahead at Blake with squinted eyes while he heavily breathed through his nose. "How can you?" Marco asked as he was referring to Dana. "You're not ready for this boy, get up on out of here," he warned.

"Nah, I don't think so. I'm going to bring you in with me, or I'll just shoot you down instead!" Blake projected.

That sentence triggered Marco to step a foot closer to Blake, and he was about to take another step, but was reluctant, and remained in place. "You don't want to die today do you?" Marco asked.

"You're going to kill me too?" Blake asked. "You're going to kill me like you killed your kids?" Blake added, attempting to trigger Marco to make a false move before his pistol could sound.

"Don't say shit about my family!" Marco demanded.

Where Blake stood, he expressed an impish grin, but it slowly faded to confusion.

If there were any room to be more ticked off, Marco was already at the top of a crammed cookie jar. "What family?" Blake asked.

Right after Blake's harsh comment, Marco began charging in as fast as his jarring right calf could let him.

Just as Blake figured he would, he hesitated to fire a shot directly into Marco's chest, as that would have ended it all there.

Alternately, Blake had swiftly shifted his fire line of sight to his right and shot Marco in his left shoulder. It skidded through. It was enough for a blood gushing blow that jolted his shoulder back.

Surprisingly, it did not seem to have affected Marco much. It was almost like he was a walking shield. The man was still charging in fast with only a yard away from him with visibly clenched teeth and pinched eyebrows.

Blake Anderson quickly lowered the gun and fired just below the right kneecap. Marco grunted at the moment of impact but still kept charging in, although he was much slower. Marco was in arms reach and tempted to get a hold of Blake's weapon.

With a rapid-fire extent, Marco got a firm grip on Blake's forearm. Shortly, Blake was feeling the excruciating pain that was filling his bones as Marco used all of his might to free the weapon.

"If you wanted to kill me, you would have done it by now," Marco spoke through his gritted teeth as Blake felt a drop of spit plummeting onto his forehead.

Fearfully, Blake's eyelids stretched as he sensed a fit of anger that only a killer could have by the way Marco looked at him. And for some strange reason, Blake was losing feeling in his legs. He slowly began kneeling down as Marco continued to press down on his veins.

Then all of a sudden, Marco head-butted Blake straight in the nose, but Blake hadn't lost the hold he had on his weapon.

As he had struggled to see while the agonizing pain had his face scrunched, Blake proceeded to lock his fingers on the pistol from getting it snatched.

With guidance from his free hand, Blake pushes his occupied hand upward, having the pistol point about a centimeter away from Marco's face, then fired a shot. The sound was loud in Blake's ear, and the flash that had come from the last discharge threw them both onto the floor.

But just before that, Blake was able to see a chunk of Marco's nose as it was blown to bits. At that point, Blake knew his gun had slid somewhere off into the distance. It didn't matter to him. He knew for a fact he'd been out of bullets.

Marco roared as he leaned in with his knees, keeping himself halfway off the floor. "You bitch! I'm going to kill you!" Marco spoke with his teeth all bloody from a red stream gliding down his nostrils.

"I'm right here," Blake called out.

Marco soon hopped up on both feet just as Blake did. "You just can't stay down can you?" Blake spoke with a smile that was quick to falter away when Marco gave him a hostile stare.

A vibe from both of their faces proved that someone was destined to undergo the worst pain that neither of them could imagine, and not much time had passed until the two went charging in at each other.

A substantial hit sounded as Marco and Blake smacked into each other, and a split second after the collision, Blake threw a quick punch, but Marco somehow managed to duck it out. The force of Blake's swing nearly took him off balance.

Marco, on the other hand, had found the perfect opportunity to retrieve a couple of clenched fists as well. With all the block attacks, there were more blows to their knuckles than at each other's faces. That was until Blake had somehow driven up a more powerful force, and threw a hard punch that sent Marco smacking onto the wooden floor.

Marco quickly rolled onto his side and hollered out, "Aye, get this fool!"

Blake picked up that it was Marco's cue for his most desperate situation. In an instant, it was like a red light had gone off. Suddenly, two men in all black clothing rushed out of the shadows with pocket knives in their hands and began swinging at the young male. A slim, yet a tall fellow nearly slashed through Blake's abdominal area, leaving a tiny incision on his new sweater.

As for the other guy, a somewhat meatier, yet shorter man with heavy arms had made Blake put his quick reflexes into effect as he had dodged out the way of the rapid oncoming movement of his arm that clenched a blade in his palm.

Blake promptly stepped about a yard away from the two and quickly analyzed them. He soon realized they were the two men that Agent Johnson had mentioned to him about back at the apartment. The ambush scene with the rusty blue vehicle for their escape route; Tony Garcia and Tommy Banks.

After they advanced up close, the two criminals continuously jabbed the steel in Blake's direction. The young male was in fear for his life as he had many close calls. He could practically feel the wind from their swings brush through the hair on his head.

Marco was still on the ground, taking his sweet time to get back up on his feet again. And as for the muscular man in black, Tommy rotated his wrist, confronted with the sharp point downward, then rapidly swung his arm back as Blake quickly ducked out the way.

Tommy powerfully chipped a chunk of wood from the column beside them when his knife had made an impact. That's when he realized his hand became stuck inside the damaged column along with the blade he held tightly. Blake was undoubtedly thankful he hadn't gotten hit as that was another close call to the side of his head.

As Tommy Banks attempted to pull his knife away, Blake quickly leaped forward and threw a solid punch to the man's throat. That was for sure when the thuggish fellow gasped for air with an instant blue face.

Blake launched several more punches in his jaw like a punching bag. The surprising thing was, Blake's immediate instinct told him to kick his feet back in a horizontal position, and that's when he'd hit his foot directly in Tony's groin. It threw the scrawny male a few feet back while Blake proceeded with his rapid-fire swings in Tommy's ribcage. Quickly, Blake was grabbed by the shoulder threads of his new sweatshirt by Tommy's free hand and had taken a great head-butt to the nose that sent him falling straight down to his bottom.

While on the floor, his eyes became blurry from the instant welled up eyes that followed with a bloody nose. That blow gave him an instant headache but faded within' seconds that felt like minutes.

During the process of getting up, his vision was clearing, but it was still faded and digitalized like he'd been rubbing his eyes for a solid minute and had been traveling in another dimension.

Blake hadn't realized the large man was released from the column, let alone seen him come charging in, but he sensed it through the man's loud approaching footsteps, but it was too late.

Next thing Blake knew, he'd been grabbed by the collar and was thrown off to the side, slamming into that same column.
Tony came running in and clasped one of Blake's arms beside the post. Tommy did the same with the other.

Pinned. Blake had no hope of being able to free himself, and Marco was soon up on his feet again to stare directly into the young male's eyes from yards away. Blake stared right back, furiously; uncertain of Marco's intentions, but he knew it wouldn't be pretty.

Marco stepped in closer and began ranting on about his lifelong situation. "You know," Marco began. "My family was killed while I was out. I didn't kill my family, you bitch."

Shocked, Blake kept quiet to see where Marco planned on taking his story.

"My family was murdered by some weak ass, punk in a mask. Veronica's ex-boyfriend. That fool shot up the joint because my crew stole money from him. Aaron took all the money back that I had stashed at my ma's crib," Marco explained.

It wasn't long before Blake's eyebrows pinched with confusion. He had glanced over at Tommy, then to the right at Tony.

"She goes and calls the pigs and told them that I killed my mother, and my kids. It made me more upset that my girl never believed me. She put me through so much shit that past week. She looked at me like I was the murderer," Marco's lips quivered. "When I came to the house and saw what Aaron Ramirez had done, Veronica told me that the five-o were on their way to get me, so I took off running."

At one break point, Marco hawked a huge spit-ball of blood and released it onto the floor. "I almost took the man's life two weeks later…I found him in an alley one night, and some other guy came in with a gun, and helped his ass get away. Jose Gonzalez is his name. He's working with some bomber who goes by, Delgado… It pains me to see the morning papers, or to hear the news putting the midtown explosion on me, telling the world that I've murdered the most important people in my life. And now, Veronica will forever have her trust buried deep within my family's ashes."

Marco again, paused for a moment, and spat onto the floor, then threw in another statement. "That woman that was killed that night near her office… yeah," Marco laughed. "You cops are just as much of a killer as people say I am."

That statement threw Blake off, but with what Marco had been telling him beforehand had made sense. Blake had trouble believing the situation entirely. *Is Marco as bad as the public had led him to believe?* The young male wondered.

"What about your son in Mexico? You killed him, though, right?" Blake wondered.

As Marco stared at the floor with anger and sadness in his eyes, he said one thing, "Delgado's Cartels."

Those two words sparked rage in Marco's eyes. The name 'Delgado' had actually flashed the memory of the traumatic death of his son in Mexico.

"This is for the media," Marco projected as he jabbed his fist into Blake's abdominal.

Blake groaned with every desire in wanting to be set free onto the floor, and curl into a ball until the excruciating pain went away.

"Here's what I wish I could have done to my family's killers," Marco demonstrated again with his skeletal knuckles.

The helpless man received multiple blows to the face and immediately got drenched in his blood.

"Here's for the stupid cops, and the wannabe's." Marco struck at Blake's abdominal. "This is for my mother," he punched again. "This one's for my sons, and my little Amelia," he lastly launched a hard one to the ribcage.

For what felt like an extensive amount of time, the two guys had given Blake a slight break and forcefully shoved him onto the floor.

While he gripped onto his belly, Blake listened in on the hurried footsteps approaching from behind. Blake quickly slipped up a pocketknife from his ankle strap underneath his dress pants and swung his arms to the left, beside him, like he'd been batting up in a game of baseball. The knife then pierced Tony's groin.

To Blake, it sure was a good thing he stole the blade from the apartment him, and Richard had that exchange of fist and kicks.

Then swiftly, Blake yanked it out and shoved Tony off to the side, watching as the man collapsed onto the floor. Hurriedly, Blake got up on his feet as he had rapidly swung his blade without aim. He ended up hitting something. The young male soon realized the knife made a direct hit in Marco's left eye. Marco groaned loudly in his ear, then he staggered.

The pain sent Marco crashing into the column Blake was pinned against seconds ago. His body glided down the post until his rear reached the floor. Blake too had fallen on his bottom while he took a breather against the column straight across.

It was a solid hit, and Blake loved it as much as it was making him feel sick. The blade remained in Marco's eye socket, and hearing the whines as he projected to the ceiling was something Blake would not forget. It was a little taste of victory resting on his tongue.

Tommy Banks remained still, slightly disgusted at all of Marco's visible punctures along with the projected memory in his head of the knife shot to Tony's groin.

Tommy then lurched forward like he'd been trying to charge in at Blake when suddenly, everyone from the room heard a loud crashing sound that came from the lower level of the diner; A sound as if someone had broken in.

The four turned their attention over to the staircase entryway as a dozen footsteps were approaching their way. Next thing they knew, several men in blue uniform swarmed in with guns and flashlights in their hands.

Police officers. They scattered all over the room like bugs. They immediately began cuffing the hands of the four behind their backs, aggressively. One of the men in uniform cringed at the knife in Marco's eye socket during the process. While on his knees with clipped handcuffs on his wrist, Blake had a policeman press down on his shoulder to hold him in place.

Marco turned his head over to Blake, staring at him from a distance to see what he could only see with one eye, and said to him, "I warned you to stay away from shit you don't know about."

Blake stared straight back with an impish grin. Justice seemed to have been serving a lot for the public that night. Once they were all handcuffed, a surprise visit had come through the staircase entryway along with two men in uniform. The young male's eyes widened as soon as he saw Emily reveal herself from the doorframe. She'd been looking as good as ever, although she appeared angry. The way she was staring at Blake as she motioned closer to him showed she knew just about everything.

Emily got on one knee in front of him as she looked into his eyes. From what Blake had picked up, she was still shaken up, and about to unload some rage.
She expressed the tension on her eyebrows as well as a clenched fist.

Staring into his favorite set of brown eyes had broken him. He felt for sure it would be the last time he would see her.

Emily's lips quivered as she wanted to project something, but hadn't. Instead, she'd given Blake a sharp right hook to the jaw, knocking him off balance and had him crashing to the floor. His left shoulder broke the fall. Then a rounded man in uniform rushed in to get a hold of her before things escalated.

The scrawny police officer in orange hair curls came from behind and guided her back. Luckily for Emily; the men let it slide. Discreetly, those two men were proud.

Meanwhile, Blake was feeling a tug on his shirt as a bit of guidance to help him back up on his feet, giving him the indication that it was time to exit the premise.

One by one, they were escorted out front where multiple police vehicles were parked all around with the lights flashing.

Each of the four men sat in their separate vehicles, anticipating a visit downtown.

A camera crew had even made an appearance, taking up close and personal photos.

Unexpectedly, Blake's number one friend, Terrence Patterson had shown up to the scene where he was being pushed back into the crowd by police officers. Blake could hear his old buddy worriedly calling out to him from within'. He wasn't able to see him, but he could listen to his voice. Perhaps it was better that way, for he wished he could not be seen in his current condition.

As Blake sat alone in the back of a police car, he was discouraged that things had to have gone the way they did. The thought that Dana had died for nothing seeped into his brain. All Marco wanted was to avenge his family, and Blake believed him halfway. Blake thought for one moment about being in Marco's shoes, certain he would have done the same for his family.

All I have done is made things worse for everybody, Blake thought to himself. *I'm the bad guy.*

.

CHAPTER THIRTY-TWO

Christmas Day

In court, with gauges placed in his left eye, and a stitched nose, Marco along with his fellow partners, Tommy Banks, and Tony Garcia received a sentence of forty years to life in prison with no probability of early leave. Marco's been charged with first-degree murder and battery, and other additional charges. The crowd sitting in the courtroom maintained a smile with the knowledge that more criminals were off the streets.

Apparently, on that day, Marco had just found out the two people that had his back were crime suspects of child rape. Some could see it in Marco's facial expressions that he was infuriated. He had been keeping himself from running across the courtroom to sock them both.

As for Blake, the young male got placed with second-degree murder, with some other similar charges. And with the crimes Blake had been said, committed, he was given a sentence of thirty years in prison.

As for policemen in the room, they were quite convinced the case was off their hands and was then sealed. It was just a weight, a massive weight that was lifted off their shoulders.

It was a shame for Blake, a person his age standing in the middle of the courtroom in an orange suit, handcuffed with his wrist directly out in front of him while his mother teared up in the back row of the crowd.

Also sitting in the packed room was a person that was last seen at the breakfast diner where Emily used to work. Trevor Banks. With bloodshot red eyes, Trevor had looked beyond the crowd as he was witnessing his father, Tommy being set for his jail term.

Meanwhile, conceiving in the mind of the young male, the majority of the most valuable years of his life are set to be wasted away in a single cell. No vacations, no beautiful kids, and a big wedding Blake had hoped for, but worst of all, he would have no idea where Emily will end up. And as much as Blake had grown to believe in Marco, it didn't matter anymore.

In his first week, as Blake was sitting on a flattened mattress, in which he could even feel the springs from underneath, Blake was leaning his head against a cold wall where he shivered, thinking about the memories he partook with the most important woman in his life. Seconds felt like minutes, minutes felt like hours and hours seemed like days, and he was in for the long haul.

He couldn't handle the fact that he will be stuck in a four wall while Emily was out, living this free woman's life, being able to feel the beautiful weather the way Blake desperately wished he could.

While things had to have gone out that way, there was nothing more he could expect. All the running, the hunting, and the secrets are behind him.

On Christmas day at the stoner's residents, Emily sat on the headboard of the living room couch as she watched the snowfall from the large living room window. Her father, Richard had been sitting in the recliner on the opposite side of the room, sipping coffee from his mug as he read through an old morning paper while Christmas music played in the background. Emily seemed to be doing better; still, saddened.

She just hadn't pictured her holidays with her father due to her mother's incident, and lose the one person she imagined walking down the aisle for.

Shortly, her father opened up that morning. Richard decided to stick around rather than going back to his condo in New York, and immediately, Emily had this great big smile on her face.

"Oh, my-" She covered her mouth. "Are you serious?"

At that moment, Richard hadn't said a word back; he just expressed a broad smile.

With a hard month passing her by, having him as company surely made things much smoother for her.

She accepted him to be the owner of the house and realized that he had been the only guy she needed in her life.

Emily was quick to have gotten onto her feet to run over to her father for a firm hug. Richard wrapped his arm around her and kissed the top of her head. "Merry Christmas, darling," he said.

And that's when she realized her father became the best gift she could receive.

Hours later, Emily had visited a cemetery alone to visit her mother's headstone. She wasn't alone long until a man had approached up beside her. The snow crunch of each step behind didn't make her turn around, but the shadow of a man in a top coat and a fedora hat that had cast onto the headstone, did.

"It's nice to see you, Emily," Agent Johnson spoke down. "I know it wasn't easy for you to help me track Blake. I know he didn't mean for any of this to happen."

"He never told me he worked for the cops," Emily shivered.

"Well, he did some parts of his job right," Allen clarified. "But anyways, I want to thank you and your father for helping us out. And I'd like to give my condolences to the family. I am truly sorry."

Allen then began stepping away slowly. Emily remained for a while as she turned back to look at the man in the suit strolling further down. She noticed he had stopped beside a headstone for a moment to take a quick glance, which indicated he had someone special buried in the cemetery as well. Then he proceeded walking.

EPILOGUE
NEARLY TWO YEARS LATER

[Two buildings north of Belmont Avenue]
A late spring evening.

A short bald and pudgy building owner of the high rising Zeneca hotel stumbled across the sounds of some keyboard clicks and a desk chair hurriedly wheeling inside the media room. The rules are strict with who could access it, and strangely someone, somehow was on the other side of the door.

With a lot of rummaging coming from the inside, the hotel owner pressed his ear against the door for certainty. His eyes had bulged, wondering how could anyone get in. The owner reached underneath his tropical button up shirt as he flared his thick mustache and quickly pulled out a pistol he'd bought from an antique shop in a small town in Arkansas. He slipped up a key card from the pocket of his gray dress pants and faced it towards the wall to have it read, then right away, bounded into the room with the gun that was cocked, loaded and placed in the back of a masked man's head.

With arms immediately raised, the crook slowly rotated around and stared at the owner's green eyes.

"How'd you get in?" The man asked.

Without a word said, there was this awkward and intimidating stare down between them while the screens were playing back an old surveillance footage above them.

The Zeneca hotel owner glanced beside him while his gun remained elevated to see that a long filing cabinet he had on the far right of the room was broken into. There was nothing but tapes from security camera footage that dates back to as long as the building's been open.

Unexpectedly, the intruder swept his arm across so quickly that the man's pistol went flying across the room. Right then, the trespasser hurriedly got up off the chair and roughly shoves the owner to the side and made a run for it down the hall, leaving the man breathless with confusion.

At that moment, he glanced over at the security footage where the screens displayed someone with a rifle walking across the rooftop of a hotel from a December night. Not Blake, since Blake was stated to be on the building across the street.

It was someone else, actually.

It seemed that the intruder had done a fair bit of backtracking, like two years he'd gone back on the service. All the way to a date that seemed familiar to him; the day that the woman, Dana Stoner was murdered.

To Be Continued.

www.ingramcontent.com/pod-product-compliance
Lightning Source LLC
Chambersburg PA
CBHW030915120626
46554CB00001B/159